On the Hana Coast of Maui . . .

Lucia Gray, granddaughter of a New England missionary, seeks solitude but embarks on an interracial marriage with a Hawaiian cowboy

Novels by

MARJORIE SINCLAIR

KONA

THE WILD WIND

MARJORIE SINCLAIR

The Wild Wind

A NOVEL

MUTUAL PUBLISHING PAPERBACK SERIES
TALES OF THE PACIFIC
HONOLULU · HAWAII

TO MY MOTHER AND FATHER

Old Times on the Valley Isle

FORTY YEARS AGO I stayed for a while at the Hana Ranch Hotel on Maui and started *The Wild Wind* at a small desk in my room. I was lucky enough to be in Hana when it was still possible to meet comfortably the people of the region. Many of them were Hawaiian. Most of the Hawaiian details of my story came from them.

The Makaniloa of the novel is an imagined location somewhere between Hana and Kaupo. In Hawaiian, Makaniloa means "the long wind." The long wind is there—those who have traveled in that country know how it sweeps out of Kaupo Gap on Haleakala and moves down the mountain, spreading out along the shore and lasting for days. Makaniloa also is a dream place—or perhaps the real place—for several of the Hawaiians I met on that coast.

I had hoped the title of the novel would be *Makaniloa.* But my New York publisher those four decades ago felt that it would be too mysterious for the mainland reader. I suggested *The Long Wind.* And he asked: What is a long wind? So we settled on *The Wild Wind.* I am still not comfortable with it. In my mind I still think of this novel as *Makaniloa.*

The Hana side of the island of Maui is remarkably beautiful—the jagged coastline interrupted by small stretches of sand, the luxuriant vegetation, and the slopes of Haleakala, in which valleys have been carved through millenia. The rain keeps things green and often covers the slopes and fills the valleys with luminescent grays. Such a landscape cannot but shape the lives of its people. The very alternation of brilliant light and shadowy darkness suggests something of the quality of life there—the light and the dark in twentieth-century Hawaiian life.

I can remember driving to the Lahaina side of Maui in those days and marveling at how very different it was. No wonder the chiefs of the nineteenth century selected Lahaina for their homes, away from the bustle and politics of the royal court. In Lahaina, which had once been the capital of the kingdom, there were gentle winds, the warm sun, and the green slopes of the West Maui mountains—there was tranquility. Beyond Lahaina lay the sweeping empty beaches and vast green fields of cane.

The Wild Wind is, in a sense, a celebration of a way of life which has largely disappeared on windward Maui. It was a life closely bound to the mountain Haleakala, the weather, the valleys, the sea. It was a life in which many of the old Hawaiian ways were still practiced. I remember the day I called on the kahuna recorded in the story, who dropped the contents of a mysterious vial into a bowl of water so that she might tell where and when a lost fisherman's body would be found. I remember the old Hawaiian woman who had, in a trunk, rolls of yellowing paper on which genealogy chants and meles had been written in lead pencil; and the thoughtful man in his mid-eighties who had a fine collection of Hawaiian books. It was he who said to me: "It wasn't taking the land from us that was the worst thing you haoles did. It was calling us heathen and primitive. You took away our dignity." I have never forgotten this statement and the gentle melancholy manner in which he said it. *The Wild Wind* is my attempt to show the struggle of the Hawaiians forty years ago in their lovely landscape of Hana and Kipahulu and Kaupo. The struggle continues today— but now the focus is on the land, the *aina*. In actuality, loss of dignity and loss of land are part of the same grim deprivation for the Hawaiians.

I didn't, however, want *The Wild Wind* to end in bitterness. The novel concludes with the hope that some things can be resolved in the beautiful land of the long wind on the island of Maui.

MARJORIE SINCLAIR
Honolulu, 1986

I.

THE two men rode to the bent lehua tree; there at the beginning of the gap the trail debouched from the crater and followed the ancient sweep of lava down the mountain. As though struck with the same commanding impulse, they pulled up their horses and gazed at the huge landscape of Makaniloa below them: the spreading gray-green slope darkly lined at intervals by spills of black lava, the misty ohia forest to the east and the reddish, barren earth to the west, the shore line sharply etched in the black of stone and the white of sea foam, and beyond, the pale blue musing sea, interrupted in its flatness by the faint violet forms of Mauna Loa and Mauna Kea across the channel on the island of Hawaii, mountains which seemed more like emanations of the mist than the stuff of earth. The wind was harsh at their backs and pressed the long grasses into great waves as it poured out of the crater and down the slope.

"Jees!" Johnny exclaimed and whistled softly. "Every time I see it's different."

"Yeah," Kaupena breathed. "Number-one kind."

"Funny, though, how every time it change." Johnny's pidgin intonation was rhythmic.

The wind charged past them, shifting the clouds, shaping the trees and low-lying shrubs, vibrating in their ears with the roar of a storm-driven surf. The pastures lay softly on the rugged broad path of the lava. Kaupena, thinking of the adventurous, proud Hawaiians who once lived on this mountainside, said, "I guess the old people knew."

3

Johnny, grasping it, nodded, "Yeah, they knew all right. They knew what all good things were. We forget."

"Sure, we forget," Kaupena said bitterly. "We no give up only this," and he made a sweeping gesture including the island they stood on and the island of Hawaii, "but damn it! We even give up ourselves."

Johnny glanced wearily at him. "Whassa matta you? Every time you burn up on these things. Waste time think about that!"

"Too many guys like you say waste time. What you think going be?"

"Jees, whassa difference! We got Makaniloa still, yeah? My mother say more better forget some things. Jus' live, that's all."

Kaupena's burst of anger ebbed as quickly as it had risen. He knew how futile it was to argue with Johnny. He was the kind of Hawaiian who purposely overlooked the adversities that had come upon his race and had learned to slip effortlessly through his days. Although Kaupena envied him this ease of spirit, yet he regretted that there were so many like Johnny who added to the white man's pleasant myth about the Polynesian.

Shrugging his shoulders, Kaupena shifted the conversation. They continued their talk in the intimacy and good fellowship of pidgin. Although they both knew correct English, they seldom used it between themselves or in their families. Pidgin had about it a warmth and quality of direct expression which no other manner of speaking could establish. It carried with it overtones of the past, tendernesses of childhood, and a rich possibility for gesture. Pidgin was for them more than just a means of communication between men; it signified a whole way of life.

Johnny asked, "Say, what you think about the new people at the ranch? That wahine, Kitty!" And he made a little clucking noise with his tongue.

"Ah, funny kind!" Kaupena waved deprecatingly with his hand. "But that other wahine, Lucia—I no can understand.

Every time she ask me question. She like know about kanakas."

Johnny laughed suggestively. "Lucia like know about you. Thass why!" He rolled his eyes.

"Shut up!" said Kaupena. Then quietly he continued, "Only since she know my name Waiolama, she do that. Just like I was one old friend she can tell any kind to. Every time she ask me about our family. Funny, yeh! She know about old-kind stuff. She ask about one girl, Piilani. I go ask my grandmother about that, and she say yeh, my grandfather used to get one sister like that name. When I tell the wahine about that she get all excited."

"Lucia get excited quick. You know I hear she had one breakdown."

"Yeah, me too. She tell me that her great-grandmother was a missionary and that she *make* here—her grave stay by the Protestant Church."

"Funny kind, no!"

"She no like the other wahines who stay at the ranch. They like play around with kanakas. You know what kind. But this wahine, I think she really like kanakas. She talk nice kind."

"You better watch out, eh?" Johnny warned and grinned.

"Ye-ah," Kaupena drew out the two syllables thoughtfully. Then brusquely he ordered, "You go and see Pia's calf. If she get more sick, go call the vet. And then by-'n-by I come."

They spurred their horses and started along the trail. About a mile down, Kaupena called good-by to Johnny and veered to the right across the pasture. Ahead of him lay the gray shadow of the ohia forest. He knew that the ieie vine was in bloom, and he had thought of taking one of its sweet, salmon-colored flowers to Lucia. In the old days the ieie had been one of the plants offered upon the altar of the goddess of the dance, Laka. Not many people knew this, and he was sure that Lucia did not. That would lend his offer of it a little secret excitement, a special emphasis he wanted no one to suspect. For he had observed

Lucia's grace of body, and he had responded to the sensitive, tender way in which she regarded Makaniloa.

At the edge of the forest he dismounted and lit a cigarette. Lucia's questioning about his family and the early days of Makaniloa had been upsetting; it stirred in him old movements of thought and feeling concerning the Hawaiian people, thoughts that had first come to him when he was a student at the University of Hawaii.

University life had been an awakening, exposing him as it did to all the subtleties of condescension which many felt toward his race, and to the awkward fumbling of those who, remembering in what fashion the Polynesians had been brought low, both tried to love him and envied what they considered his freedom. He had returned home with two strong intermingled emotions, love for Makaniloa and concern for his people. Gradually as the months advanced, this fervor had been dissipated in the quiet routine of the ranch. At times his grandmother prodded him, for she had this same passionate regard for her people, and she wanted him to follow in her footsteps. But her proddings had only a momentary effect. Now strangely, Lucia was rousing him as his grandmother had been unable to do and was creating a flaming-up in him. Before her arrival he had sunk into the lethargy which had come upon so many of his people, a lethargy growing from the confusion and despair that lay deep in the background of their lives.

Even in his darkest moments, however, his love for Makaniloa was never quenched; it ran in his blood. His family, the Waiolamas, had lived for generations among the lava flows and forests of Makaniloa. Their lives had molded its history and their bones had rotted in its earth. If anyone had tried to force him away from it, he would have fought violently. And as he lived in its beauty and its loneliness, his life had grown dreamlike with the curious unreality of a pattern half ancient, half modern. In this last week Lucia was forcing him to think on these things.

The crux of the matter, of course, was that he was in love with Lucia and that he was afraid of this love. His grandmother had often warned him: "Makaniloa and a haole woman won't mix. You will have to choose. And you know there is only one choice for you," she had said in her sonorous Hawaiian.

"But it is possible," he had argued, "that there might be a woman who loved Makaniloa and found it beautiful."

"There is a point in our lives beyond which they cannot go. When they reach that point they turn away in fear, or disgust, or even amusement. If she did that to you, you would be lost for all time. There are some hurts from which we never recover."

He knew what his grandmother meant. There was that line through all Hawaiian life, on one side of which lay the happy warmth and on the other side the uncertainty, the darkness, the sorrow. Although most Hawaiians would say that all that really matters is what one has in the heart, yet they know that even in the heart is this duality of pain and love.

He stamped out his cigarette and after looping Panini's reins around a stump, entered the forest. The fragrance of ieie clouded the air, and the intricate twining of its branches, topped by shocks of spiny, slender dark green leaves, wove a coarse mesh among the trees. Occasionally, like a bright, long-tailed bird caught in the mesh, a blossom rose from a cluster of fronds. Kaupena, sniffing the fragrance, strolled contentedly among the trees until he came upon a flower perfectly formed. He cut it and carried it directly back to his horse, where he tied it securely to the pommel of the saddle. He mounted and returned to the trail that led down the mountain.

As he neared the ranch, his mind began to move among the difficulties of presenting the blossom to Lucia. How could he do it without embarrassment to them both and how could he avoid being teased by Johnny and Bill Perkins and that sharp-tongued Kitty? The delicate feeling he had about making the gift curdled into irritation. He snatched the blossom from the pommel and tossed it down. Panini's hind feet trampled it.

As he approached the highway, he noticed in the yard of the Protestant Church the figure of a woman. Lucia, he was sure. She moved with that soft rhythm which revealed the fastidious restraint of her sensuousness. Her hair had its fine color spread in the wind, and her clothes were molded close by the wind against the tender lines of her body. In the way the light fell upon her he could see the outline of her breasts and the graceful form of her thighs. She was not, he had decided, a really pretty woman, but she had a charm that made one notice her. Her blue eyes were round and moist. Her skin was tanned, and did not have that peaked look which washed out the loveliness of many mainland women. Her hair was truly beautiful, streaked in some places a rich reddish brown like guava bark and in others the creamy color of the pua kenikeni flower. When she was not absorbed in some moodiness within her, she reached out with a gentle, hesitant manner, offering a delicate friendliness. She had never made him feel, as so many of the other mainland women had, that he was Hawaiian and therefore Exhibit A.

He tightened the reins against Panini's neck, gently urging him around until he faced the mountain. Little clouds were gathering in the crater; their shape and motion told him that nightfall would bring squalls thundering on the roofs and slashing through the trees. His heart warmed at the sight of the broad flow of green down from the gap, at the up-thrusts of lava like ragged black flames against the grass. Panini too responded, tossing his head at the smell of freshening wind.

Kaupena prodded the horse's ribs gently and made toward the ranch house. Cocktails at five, and the boss expected him to be there; he was head cowboy and had some social duties. The boss liked to brag to his guests that he had the only university-educated cowboy on the island.

He caught another glimpse of Lucia pushing her way against the wind toward her car on the road. Her slight figure hunched against the cold, lonely in the vast landscape. A spasm of tenderness filled him. He knew of her marriage and divorce and that she was still struggling against this distress. Perhaps after that unhappy marriage with one of her own kind, she would consider . . . Perhaps . . .

It was the first time in the week she had been at the ranch that Lucia Gray had been able to slip away alone to the one spot in all Makaniloa she wanted most to visit. Kitty kept a sharp watch over her and had whispered to the others that Lucia was recovering from a nervous breakdown. That was not quite true, for the doctor had dismissed her a year ago. But she still had moments of uncertainty and confusion, which she tried to conceal and which she was certain would disappear as soon as she could form some pattern for her life.

She stepped carefully among the grasses and markers of the churchyard; any stone might be the one she was hunting. How lucky she was that Kitty, her friend, should be a cousin to Elizabeth Perkins! For it meant that Kitty could bring her here, the place of all places in the world she had most wanted to visit. Makaniloa, which had once seemed so remote that it must surely be fabulous, was now beneath her feet.

She was searching for the grave of her great-grandmother, bending at each tombstone to read the inscriptions, many of which were in Hawaiian. Presently, on a white marble stone, she read of Lucia Breckenridge, wife of the Reverend Ezra Appleton who had been born in Greenwich, Connecticut, on May 23, 1818, and who had died in Makaniloa, Maui, November 16, 1845. With trembling fingers Lucia Gray reached out to touch the letters graven in the rock. Confusion trembled in her mind, and tears welled to her eyes. But the core within her remained cold. There was no quickening of the heart, no deep thrill of the mind.

She turned away from the tombstone, bitterly disappointed with the emptiness of this long-awaited moment. Where was that full pulse of love mingled with sorrow which she had felt for her great-grandmother? It seemed to have been dwarfed by the gigantic landscape of Makaniloa and by the utter loneliness of the white marble slab in the deep grass. All the emotions she had ever had seemed small in this place; it was as though she had never really tasted of the deep flavors of life.

She faced the broad green ascent of the mountain, which had been so loved by her great-grandmother. "Makaniloa," she said aloud, "the long wind." It was the fitting name for a spot where the wind constantly hurled itself out of the crater gap and swept with fierceness down the ancient course of lava.

Time enough had passed for grasses, ferns, sisal, lantana, and even a few stunted koa and kukui trees to grow richly upon the lava flow. Their green was intense where it was contrasted with outcroppings of black rock. The vastness of the flow and the barrenness of the slowly rising mountain gave a tone of crude force and desolate freedom to the landscape. The slope was cut by two sharp narrow valleys, both rich in foliage—coconut, hau, breadfruit, ti, kamani, ginger. Behind each valley was a cliff over which spilled slender waterfalls. The mouth of each valley led by long, gentle, grassy slopes to the sea. Much of the shore line, formed originally by lava, was jagged and fantastic, and offshore strange frozen driblets of pahoehoe jutted up through the waves like beasts from an old legend. The water frothed about them, often lunging over the crests and spilling into cascades of white and green-gray and blue-black. Although she had never been in a spot so wildly and desolately beautiful, she did not feel strange or alone.

The wind against her face dried the tender, city-sheltered

skin. In gusts it traveled down the slope, lashing the tassels of the grasses, cutting the tough little fern leaves, twisting the koa trees into fluid patterns, stirring up eddies of dust where it had managed to sweep the soil bare of vegetation. Its noise poured into her ears, and in a sudden vague impulse she flung her arms out to test the strength of it. She shuddered under its cold and its power. Then quickly she moved to the sheltered lee of the church. There she sat in the sun and pulled from her bag a small, faded brown book. She opened it at a place marked with green ribbon and read the tiny, perfectly formed handwriting of her great-grandmother.

Wednesday, Jan. 25. The wind has been violent all day. My dear husband left at dawn for the church at Keanae. I conducted the school as usual today. One new pupil, Piilani Waiolama. She is a pretty girl but very shy and knows no English.

Tonight the children were restless and couldn't sleep. Willy was frightened when during a horrible blast the whole house shook and the thatch seemed about to be lifted off. I held him in my arms and sang a hymn. That seemed to quiet him. After he was in bed, I had Charity kneel with me and together we prayed for the safe return of our dear husband and father.

Tomorrow I must walk up to Mrs. Waiolama's. The girl, Piilani, told me her baby brother had been sick with fever for four days, and they thought he was going to die.

Just a moment ago I stepped outside. Oh, the wildness and strength of the wind! It is like the voice of God. I knelt in the darkness and asked Him to grant me strength to do all the things which I see must be done among the women and children of beautiful Makaniloa.

Lucia looked away from the journal, resting her fingers on the pages. "Oh, the wildness and the strength of the wind!" she whispered. "It is like the voice of God." The emotion she had expected was coming now, stirred by those words, and again tears flowed into her eyes. She rose, facing Makaniloa, and became aware of the increased wind blasting down from the gap and smelling of cold rock and thin air. She arched her back and walked slowly across the churchyard, her head thrown high, her lips parted, her eyes glimmering. She remembered the fire which had once flamed in the core of the mountain; she remembered too the passionate love her great-grandmother had borne for this place. A strange trembling came upon her body. She felt herself drawn in, gathered up, reaching a focus, for something of deep, puzzling significance was happening to her. She laughed suddenly and broke into a run.

Lokalia Waiolama, Kaupena's grandmother, stepped slowly down the rocky path choked with decaying leaves and snarled with jutting roots. She was on her way to the mouth of the valley to cut some bananas from the bunch that she had noticed ripening two days ago. The falls at the back of the valley were swollen, echoing against the precipitous, enclosing cliffs with a portentous roar. Wind passed far above, whistling and shaking the treetops. Lokalia noticed a certain sharp, fresh, warning odor to it and thought she must be sure to take her drying hala up onto the lanai of the house so that it would not get wet in the night rain.

At the mouth of the valley the path moved out into the open and was neatly graveled—work done two years ago by Kaupena. She went faster on her aching old legs. The dampness and the wind—if only she could keep dry and warm all the time! The family was constantly trying to get her to move down to the beach. But she could not leave the house where her children had been born and in which she had reared Kaupena. She could not desert the place of her mana, her power.

In that house, when she was only a bride she had first learned of her special talent with the gods. Her husband's grandmother, dying on a pile of mats in the back bedroom, had whispered chants for her to write down and had explained certain ceremonies of ritual. "Learn them, Lokalia. Never forget. Teach one of your grandchildren so that they will not be lost." Lokalia had felt within her a vivid strengthening of will and sharpening of intuition. It was as though this woman in dying had passed on her power. And she was certain that it was because of this that old Hoopai, years later, had given over to her his position as counselor and kahuna.

Suddenly Lokalia sidestepped awkwardly, her heart plunged into fear. So deep in reflection had she been that she had nearly stepped on a lizard sunning himself in the path. She shuddered at the thought of harming a lizard, the aumakua, personal deity of the Waiolamas. Her breath came harsh and hurting and she had to sit and rest for a while. She remembered tremblingly the occasion in her early married life when she had inadvertently frightened a lizard. It had lost its tail. For weeks she had brooded, wondering what would come to her for harming her protector. And surely enough, that was the winter she had had a painful sickness in the lungs and had almost died.

She went on in the sun, murmuring under her breathlessness old Hawaiian prayers, some of the words of which people no longer understood. The rhythms gradually soothed her nerves into quietness. At the banana patch she cut herself a hand of the fruit. Laying it aside, she climbed a little promontory, which gave a view of the massive sweep of Makaniloa. The power of the landscape moved into her, as it never failed to do. The pain of her seventy-six years fell away and briefly she knew strength and exultation again ruling her body. She thought proudly of the men in her husband's family who had gone into Hawaiian history, the chiefs, the priests, the fishermen who ventured farther upon the sea than anyone else. Such a land made such men.

She hoped that some day Kaupena would follow in the legendary path of his ancestors. Everyone from Kaupo to Lahaina knew of the Waiolamas. Though the family had dwindled sadly—as had most Hawaiian families—there was still Kaupena. His sister Hannah, who had married a haole man and lived in Honolulu, did not count. His brother Joe, who had had both legs shot off at Iwo Jima, was a poor sad man, not one in whom to place the hope of the family. Yet, he had given the Waiolamas some little fame, for his Hawaiian songs were sung by all the young people.

Just as she was about to turn and carry her bananas home, her dim old eyes saw a man on horseback far down the slope. She studied him. It must be Kaupena. She watched him stop and stare down the hill. Slowly he moved from a slouching position in the saddle, throwing out his chest, moving his head slightly to one side; she knew the significance of that attitude, that there was devotion and compassion moving in his heart. He was a man of deep feeling, and his hot temper was often submerged by the tenderness within him. Her eyes watered as she strained to find out who was below him. Then she saw the yellow coupe start up from the road near the Protestant Church and speed off toward the ranch house. Mrs. Gray's car. Lokalia felt fear move through her like a wave. "No!" she cried aloud, and clenched her fists. "No, no, no!" She saw all of her life's work vanishing. This woman would take him away from Makaniloa. She would fill him with that subtle poison which infected so many Hawaiians and made them try to be what they were not. His place was here in Makaniloa; this woman could never understand the meaning of that!

Back at her house deep in the valley, Lokalia threw the bananas listlessly onto the lanai stairs and sat down. Loneliness moved in her vitals like a sickness. She was used to being alone. But this sense of abandonment was something else. She held her head in her hands and sat quietly. The roar of the waterfalls contended with the throb of blood in her ears, and she was dizzy. Presently she went inside and knelt at the old cedar chest. She opened it and from under the pile of Hawaiian quilts worked by herself and her mother, she pulled yellowed sheets of paper that held the genealogy chant of the family. She murmured the words softly, starting at the beginning which told how the lizard-god had come down to Hawaiki and married a beautiful chief's daughter. This daughter had borne to the lizard-god a son who was destined to travel thousands of miles alone in an outrigger across the seas until he came to Hawaii. Sailing around all the islands, he finally settled upon Makaniloa as the place for his home. He landed there, planted in the valleys his shoots of breadfruit and cocoanut from Hawaiki, and at the shore his shoots of pandanus. Then he married the most beautiful daughter of the Anuenue family and thus started the Waiolamas of Makaniloa. . . .

2.

LUCIA, reaching the ranch house, parked her car under the mango tree, slipped through the kitchen and up the back stairs to her room. She went directly to the window and stood gazing down at the church, which from this distance looked like a dark toy set in an overwhelmingly wild landscape of rough sea and wind-swept pasture. In the fading greenish light, it was infinitely sad. Suddenly she turned away, took her great-grandmother's journal from her bag, and hid it under a pile of scarves in a drawer.

She examined herself in the mirror, running cold fingers through her tangled hair. She pulled it tight and then swooped it up in the back, twisting a loose, old-fashioned knot. It was always said in the family that she looked much like her great-grandmother. Could it be, she cautiously reflected, more than that? Today the emotion that had filled her at last down in the churchyard, an emotion that brought a sharp focusing of life, a concentration in her being—was that what Great-grandmother had felt in Makaniloa? Abruptly Lucia shut off this channel of thought; she was not yet ready to accept all the implications of a journey that was becoming in some curious way a return to home.

She went from the mirror to the closet and removed her slacks. In the bathroom the pelting hot water of the shower felt good on her chilled flesh. She dressed in her new silk print and pulling some ginger blossoms from the bouquet on the bedside table, fastened them in her hair. She put on the pale green cashmere sweater her mother had knitted for her.

Poor Mum, she thought as she rubbed the soft sleeves of the sweater. She's still so concerned about me; ever since the divorce from Ted, and then the nervous upset. Mum liked Ted. But she couldn't know how afraid he was of everything but his safe little world of proper people and golfing and making love and selling bonds. He put tall barriers around his world, and that was the total of life for him. He didn't want anything else, nor did he want to know about anything else. She couldn't make Mum understand this part of Ted. Daddy, in dying so early, had filled her with a romantic attitude toward all husbands. They were all good and strong and dependable and liberal as he had been.

After a year of marriage with Ted, Lucia had begun to stir out of the happy spell of the physical experience. She saw clearly—and it brought even now an acrid taste to her mouth— the strangely artificial, holiday life in which they spent their days. What could such an existence possibly mean in a world of suffering and anxiety? Was not their ivory tower far more shameful than that of the calumniated artist? At least the artist was trying to preserve beauty in a world that had only a craving for security and food. When she tried to get Ted to talk about it he had laughed and said that she sounded like a college sophomore who was taking her first course in philosophy. And then for a week he made a special effort to be attentive. He had seen that her questioning came from a rift deep within her. But his gay laughter and tenderness only engendered her awakening. Life grew emptier and emptier as bridge parties and golfing parties and drinking parties increased in number. She yearned for children, but she never became pregnant. At the end of the third year she had asked Ted if they could adopt a child. He grinned and called her his "little mother"; then quite soberly and sadly he added that he had had enough responsibility in the war to last him for quite a while. There was plenty of time to have kids, in a few years maybe. . . .

Ted had not been wounded physically in the war. But she knew he had other, deeper wounds. He felt that his experience on the battlefield excused him for a while from all social obligations or from unhappiness or strife. Understanding this, she had tried desperately to play his game.

In the midst of this effort two things had happened. First, her mother had given her great-grandmother's journal. "You are named for her, darling. And now you are old enough to appreciate what a precious family document it is." Lucia had read it at first rapidly to refresh her memory of the romantic story of a shy, sensitive Connecticut farm girl who had married a missionary and had gone out to the savage south seas to convert the natives to the ways of the true God. In little more than a year this girl, in her suffering and loneliness, had become a woman brilliantly aware of her social function and spiritually alert. Makaniloa, its physical beauty and its people, had made this change, and on Makaniloa she had lavished her devotion. Lucia had read the journal slowly for a second time, constantly reminding herself, this is my great-grandmother who writes; her blood runs in me; her emotions are probably in me. She found herself turning to the journal when nothing else satisfied her. Presently she recognized that her great-grandmother was a woman who in only twenty-seven years had molded a life with firm direction, a life significant and warm in humanness. Notwithstanding all her fears and anguish, her worry and heavy work, her physical pain, she had been happy. For the first time Lucia understood that true happiness was not always something happy in itself.

Then in turning the pages of a magazine one day she came across a photograph of the tragic blank eyes of an European child gone mad from bombing. The picture had aroused deep within her the distress of profound compassion for suffering people. Her great-grandmother and the child—they made impossible the kind of life Ted provided. Barriers must be broken down, not built up! Men must approach each other openly and in sympathy. There must be no more shutting off of people for any reason.

On that day she had simply packed her things and left the apartment. She had gone to volunteer her services in a settlement house. But within a few months the illness had come upon her. The mingling of her own confusion with that of those who were caught in the pitiless turmoil of the city upset for a while the even temper of her heart and mind.

"Lucia, Lucia!" It was Kitty's voice calling from below.

"Yes, Kitty." She started up. "I'll be right there." And she hurried down the stairs.

She paused in the doorway of the big room, now filled with the falsely brilliant golden light of early evening. The room, although of large and fine proportions, was always disappointing to her: the bright chintz covering lumpy furniture, deer horns above the mantle and reproductions of hunting prints around the walls, a heavy fireplace of porous lava rock, blue linen drapes, bouquets of such unexotic flowers as sweet peas, snapdragons, and pinks. Elizabeth Perkins had tried to make it seem as much like home as was possible, for Elizabeth had grown up with Kitty in Indiana. The room was pleasant and commonplace, with nothing of Makaniloa in it.

Bill Perkins, Elizabeth's husband and owner of the ranch, had been born and reared in Makaniloa. He had that fierce attachment which island-born people often have for island earth. Bill could never leave Makaniloa for more than a month at a time. Elizabeth had to accept this, although she went alone to Indiana once a year for a visit. After ten years she was still regarded as a stranger by the ranch people. She had never been able to achieve the manner of casual yet warm friendliness that endeared Bill to everyone of every racial background on the ranch.

Bill was standing near the large plate-glass window which gave a broad view of mountain and sea. He was talking with George Lambeth, the visitor from New York. Across the room Kitty was talking animatedly to Elizabeth, Kaupena, and Alec Johnson, the cattleman from Wyoming. The four of them stood near the mantle, where the rainbow colors of a driftwood fire blazed in the grate. In a corner near the door was a small bar paneled in lauhala; there Toshi was handing a drink to Margaret Campbell, Bill's cousin, unmarried, and a painter.

"I'll have a Manhattan too," Lucia said.

"Where've you been?" Margaret asked. "We'd almost decided to send out a search party when we discovered your car hidden under the mango tree."

"Lucia!" Kitty interrupted and started across the room to greet her. "Where have you been? Honestly. We were getting worried."

"I was just driving around," Lucia said lamely. She noticed that Kaupena was gazing at her with a warm look that roused in her an uncomfortable shyness.

"Driving on these roads!" Margaret exclaimed. "You must be crazy."

"Better take a horse next time," Elizabeth suggested.

"I can find the roads! But the trails—they're hidden."

Alec laughed. "They're hardly as well marked as the bridle paths in Golden Gate Park."

Kitty took her arm, and pulling her aside whispered, "Honestly, Luce, you've been behaving queerly. Snap out of it."

"There's nothing wrong. I love it here."

"Well, you don't act it. You're so queer."

"Kitty darling, don't worry. The old trouble isn't coming back. It's just—oh, everything is so beautiful, so exciting!"

Kaupena overheard and said, "It's Makaniloa." His eyes

were sharp on Lucia now, his voice penetrating. "Sometimes it does that to people. It casts a spell. Those of us who are caught find it hard to escape."

His words sank into Lucia, subtly influencing the thoughts and moods of the afternoon in the cemetery. "A spell," she murmured. "Perhaps that's what it is."

"Yes," said Margaret somberly. "There is a spell. I'm an old maid because of it. The only guy who ever asked me wouldn't live here. But I'm not sorry."

Lucia searched Margaret's eyes, puzzled by the contrast between the seriousness of her tone and the flippancy of her words. When she found the truth, she masked the expression on her face by gulping down the rest of her drink. Her own decision flashed upon her. She would stay in Makaniloa, yield to its spell, even as her great-grandmother had done. After all, she was coming home.

The drink flowed warmly within her and relaxed the tensions of the afternoon. "Toshi, another one," she said. Tonight she would be gay in the old artificial way she had practiced for Ted's sake. She took the drink from Toshi. "Let's put some music on the victrola," she said to no one in particular. "Hawaiian music."

Alec obliged her, and she went up to Bill and George, absorbed in their conversation.

"What are you two talking so solemnly about?"

"We were waiting for you to come over and cheer us up," Bill said.

"Oh, Bill, I wish I could always believe you." She sipped at her second Manhattan. The last time, she thought jubilantly, to pretend this casual sociability. In her new life she was going to be honest with herself.

Bill was watching her closely, and she smiled up boldly at him.

"What did you do this afternoon?" he asked. "Your eyes sparkle. You're absolutely dazzling tonight."

"I met an old friend out on the hillside," she said, not realizing what her words would be until they came out. Then she held her glass high and said, "To Makaniloa!" She would have to find a reason for staying; these people would never understand without a reason. The income Ted had settled on her was, thank heavens, enough to live on here.

"An old friend!" Kitty cried. "Who?"

"A ghost," Lucia teased.

Kaupena took her arm suddenly and led her toward the fireplace. Just as he touched her, a squall hit the house, roaring on the tin roof, pushing at the windows, and sizzling in the fire. "It's a sign!" she exclaimed, realizing that Kaupena would understand her.

He nodded and whispered, "I saw you this afternoon. In the cemetery."

"Come, let's sit down," she said and pointed to the sofa facing the fire. She spoke seriously. "What work can a woman do in a place like this?"

"Work?" he asked.

"I mean for an excuse to stay. I want to stay here. To live here forever!" She enjoyed the touch of melodrama she gave to her words.

"And moon over your grandmother's grave?" he said lightly, smiling. "You'll get over that quickly enough."

"My grandmother loved Makaniloa. She wanted to be buried here and not carried back to Connecticut. But it isn't because of her grave that I want to stay. It's because of what she found here and of what I too will find."

"Things are a lot different now than then. Not so many people. No heathens to convert."

"Oh, Kaupena! Don't make light of it."

He turned away from her to face the fire. "If you're wrong

about this, it'll be hard. We've had others who thought they could bury themselves here. It's a bitter thing to find out you can't."

She disregarded his words. "What can I do? What excuse can I give? Please help me think. These people have got to have a reason."

"There's no reason for a woman to remain in Makaniloa. There's no work for a woman."

"Are there any empty houses?"

"A few. Hidden away here and there. Most of them not very livable. They belong to people who felt the lure of Honolulu. They'll be back next year or in ten years or twenty years. It always happens that way. Makaniloa loses few Hawaiians forever."

"Could I rent one?"

"I suppose. And pretend you're writing a book or some such thing. We had a writer here a few years ago. He wrote a mystery."

"A book," she said slowly. "A biography of my great-grandmother. I could pretend I'm editing her journal and adding an account of her life. Or maybe I'll really do it!" She paused briefly; and then decisively, "I'll tell them about her."

"You really mean this?" he asked.

"There's no other place for me!"

"It's lonely. Sometimes Elizabeth is beside herself with loneliness. Margaret isn't always helpful. She goes off painting."

Lucia looked at him in amazement. "But they aren't the only women here! Look at all the Hawaiian women. The few I've met have been wonderful. I want to know them too."

"Yes," he blushed. "The Hawaiian women—"

"Dinner is ready," Elizabeth broke in.

"I'll tell them at the table," Lucia whispered.

The table, a shining one of polished koa wood, was lighted with four fat candles, and as Lucia sat down their flames dazzled her eyes. A nervous exhilaration gripped her. Before they were all properly seated, she burst her news among them. "I'm staying!" she cried and flung her arms out.

George Lambeth said, "I think those two Manhattans were too much for her in this pure mountain air."

"No!" she denied scornfully. But she smiled and patted his hand. "It's just that you don't know my secret."

Kitty squealed, "Your secret! What is it, Luce?"

She waited until they were all looking at her. "My great-grandmother lived in Makaniloa. She is buried in the cemetery!"

Bill let out a "My God!" And then, "Of course. Lucia Breckenridge Appleton. How often I've looked at her tombstone, thinking how lonely she must be with all the rest of her family back in Connecticut."

"She isn't lonely. She wanted to be here."

"So?" he said incredulously.

"Yes. Her journal says so. That's why I'm staying. To edit her journals and work up an account of her life here."

The table bristled with talk about Lucia's revelation, but she herself scarcely listened. Once when probed she said that she hoped to find a little house. Elizabeth insisted that she stay at the ranch, and she answered vaguely that she might for a while. But eventually she must have a place of her own.

Later, after they had gone upstairs, Kitty came to her room. Lucia was already in bed reading a volume of Hawaiian legends.

Kitty curled herself up on the foot of the bed and asked, "Luce, did you really mean all you said tonight? Or was it the Manhattans?"

"I meant it. It all came to me when I visted my great-grandmother's grave this afternoon—although I didn't quite realize it then."

"But whatever will you do? You'll go crazy staying on in a

place like this. If you want to write, you can do that better in New York."

Lucia laid her book on the bedside table. "Oh Kit, try to understand. You know how I've floundered since Ted. First the settlement work and then that awful time in the hospital." She twisted her fingers together, her eyes fixed upon them. "Then I tried a little of everything! Business college and being a secretary; a summer of painting at Woodstock; then, at Mum's suggestion, travel. But nothing worked. I didn't seem to belong anywhere. No one seemed to need me. It was an awful feeling —like being forever lost."

"I know, darling," Kitty murmured. "You always take things so seriously. And that's what you need to get over. Not burying yourself in a place like this. You'll do nothing but brood."

Lucia mused, "This afternoon on that hillside I felt for the first time since I've grown up and left my family that I really belonged somewhere!"

Kitty hesitated and then began softly, "Lucia darling, you are just romanticizing over your great-grandmother."

"Perhaps. But maybe it's my nature." She flung off the covers and walked to the window. Rain streamed down and she smelled the sharp, strong odor of wet night. She turned to Kitty and said, "This rain! I love it! Just standing here and hearing it, smelling it, is a moment of real living for me. I don't know why it should be, but it is. For some people place makes as much difference as friends. Perhaps I'm one of those."

Kitty stood silent in the middle of the room.

Lucia held out a beseeching hand. "Oh Kit, forgive me! You know how I talk."

"Luce, I forget so easily that there are people in the world like you. It kind of scares me to remember it. Human beings sitting around with their nerves tingling . . ."

Lucia laughed and put her arms around Kitty. "Come, let's

read to each other as we used to. I have some legends of Makaniloa."

When Kaupena left the ranch house, he heard the fuming of
water and wind in the valley, and he thought of his grandmother up there alone. He would go and spend the night with
her. There in the solitude, he could think of Lucia and how inevitably they were being drawn together. He stopped briefly at
the bunkhouse to change his suit. At the stable he saddled Panini and rode for half an hour through the wet darkness.

The kerosene lantern in the window of the remote little
house shot a beam of glittering light down the streaming lanai
stairs; it was like an arm stretched in welcome through the
stormy night. He unsaddled Panini and tied him under the
lean-to. Then he followed the path of light up the stairs.

Pushing open the door, he called in Hawaiian, "Hello! It's
me!"

His grandmother sat in her rocker reading; she did not look
up or acknowledge his presence. The room seemed to have
shrunk to the small space bathed in the lamplight. Lokalia continued rocking back and forth. The rockers squeaked across a
weak board in the floor; the windows rattled under the impact
of the wind. A gust blew in and picked up a corner of the skirt
of her muumuu. She shivered slightly, but her eyes remained
on the book. Kaupena closed the door.

"Hello, Grandma," he said softly, endearingly.

The board creaked under the rockers. The lighted area, he
sensed, was on this evening tabu to him and sacred to her. The
rest of the room remained dim and mysterious. The paper kahili
he had made years ago for a school pageant threw an odd
shadow on the wall behind it, like a huge club raised in striking
position.

He moved to the hikie and sat on it in the darkness. He saw
anger stiffening Lokalia's body, making the rocking more jerky

and intense. He in turn became angry. He burst out, "I come to stay with you, and you treat me this way!"

Dramatically she closed her book. "I saw you looking at that Lucia Gray today!"

Kaupena laughed loudly. "You're a jealous old woman."

Lokalia left her chair and went into the bedroom, slamming the door behind her. Kaupena watched the chair as it continued to rock. He rubbed his fingers across his cheeks and in his own loneliness pitied the old woman in the bedroom for hers.

Presently he took off his boots and blue jeans and going to the cedar chest took out a quilt. He turned off the lamp and sprawled across the hikie, pulling the quilt close around him.

He could not sleep, and so it was that he heard the bedroom door open and the soft shuffle of footsteps. He pretended sleep. In a moment he felt a hand caressing his hair and the lightest of kisses on his forehead.

3.

ON SUNDAY in the third week of their visit, Kitty and Lucia drove down to the Protestant Church built by Lucia's great-grandfather. They faced the sea all the way, and light glittered on the water, burning their eyes. The sun in its bright intensity had drained the color from land and water, and the church rose dark and sharply drawn against the brilliance. Its harsh opaque quality gave it a semblance of rigid austerity.

Kitty and Lucia walked arm in arm down the path toward the church. Kitty said quietly, "I can't imagine your wanting to live here."

"You don't think I'll stick, do you?"

"Oh, maybe for a month or so. Then you'll be rushing back to New York."

"You don't really know me, do you?"

"Do you know yourself?"

"Yes," Lucia replied firmly. "I do."

They stepped shyly into the foyer and made their way through the throng of smiling, chattering Hawaiians. A large, handsome man in a rusty black suit showed them to a pew. They sat close together, Lucia's hand slipping over to clasp Kitty's fingers. The gray walls rose sturdily, gauntly above them; the koa lectern, with two little fern stands on either side, glowed soft gold against the dusty floor.

The choir, followed by the deacons and the minister, paraded in and stood before their chairs lined up on the platform. The minister, a thin blond young man from the mainland, moved forward to the lectern. The deacons opened their hymnals. They were all elderly Hawaiians, their faces so chiseled as to suggest a life filled with deep moral problems and profound sadness. They all had thick white hair and burnished brown skin, and their resonant voices led even the choir in singing. Before them the minister seemed a pale, serious boy.

During the hymn, Lucia tried to imagine her great-grandmother seated in the first row with her class of Hawaiian girls clustered around her. She had sung in a high clear soprano, leading the voices of the children. And she had spoken the Psalm responses softly in Hawaiian.

When the lesson was being read, Lucia noticed that Kaupena and his crippled brother, Joe, were a few rows ahead. She could see the shining brass knob of the cane which Joe used to help his artificial legs. The two brothers were alike physically. Their hair, black and luxuriant, curled crisply back from the forehead. Their noses were straight, their mouths full and firm. The difference, so obvious in their personalities, was expressed in their eyes. Joe's eyes were either laughing or dreamy. But Kaupena's reflected a wide range of feeling and often had a dark in-looking glaze which shut off all communication with him. She reflected anxiously on the attraction he had for her, which had grown rapidly in the three weeks she had known him. Always at the ranch parties she found herself sooner or later in a tête-à-tête with him. She had tried to analyze this attraction, wondering what it was that brought them so constantly together. There seemed to be many facets: the withholding of a part of himself, which stirred her interest deeply; his warmth of spirit; the tender love she felt in him for his people; the fact he was a Waiolama born and bred in Makaniloa; the troubling power he had of conveying without a word that he knew a great deal of what she was thinking and feeling. It was as though she and Kaupena were not new friends, but rather friends of long standing, perhaps even mysteriously through generations.

The young minister stepped forward to deliver his sermon; a sober melancholy settled over the congregation, a melancholy that made them seem quite alien to the happy laughing people gathered outside the church before the service. Lucia did not listen to the sermon but turned her attention to the windows. Through the spray-fogged glass she watched the brilliant landscape; her eyes, now sheltered, could perceive the vivid colors. The sea was an opaque rich blue, the grass at the shore a translucent yellow green, and these colors shimmered together as though mingled in a jewel. As she watched, she went again over the pattern of her life in Makaniloa, which in the last week had shaped itself in her mind: a little house shaded by coconut and mango trees; the sea and mountain-scented air blowing in at the windows; a deep quietness in which the wind sounds and the clashing of palm fronds and the hum of waterfalls were a part; the peace of her own spirit as she boiled a pot for tea or weeded in her garden or washed the linen and hung it on the line, smelling the fresh soapy scent of it; the slow piling up of proper tone for the writing of her great-grandmother's life; the casual timid calls on her Hawaiian neighbors and their friendly welcome; perhaps an occasional ride with Kaupena or Elizabeth up the pastures toward the gap. . . .

Abruptly a Hawaiian girl of about ten brushed past her knees and slipped into the seat next to her. The child carefully arranged her skirts, crossed her legs decorously, and flipped the long dark tresses of her hair so that they fell neatly at her back. She watched the minister intently, seeming to be absorbed in all he had to say. Her eyes, large and sad, glowed in her pale little face; she had the classic Polynesian beauty. Lucia wondered why the girl had come in from the sunshine, why her little throat quivered with emotion. She wanted suddenly to put her arms around the thin shoulders and make the child hers. This was an old familiar ache, and as its pain grew in her the frail pattern of her life-to-be in Makaniloa dissolved. She had left out of it the need of close, warm, human relationship! Next week Kitty would be gone! Without Kitty there would be only Elizabeth and Margaret, absorbed in their own lives. Lucia looked breathlessly around her. There were also these people, but she was the stranger, the outsider. There was no one else on all this great lonely mountainside, so far away from everything! Her breath came short as the panic swelled in her. She gasped slightly. Kitty whispered, "Are you all right?"

"O.K." Lucia managed to mutter. Sternly she held back her tears. But she could not keep the flush from her face or the dizziness from her head. She hated herself for this revolt of the nerves.

The minister announced the closing hymn, and Lucia sang jerkily with the others. By the second verse, she had steadied her voice and imposed a carefully balanced calm upon her mind. The child edged closer to her, peeking as best she could at the hymnal. She held the book down and presently heard the sweet, small tones mingled with her own. Tears came this time in spite of her, but they were happy ones. The child's gesture of friendliness had brought back the possibility of Makaniloa.

The minister spoke a short benediction in English. Then a deacon stepped forward, and leaning his arms comfortably, intimately across the lectern, closed his eyes and intoned a benediction in Hawaiian. His voice filled the large old church with the ring of richly spoken vowels. The congregation straightened up in their pews and lifted their heads, and as they responded, so did Lucia. The prayer was offered to the God of her great-grandmother, the passionate, wrathful, and very human God. He was different from the cold, intellectual God she had grown up to know and who had abandoned her when she had turned to Him. Or, she suddenly wondered, was it she who had abandoned Him in her smallness and incapacity. Her great-grandmother would not have committed that selfish folly.

When Kitty nudged her sharply to point out that the service

was over, the people were already moving slowly from the church, nodding heads and greeting each other. The Hawaiians politely shook hands with the minister and clustered around the deacons to exchange family news and friendly gossip. They smiled shyly at Kitty and Lucia, trying with these smiles and a faint indistinguishable murmur to make them feel at home.

On the threshold, Lucia gazed at the pastures sweeping up the mountain. There was something remote now in the landscape, withdrawn, as though it were sheltering its ancient secrets. The green was cool and crystalline, strangely without warmth, and the rocks a glittering black. The crater was filled with blue and tawny clouds reaching softly down to the ledge from which the waterfalls started their plunge. She had never known so shifting and changing a place.

When they were in the car, Kitty said, "Honestly, Luce, how can you plan to stay here? When there's only this!" And she made a sweeping gesture. "You'll go mad."

Lucia, her face quite pale and her lips tensely drawn, said, "I'll do it somehow. It will be all right. It has to be all right."

After dinner when they were having their coffee on the terrace, Bill proposed that they all drive to Kipahulu Ranch. Margaret said that she had a model coming to pose, and Lucia said that she thought she would take a nap.

Elizabeth urged Lucia, "Come along, dear. You need getting out more than a nap. You've kept rather close these last few days."

Lucia smiled, but a little bitterness welled up in her. "My goodness, people still fussing over me! You know, I'm supposed to be cured now." She sighed and then in good humor said, "I'll tell you a secret. I've decided at last to be myself." She laughed at the puzzled faces peering at her over coffee cups. They had all the doubt and suspicion with which so many had regarded her since her breakdown. The nervous trembling of a faint hysteria pushed up in her. Her voice was shrill. "You look as though that's a terrible thing to say!"

Bill asked tenderly, "And what, dear Lucia, are you other than the delightful, intriguing girl we know, who sometimes sparkles with gaiety and sometimes seems to brood quite charmingly on hidden problems?"

"Perhaps I'll tell you," she said lightly, now able to pull herself away from the threat of hysteria. "But you'll only be bored." She shifted to a grave tone. "I pretended so long for Ted's sake that I'm not always quite sure. That's what's hard. But I think . . ." She laughed. "But you want to know what I really am!" Her eyes glistened as she counted off the points on her fingers. "First, I really like to be alone. Honestly! Second, I don't want to have to be in a cloud of social merriment all the time. Third, I really have a grim temperament, inherited from my missionary ancestors. Fourth and last," she paused to wave her arms dramatically, "I feel the pangs of the modern guilt complex!"

They laughed and Elizabeth said what a dismal person she made herself out to be when she really wasn't.

Kitty hooted noisily. "The modern guilt complex! Behold, the modern man mooning around among his atom bombs and his crackpot ideologies! We're all as guilty as hell. But it doesn't help to brood about it."

Lucia asked gravely, "What can I do to help?"

Bill put in brusquely, "Just be a nice ordinary human being. That's what we need more than anything. After all, you're going to live in Makaniloa, and you won't have to worry. Life is simple here."

"About as simple as it is in the rest of the world," Margaret retorted. "All the tensions are here. As a matter of fact I've just about come to the conclusion that Makaniloa is one jump ahead of the world. Here people have had the emotions and trials of the dispossessed for a hundred years. They know what it is to despair about the future of their race; they know what it is to lose dignity because they can't work out their own salvation."

Bill looked in amazement at his cousin. "Whatever are you talking about!"

"I'm talking about the glorious present. Men rushing from one ideology to another, men jostled in a political stew pot, men dispossessed of their land and things and of dignified identity as human beings. The Hawaiians have known these things for a long time. And they've responded in all the typical human ways—despair, religious fanaticism, war, political agitation, in the eat, drink, and be merry mood."

"Why Margaret!" Elizabeth exclaimed, her delicate face flushed with worry. "You've never said such things before."

"I tried to keep my mouth shut."

"Oh God, Margaret, let me have my simple Makaniloa!" Bill said in mock despair.

"There's a simple Makaniloa too. That's the genius of Hawaii," she said wryly.

Bill stared at her in confusion, then he turned to Elizabeth and Kitty. "'Come on, let's get on our tin horse. It's a beautiful day, and time's a-wastin'."

When they had gone, Margaret said wearily to Lucia, "There are those of us who have to try to make sense out of the mess of things and there are those who want to avoid the heartache. You and I bear the curse of caring, I'm afraid."

Lucia gazed at Margaret. "I wish I had your knowledge of these people. . . . I could even wish I had been born one of them. It's a strange thing that I feel so much at home here."

"I know what you mean. It's something that seems to come right up out of the earth."

"It does."

In her room Lucia stretched out on the chaise longue. It was, she knew, the simple Makaniloa that she needed now. Later on was time enough for complications. She felt her muscles slowly go soft in relaxation, and watching the wind in the misty foliage of the ironwood trees, she drifted into sleep.

She awoke refreshed and with a yearning for the hillside. She dressed in slacks and a bright print blouse, and tied a sweater around her hips. Halfway across the lawn she saw Kaupena coming from the stables. She had a sudden suspicion that he had been watching for her.

"Going for a walk?" he called.

"Yes."

"May I go along?"

"Surely. Maybe you know a good place to go."

"There's a waterfall up a little way."

"I'd love to see it."

He led her to a trail that seemed to go straight up the mountain. When they had walked for some time in silence she asked, "Are we going to the top?"

He laughed. "No. That's a little far. Some day though, we'll ride up there, if you like."

"Oh yes! The crater seems so mysterious."

"This mountain has a power about it."

"I think I've already felt it."

"But when you've lived here all your life and watched it and known it—" He broke off. "How about stopping for a cigarette?"

He lighted a cigarette for her and one for himself.

She sat down on a flat rock. After a few moments, she began tentatively, "We were talking after dinner today. Margaret said Makaniloa is not as simple as it seems."

"You mean the people?"

"Uh huh."

"I guess that's true. You know, people haven't had an easy time here. We look at it and say it's beautiful. We forget it's also hard. But if it were only beautiful, there'd be no spell to it."

"No spell," she repeated softly. She leaned over and crushed her cigarette in the gravel of the trail. Abruptly she asked the question that had been weighing in her mind. "Do Hawaiians feel dispossessed?"

He stamped out his cigarette. "Why shouldn't they? They are."

"And are they unhappy?"

"Some. Some think about it all the time. Others forget—or try to forget. Others are ashamed."

"Ashamed!"

"Yes. There is much shame in a people who have been swallowed up in their own homeland."

"Oh!"

"Just as many are proud."

"They should be proud!" she said fiercely.

"I think, though, we're doomed as a pure race."

"You do!"

"I've come around to accepting it. There are other ways for us. We can mingle our blood with strains that will accept it. We can, in a way, make a new race. Already we see it coming. The part-Hawaiians are people to reckon with now. And they're growing faster than any other group in the territory."

He pulled her up. "The main thing is that we mustn't forget the fine things of our Hawaiian heritage."

She followed him along the trail. "You've thought a lot about it, haven't you?"

"Some of us do."

The trail plunged into a little valley. He took her arm and faced her toward the sunny, wind-swept mountain slope. "Here you see the light and the warmth," he said. "Remember it."

Then he turned and descended the trail into a grove of thickly overhanging pandanus. The wind sound was gone and in its place was the hollow roar of water. The air in the grove smelled of dankness and was green-gray with shadow. "And this," he exclaimed swinging his arm in a broad gesture, "is the dark and the mystery. In all the islands you'll find both. And you'll find it in the Hawaiian people." He looked at her with the expression of one who has offered the core of his thinking. Then abruptly he started off again.

She clung to his hand as he led her over the slippery, mossy rocks of the trail. Presently they reached the waterfall. Sheer green cliffs towered on three sides of them; the water plunged hundreds of feet into a still, dark pool. Lucia gazed up at the small patch of clear sunny sky framed by rock; it seemed remote and unreal. She was oppressed by the dampness and the heavy, overhanging quality of the cliffs. There was something frightening and lonely in the atmosphere, something that was palpable as a seen ghost. "It's eery," she said.

He put his arms about her shoulders. "If you live in Maka-niloa, you'll have to learn to love this sort of thing too."

"I wonder if my great-grandmother ever came here. She writes often of visiting 'her waterfall'."

"Probably. It's the closest to the church."

"She didn't think it was ghostly. She loved it. . . ." She turned in his arm to face him. "Do you think it really could be the one she mentioned?"

He gazed down at her and his eyes grew darker. He stroked her hair softly.

Then slowly and reasonably he said, "I don't know how you'll take it—there's so much dividing us—but I love you."

She started to speak, and he laid his hand across her mouth. "Don't say anything about it now. I'm afraid to know how you feel. Give me a few days, anyhow." He bent down and kissed her cheek.

"We'd better go back," he said. "Wednesday I want to take you to a place much more beautiful than this. We'll have to go part way on horseback. I'll come right after breakfast with the horses."

She had never had such gentle, hesitant love made to her. It was singularly appealing against this background of darkly beautiful landscape, and from one of his race. She knew that if he had pressed her she would have yielded, but he did not want to take her in that way. Before Wednesday there would be time to probe deeply into her mind, her heart. . . .

At nine o'clock on Wednesday he was waiting at the ranch house with the saddled horses. She saw him through the window as she was helping herself to sausages from the breakfast buffet. She ate with an elaborate leisure, and Margaret watched carefully. Presently she said, "Is Kaupena waiting for you?"

"Yes. Why don't we ask him in for coffee?"

"He won't come. I've already asked him. There's something on his mind."

"Uh huh." Lucia cut a sausage into tiny bits, but she did not taste it.

Margaret smeared a piece of toast with poha jam. "He's a fine young man, sensitive, intelligent. Perhaps sensitivity is his great fault; it makes him grope for things he can't quite define."

Lucia took a sip of hot coffee. "Margaret," she said just above a whisper, "the thing I want to do is break down a barrier. We're all putting up barriers these days instead of breaking them down—against ideas, races, nationalities, gods. I want to break down even one little insignificant barrier."

Margaret said quietly, "You'd better go along. He's waiting."

Outside, Kaupena said, "We're going down to an ancient village on the shore. Several of the stone platforms are still there."

"It sounds wonderful," she said and with his help mounted her horse. She trembled a little as she pulled the reins. Events were shaping swiftly and inevitably, and it took all of her courage to remain abreast of them.

They cantered down the road a half mile and then turned abruptly through a pasture toward the sea. Across the channel straight in front of them Mauna Loa and Mauna Kea rose like two blue ghost mountains. Broad yellow-green Makaniloa pastures stretched out on either side of the trail. At the east the pastures were cut off sharply by a waste of old lava flow on which only lichens and a few ferns had managed to grow, and at the west by a forest region that reached down the mountain almost to the sea. The wind swept steadily from the crater gap.

Kaupena held back until he rode at her side. "When I was a kid my grandmother grew gourds. And one year we had two huge ones on a vine. We called one Mauna Loa and the other Mauna Kea. Grandma kept those gourds; she uses them to this day to store dried fish."

"Is she still living?"

"Oh yes. She raised me."

"I haven't met her yet?"

"No, she doesn't get about much. She's pretty old."

"Doesn't she go to church?"

"Not any more. Anyhow, she lives way up the valley. There's no road, and she'd have to walk."

"She lives alone?"

"Uh huh. About once a week I go up and stay with her."

Lucia felt that he was eager for her to know about him; it was necessary that all happening between them should have a sound base. So she asked him about himself, his brothers and sisters, his education, how he liked being a cowboy. At the end of her questioning, he shrugged his shoulders and said he guessed she knew all about him.

She laughed and said she supposed there must be some hidden things. There were always hidden things about people.

He denied it, growing tense and nervous in his denial. Then

he burst out, "Do you think you could—that is, considering I'm what I am and you're what you are—" He cut off his words and spurred Panini to a gallop. All the way to the shore he kept ahead of her.

By the time she reached the beach he had dismounted and tied Panini to a stump. "We have to leave our horses here and walk from now on." His voice was stiff. He pointed, "There it is."

She saw, at some distance down the coast, a small beach of black pebbles abutted on each side by lava cliffs. Back of the beach lay a valley thickly overgrown with hau and coconut trees.

"Can we really get to it?"

"There's a trail. Not a very good one. And it may need some cutting. I brought a cane knife." He unhooked a small knapsack from Panini's saddle and slung it on his back.

A shaggy grove of pandanus trees straggled along the cliff's edge, and he made his way through it, stepping carefully on the ground spongy with rotting fronds. She followed him, listening to the wind lashing the spiny, saw-toothed foliage, which crackled and roared like a rain squall.

"Careful! A puka here!" Kaupena called back to her.

She looked into the hole carved out of lava. Its edge was rimmed with a stunted fern growth, and it seemed to go endlessly into the earth.

His warning somehow restored the ease between them, and she called, "This is a spooky place."

"Yes, it is, kind of. Probably in the old days it was a sacred grove."

She saw a lonely plumeria tree struggling under the thick shade of the puhala. It stretched a few little blossoms toward the sun. She wondered if someone might have had a house there long ago.

"We go down here. Watch your step."

She reached the place he pointed out and saw the trail winding down the face of the cliff. It was just wide enough for one foot at a time, and there was nothing to grasp except the jutting rock. If she fell it would be a straight plunge to the sea, which broke into a violent froth of foam against the lava. Her heart beat harshly for a moment, taking the breath from her, and she wondered if she could possibly make it down there. But he was already fifteen yards or so beyond her and confidently expecting her to follow. She edged her way cautiously down and when she found the footing secure, her courage returned. She could see him far ahead of her now at the bottom. He had taken the knife from the knapsack and was hacking at some entangling branches crossing the trail.

When she reached him, he said, "This stuff grows fast. I was down here six months ago and cut it away. Now look at it!"

After ten minutes of steady hacking, he managed to cut a way through. He slung the knapsack again on his back and took her hand. "We're almost there."

He led her into a small clearing neatly divided by ancient mossy stone walls. At the back a thick grove of tall coconut trees slowly and rhythmically bowed their plumes to the wind. A stream edged by marshy land flowed close to the opposite cliff. A small cluster of kamani trees hung low over the pebbly beach where the stream met the sea. Behind the swampy area a snarl of impenetrable hau reached into the valley as far as one could see.

He walked to the beach, and she followed him and sat on the big drift log that he pointed out to her. The beach glittered with the wetness of the smooth ovoid rocks of which it was made. Waves reached up on it with a frothy roar and retreated in a musical clatter and clinker.

"This was a village. No one has lived here for about sixty years."

She looked at the landscape, trying to imagine the life

that had gone on there, simple life in the midst of a wild remoteness: women beating tapa, men pounding poi or fishing, old men mending nets, old women watching the babies and keeping an eye on the older children playing rowdily in the surf.

"Those smaller enclosures were for houses. In the bigger ones they grew taro. They were able to flood them by a simple irrigation system from the stream."

She envisioned the taro paddies reflecting the blue of the sky and the nodding flashes of coconut plumage. Boys, slender yet sturdily built, waded in them tending the young taro. Small children played on the rock walls, some dangling fishing lines into the paddies.

He went on, interrupting her image, "It's said my family had a place here for fishing. But mostly we lived back up the valley." He began pulling at the knapsack. "I brought along some coffee."

He took out a thermos and opening it, poured her a steaming cup.

"Have a cookie." He offered her a bag of *crème* sandwiches.

"You think of everything." She smiled at him.

They sipped their coffee and munched cookies in silence. She felt the eagerness with which he took in the landscape. His eyes darkened and his body became tense.

"Now!" he said suddenly, jumping from the log. "Our dessert." He went down to where the water washed upon the stones and bending over a big rock began pulling off small shellfish. He brought a handful back. "Have one!"

"What is it?"

"An opihi. Very good. Just push your thumb down into the shell, and he'll come out."

"Is it alive?"

"Of course," he said and laughed at her. "It won't bite you!"

He laid one of the creatures in her hand. The shell was black and fluted. Inside it looked like a small clam.

"Go on. Try it. It's really good. I've got to make a Hawaiian out of you, you know. If you're going to live here." His eyes caught hers briefly, and she saw a hope in them, and it quivered in her.

"Yes," she replied uncertainly. Slowly she pushed her thumb into the cuplike shell. The tiny animal emerged.

"Pop it in your mouth!"

She did so and waited fearfully for the flavor. It was salty and good. A smile spread on her face, and he immediately handed her another.

"Good, yeah?" he asked, with a pidgin intonation.

"Yeah," she sighed happily.

He gathered more opihis, and they ate them, hurling the shells into the sea.

"Come," he said presently. "We've got to explore." He took her hand and led her across the beach toward the kamani grove. "That grove is probably where they hauled their canoes up for shelter. Anyhow, it would make a good place."

In the grove there was an elemental freshness, a purity, and a sense of sharp emotional power compounded from many elements: the waves clattering and roaring on the big, smooth pebbles; the air pungent, salty and cold; the wind coming in unpredictable gusts, one moment whipping the large round kamani leaves and the next allowing them to hang still; the mesh of twisting dark branches fogged by the green foliage light; an animal awareness of shelter from rain and sun and prying eyes. Here was a secret, dark wild place! She folded her arms, clutching her elbows in the palms of her hands. Kaupena had been watching her; she wondered how long, and she felt a flush warming her cheeks and bosom.

"Lucia," he said. "I think you are in love too."

"I was just trying to get the feel of this place. I've never been anywhere quite like it."

He moved a little away from her. A gust of wind swept through the kamani trees and a cloud passed across the sun, shedding a true dusk over the grove. She stepped toward him. He whirled and took her in his arms. For a moment she struggled against him, but she could not resist the crying out within herself.

After he had kissed her mouth, he stroked her hair. "Sunday in church, I turned around. There was pain and fear on your face. In that moment I knew I loved you. You were beautiful and tender and sincere."

"Oh Kaupena, you saw me then!" she muttered, ashamed.

"I had not imagined that I could know love so intensely."

He bent down and gently kissed her neck. She fastened her arms tightly around his shoulders.

"Oh Lucia, my dear!" he whispered. Gently disengaging himself, he slipped off his knapsack and threw it aside. Then removing his jacket he spread it on a spot plushy with many years' falling of kamani leaves. "Here, darling," he said and drew her down beside him.

She lay on the jacket and smiled up at him. He combed her hair with his fingers until it was spread around her head like a halo. He smiled softly, "Ah, you are beautiful!" He touched her cheek, tracing with his fingers its contour and then the contour of her lips. He bent and kissed her with parted mouth. The waves were loud in her ears. The kamani leaves twirled dizzily above his shoulders. Presently she felt the long sweep of her own rising passion, and she could no longer hear the waves or see the leaves. . . .

When they came hand in hand out of the kamani grove, she knew that it had been years since she had felt such quiet happiness. Then as they walked along toward the trail a little nibble of neurotic fear began. She turned to him and said timidly, "Kaupena, do you really love me?"

He cupped his hands about her face and looked deep into her eyes. "Silly!" he said. Then he kissed her, pressing his body close and hard to hers. He whispered, "Remember your date with me. Day after tomorrow. Four thirty at the church."

"Yes, darling." She took his hand, and together they raced along to the cliff's bottom.

When they reached the ranch house it was dusk. At the stables he lifted her from her horse. "Don't forget. Tomorrow I'll take care of the license—my uncle can do it for us. Then Wednesday at the church. I'll not see you until then. Bring Kitty, if you want."

"Wednesday!" she whispered and laid a hand softly on his cheek. He pulled her close and kissed her with a fierceness which startled her. In this embrace there was none of the gentleness that he had shown in the kamani grove. A squall struck the stable, rat-a-tatting on the tin roof. She moved with her own strength against his.

4.

SHEETS of rain slapped the windows and filled the dank church with a roar of melancholy. The light was dim and shadowy, and Joe Waiolama, Kaupena's brother, had to peer closely at the words scribbled in pencil on the slip of paper he held in his hand. He was singing the song he had composed only the night before for the occasion of Kaupena's wedding, and he sent his voice out rich and full into the farthest corners of the church, ringing it triumphantly above the noise of the storm. When he had finished, old Mr. Wakinekona, the retired minister of Makaniloa, read in resonant Hawaiian the lines of the marriage ceremony.

After the benediction, Kaupena kissed Lucia, his wife. He then kissed Margaret and shook hands with the cowboy, Johnny, who had come to stand up with him. He called to Joe who was sitting in one of the deacon's chairs, "Thanks! The song is beautiful."

"I had a feeling when I wrote it that it should be special. This is not just another wedding."

"No, no, it isn't," Kaupena responded nervously. He had been uneasy all through the ceremony about the necessity of leaving Lucia long enough to tell his grandmother of the wedding. She must learn of it from him first.

Now he said to Margaret, "I've got to go on an errand. Take Lucia up to the ranch to get her things, will you, Margaret? I'll come for her in an hour."

"But I have my things, darling," Lucia said. "Don't you

think we'd better be on the way? Margaret can tell them at the house. There's a special note for Kitty on her dresser."

Kaupena said desperately, "Lucia, please try to forgive me. I must have an hour before we go. I'll call for you at the ranch. Margaret, Joe—take care of her for me."

He kissed her and walked swiftly out of the church. She called after him, but he did not turn. He mounted Panini and headed up the valley.

The earth was sodden and the horse's hoofs splashed and slipped along the trail. The foliage dripped heavily, and even though the rain had ceased, the effect was of a shower. He scarcely noticed the wetness; Lucia's face was constantly before his eyes. He saw her puzzlement growing into anxiety. He heard the pleading in her voice as she called after him.

By the time he reached his grandmother's, anger had full sway in him. For one stubborn old lady to fill the beginning of his married life with such bitterness!

He tied Panini under the lean-to and sloshed his way through the thick grass to the house. The door stood open and he saw her sitting on the floor weaving lauhala. She leaned close over her work, her gold-rimmed glasses resting on the end of her nose, her eyes peering intently, and her chin jutting out sharply. Her knobby, blunt fingers were not so deft now as when as a small boy he had watched them on rainy days. His anger was lessened somewhat by the tender pity he felt for the frail old woman.

"Grandma!" he called. "I have come to confess something to you."

She looked up from her work. "What naughtiness now? Come in." Pleasure glowed in her eyes and in the large smile curving her mouth.

He sat on the floor close to her. "Grandma, you must forgive me. You're not going to like what I am about to say." He wished he could speak to her in English. It might be easier to express himself in the language in which she herself was not at perfect ease, and it might not sound so bald to her.

"What is it, Kaupena?"

"Grandma, I am married. I got married just a half hour ago."

The old woman seemed stunned. Then she began to breathe heavily, struggling as though for air. "Whom?" she whispered hoarsely.

"Lucia Gray," Kaupena said and prepared himself for the storm.

It was a minute or two before it broke, but when it did, he thought he had never seen her more violent. He was concerned that she might be taken ill and watched anxiously as she stood up and, trembling in every limb, shrieked a steady flow of Hawaiian at him. Much of what she said he could not understand, but he did hear that he had betrayed his familiy, Makaniloa, and her. He had betrayed the purity of his race. He broke in to remind her that his mother had been half white. She disregarded his words and went on, almost in tears. She cried that Hawaiian culture must be preserved; there is so little left, and those who know must do everything to perpetuate it. Her life had been dedicated to this, and she had hoped he would help her, carry on for her after her death. The Hawaiians will come again into their own, and when they do they must have the ancient knowledge, to understand themselves. How could he help her when he had married a white woman who knew nothing and cared nothing about Hawaii?

Finally, pale and exhausted, she reached the close of her tirade. He helped her to a chair. "Grandma," he said softly, "it will not be so bad as you think. Lucia really loves Hawaii."

"Perhaps. But she can never understand. It is not in her blood. She will wean you away." She sighed. "The words of the old priest may be true. 'The hibiscus shall grow, the coral shall spread and stretch out its branches, but man shall cease.' "

"I must go now," he said. "Come to see her when we return. When you know her, it will be all right."

Lokalia stared in silence.

"Good-by," he said.

She continued to stare, and he knew by the subtle shift of lines in her face that she was thinking, planning. He worried briefly. She could be a vengeful old lady.

"Take care of yourself," he warned. "We shall be at the Fernandez' house in Hana for a week. Then we will come home to the old house."

When he had gone she rose slowly and wearily from the chair and shuffled into the kitchen. There she spooned poi into a small wooden bowl and took an orange from the window ledge. She tied these into a scarf and went out the back door. In the garden she added two gardenias to her bundle. Glancing uneasily at the sky, she started on the path that led to the back of the valley.

Heavy clouds laid a premature dusk along the tree-shadowed way, and she stumbled uncertainly among the wet stones and mud. The sound of the waterfalls echoed in a deep hollow tone. Presently her breath came short and painfully, and there were aches in her chest and head. She sat down on a stump for several moments. Her anger was rising again, this time anger that the life force should be growing frail within her. Goaded by it, she started out again. The valley narrowed and the pali cliffs rose straight up on either side. At this spot seven men with their arms stretched out, fingers touching, could span the valley. She approached the pool, dark and tensely placid, into which the falls descended. At its edge rose a slender shaft of rock twice her height. She knelt near the stone and, untying the scarf, laid the bowl of poi, the orange, and the gardenias in offering. After mumbling some verses in Hawaiian, she rose and walked three times around the shaft of rock. Then she stopped and, staring into the darkness beyond the rock, beyond the cliff, gave way to the bitterness in her heart.

The Waiolama house had long been unoccupied. Vines completely shut in the lanai and crawled luxuriantly over the roof. Grasses reached up to the window ledges, poking under the sills stiff tendrils which in time withered away to straw. At the back a mango tree spread its thick, shadowing foliage over the kitchen ell. The sense of isolation was complete; it was as though the trees and the grasses had claimed for their own this patch of land, this bit of wooden structure.

"Here it is, darling!" Kaupena said. He watched Lucia closely; her lips parted slightly and she stared, her face quite void of expression.

"Oh!" she breathed.

"It looks rather decrepit. But inside it isn't so bad." He strode forward and yanked away the vines festooning the entrance to the lanai. He mounted the stairs and continued to pull at the vines until he had cleared a large part of the balustrade. Then he put his key in the lock and opening the door, stepped in. The floor was littered with dirt and droppings and the shells of dead insects. The old koa furniture was dull and shabby under a layer of dust. Why hadn't he thought to have someone come in and clean it up?

He went back to the door. "Come on in, Lucia. It's pretty dirty now. I'm sorry."

She walked slowly up the stairs. Her body had the quiet melancholy of a figure in a Chinese landscape painting.

He saw the room suddenly as it must be through her eyes: the heavy sturdily built furniture, much too massive for the small room; the commodious chairs built for large people; the great table in the middle; the hikie filling one end and large enough to seat fifteen people; through the archway the long dining table and the cumbersome chairs of koa wood. Everything was dingy, the hikie cover an ugly faded brown, the furniture ashy with dust, the gray walls specked with lizard droppings and hung with webs, the cracks of the floor lined with little ant piles of dirt.

Together they walked across the threshold. She moved to the large round table and traced with her fingers a design in the dust. "The wood is beautiful, isn't it?"

"It's old. My mother and sister took good care of it. They used to oil it all the time."

She went to a door in the opposite wall and opening it, looked in. "A bedroom with a bed!" she exclaimed. "Such a big bed!"

"It can be ours," he said and hoped for some sort of warm response.

"I have a funny feeling that I'm trespassing," she whispered.

"Trespassing!" he repeated in amazement.

"Yes, as though someone still lived here in the dust and the dead wasps. There's a presence."

He frowned at her. "No one has lived here for five years—ever since my sister went to Honolulu."

"I've always been good at imagining things," she said, and laughed. "When I was a child I imagined that a whole family lived on our side porch. But there is something here. Can't you feel it yourself?"

He put his arm around her. "I can't. But if there is something, I'll drive it out for you."

She laid her head on his shoulder for a moment and then pulled away. She walked through the open archway leading to the dining room, paused to look at an old photograph on the wall, and finally went on into the kitchen. The mango branches scoured the roof with noises at times hollow and scratchy and at other times shrill like frightened birds. She leaned upon a window sill and gazed out at the cluster of trees and beyond to the soft green slope of the pasture.

As he watched her he wished that his grandmother were not so stubborn. She could have had the house ready for them, flowers on the tables, supplies in the shelves, sheets on the bed. Twice now because of that old woman he had failed Lucia. He rubbed his fingers together anxiously and decided that he would have to ask Bill Perkins for a room for the night.

Lucia, gazing from the kitchen window, was seeing two other homecomings. The first that trailed through her mind was the bright morning on which she and Ted had returned from their Cuban honeymoon. With great pride he had taken her to the apartment he had decorated on East Sixty-ninth Street. The apartment had been just like Ted, or like the personality Ted wanted to affect. It was gay with color, one wall painted chartreuse, another pink, another a solid panel of glass brick. On the chartreuse wall hung a reproduction of a Picasso abstraction, and on the pink an original Miro. The furniture was sleek and low slung. She had admired it for Ted's sake, kissed him, and yearned for the shabby old New England furniture in the Connecticut farmhouse of her childhood. She recalled the first evening in the apartment and the persistent feeling she had that she was living on a page in one of the ultra home-design magazines.

The second homecoming in her thoughts was one in Makaniloa. How vividly her great-grandmother had described it—the landing on the beach, the rough walk across the pebbles and up the lava cliff to the neatly sanded yard with a stone wall enclosing it. Her husband had taken her arm as they entered the house, which was nothing but a great long room, neatly thatched and smelling sweetly of dry grass. The interior was filled with the muffled sound of waves and wind. They had clasped their hands, bowed their heads, and asking the Hawaiians to join them, prayed for God's blessing on the house and on the work they would do together in Makaniloa. Afterward three Hawaiian women had come forward and pressed upon them clean new mats woven of lauhala, calabashes filled with dried fish, and goats' meat and poi. They had then shown the missionaries the little shelter at the back where the food should be stored in calabashes hung from the rafters, and beside it the outdoor oven. After Lucia and Ezra had put away their boxes of clothes, household utensils, books, and their precious small store of flour, sugar, lard, and seeds with which to make a garden, they had walked out together, looking at every inch of the plot of land which had been given to the mission. They spoke of the spot where the church should be, the church that was to be built of coral and stone and that would be sturdy enough to stand for generations to the glory of God.

And now here was she, Lucia Waiolama, homecoming in Makaniloa, feeling this flow of the past into the present and wondering what the pattern of the future would be for her. She hoped for simplicity and quietness and above all that she would grow in her sense of at-homeness in Makaniloa.

"Lucia, Lucia!"

She turned. "Yes, Kaupena."

"Let's go over to Julia Kaneloa's. She'll find someone to help us clean the place."

"Why don't we do it ourselves?"

"We've got to go all the way down to Kitayama's Store to buy sheets and groceries. There's nothing in this house. My sister certainly cleaned it out."

"It'll be a nice place when it's fixed. The furniture is of beautiful wood."

He looked at her with deep gratitude.

In the car he said, "Julia is our nearest neighbor. By the path through the woods it's only a quarter of a mile. But by car it's a mile."

"Is she related to you?"

"In a way. You see my mother only had three kids. And I

was taken by my grandmother, and my sister went to school in Honolulu. That left only Joe at home. Julia has a lot of kids. She gave my mother one, a little girl—who died later. Julia's only twelve years older than I am, but she's kind of like a mother to me. We kids were always back and forth between the houses. But my grandmother always wanted me with her. She was lonely. So I didn't get in on the fun so much."

Lucia envied the easy coming and going of such a childhood. "It must be wonderful, growing up in Makaniloa!"

"In a way it is. Of course we miss a lot—good schools and movies and such things— Here's Julia's!" He turned into a narrow roadway leading up to a clump of mango trees in which could be seen a stained tin roof. Halfway up they passed a broken-down truck by the roadside. It had been there for years, the grass grown up through the engine and a sapling twisting its way through the spokes of a wheel. Three small boys played on it. "Hi, Kaupena!" they called.

"Hi!" he called. Then to Lucia, "They're Julia's kids."

In the Kaneloa yard they saw Julia and her mother-in-law seated in the grass. A few yards behind them were the steps of the unpainted, shabby wooden cottage, the front masked by a thick growth of blossoming hibiscus shrubs, orange croton, and plumes of ti. At Julia's left stood a rusted, smoke-stained ten-gallon can. In front of her was a battered kettle of water. She was taking freshly boiled taro from the can and dipping it in the water, slipping off the peelings. Then she handed the taro to her mother-in-law, who with an opihi shell did the final scraping of the vegetable.

"Hello, Kaupena!" Julia called. She was a large woman with a luxuriance of black hair caught in a loose bun at her neck. A bruised and tattered hibiscus was thrust into the bun. Her skin, a clear golden brown, gleamed with perspiration. Her mother-in-law was a thin old lady with wrinkled yellow flesh;

she wore metal-rimmed glasses on the end of her nose, and her lower lip was thrust out in such a way as to give her a concentrated look.

Julia said, "So this is your wife!" Her voice rang with welcome.

"Yes," Kaupena answered, getting out of the car.

Lucia followed him, emotion thick in her throat and moist in her eyes.

"So at last!" Julia cried. Then she laughed heartily. "You know, we thought he never was going to get married. He's taken out all the girls in Makaniloa."

"Mrs. Kaneloa," Kaupena said to the mother-in-law. "This is my wife, Lucia."

"Have a piece of taro?" Mrs. Kaneloa held out something that looked like a gray boiled potato.

"Try it," Kaupena said.

"It's better made into poi or mashed and fried," Julia said.

Lucia bit into it. It seemed not to have much flavor, and the texture was clinging and sticky.

Kaupena was on the ground beside Julia. Chickens crowded close and noisily pecked at the peelings; muscovy ducks, more timid, kept aloof with silent dignity. Three lean dogs came as close as the mother-in-law would allow. Every now and again she would wave her arms at them and cry shrilly, "Go 'way!" A fat tortoise-shell cat slept unconcernedly on the tin roof of a shed, and three pigs rooted in a small stone enclosure. A little boy of about three came from the house and sat gravely on Kaupena's knee.

Julia said, "Sit down, Mrs. Waiolama. We'll be through here in a minute."

"Call her Lucia," Kaupena said. "She's part of the family now."

"May I help?" Lucia asked.

"No. We're almost pau. Thanks," Julia replied. Then to Kaupena, "When are you going to move in?"

"I'd planned to today. But you should see the place. It's filthy! That's one reason I came over. Do you think Mrs. Tomita would be willing to come up today and clean it for us?"

"If you hadn't been so secretive about this wedding, we'd have had it all fixed up for you."

"I know," Kaupena said, and blushed.

"I'll get Mrs. Tomita, and go over and help her. Grandma can take care of Georgie."

"Lucia and I have to go to Kitayama's. That'll take some time. But we'll be back to help. There's absolutely nothing in that house! Not even sheets or pillows! My sister took everything."

As they talked, the little boy timidly approached Lucia. She held out her arms, and after much hesitation he came and sat on her knee. He saw the moonstone brooch she wore on her blouse and with his small first finger he delicately touched it, feeling the surface, tracing the outline. Then he looked up at her and his solemn face broke into a smile. "Hello!" she whispered and smiled back at him.

"Allo!" he said and laughed merrily, clapping his hands together.

"Georgie likes you," Julia said. "He's always been kind of shy."

Lucia embraced the child lightly and laid her cheek against his. She wondered for a few agonizing moments how he would take this. But he bubbled with laughter and threw his arms around her neck.

"Well, for heaven's sake!" Julia said. "Look, Grandma, at our boy."

Mrs. Kaneloa peered up over the rim of her glasses and frowned. "You'll catch his cold," she said gruffly.

Lucia released the child and he ran off to chase one of the

dogs. Mrs. Kaneloa is rejecting me, she thought, and Julia and Georgie are accepting me. Is that the way it will be always, some friendly, some not? She remembered then that Kaupena had a grandmother. She had not come to the wedding. She felt the sharp, hurting separateness of an alien. She wanted suddenly to escape from the barriers rising around her into the protection of her own house.

"Kaupena," she said urgently, "we'd better get started. There's a lot to do if we're going to sleep in that house tonight."

"Yeah," he replied and jumped up. "Julia, off with you to Mrs. Tomita's." He took her arm and pulled at her.

Julia laughed. "I'll go right now and get that old Japanee lady out of her washtubs." Slowly and gracefully she rose, pulled her muumuu more decorously about her, put a plump, finely shaped hand to the bun at the back of her neck and deftly pushed in the hairpins.

"We'll drive you down."

"O.K. You wait. I go get my bag so I can buy some bread."

He looked at her with mock solemnity. "If you spend the whole morning gossiping in that store, I'll never forgive you."

"O.K. O.K.!" she said in a mollifying tone. "You every time suspect me."

"You're a kanaka wahine. I know what they do."

They both laughed, and Julia went into her house while Lucia and Kaupena sauntered toward the car. Lucia studied Kaupena's face as she said, "I hope when we're settled that your grandma will come to call."

A flush spread over his cheeks and sternness came into the lines around his mouth. "Yeah," he said. "She'll come down to see us. I'll go get her."

Mrs. Tomita and Julia worked hard and by nightfall the

house was clean and ready. Only the musty odor of the long shutting persisted and a cloudiness etched the windows facing the sea. At dusk Mrs. Kaneloa came shuffling through the dim path in the woods carrying steaming laulaus, poi, and half a coconut cake. She laid them on the kitchen table, smiled fleetingly, and shuffled out again.

When their friends had been thanked and had gone, Lucia set the table with glasses and forks, and she and Kaupena sat down next to each other. They clasped hands under the table.

Presently he said, "The laulaus are getting cold."

She drew her hand from his and started peeling down the ti leaves until she exposed the smoking pork and fish.

"I thought Mrs. Kaneloa disliked me."

"She disliked the idea of you. That's the trouble with some of these old Hawaiians. They get ideas and people mixed up. I guess it's from the old days. People stood for ideas, and ideas were vague with nothing written down."

She ate her laulau, but hardly tasted the rich flavor of it. She was capturing the feeling of this house. Restlessly her gaze shifted from Kaupena, to the garden, to the strange things, not yet hers, in the kitchen.

"Shall I turn on the lights?" he asked.

"No. I like the dusk. . . . It's funny; I still feel as though we were trespassing." She laughed to show him she was teasing. "Are you sure this is your father's house?"

"Did Julia or anyone say it was not my father's house?"

"No."

"Well, darling, what's wrong?"

"I just felt something invisible—something intangible!"

She was close enough to feel him tremble a little. She asked lightly, "Is there a ghost?"

"There was an old ghost. It was laid long ago by my grandmother."

"Maybe he's gotten up again. With a stranger in the house. Perhaps your grandmother . . ."

"Please, darling, let's not talk about her tonight."

She wondered at the mystery and how far she dared probe it.

She could see from the window a dark red cloud hanging over the crater. "It looks as if the mountain is erupting."

He turned to see it. "Uh huh."

She rose and stretched her arms. Then swiftly she cleared the table and put the remains of the cake in a cupboard.

They moved through the now dark house into the green-gray light of the lanai. She sat on the step below him and leaned against his knee.

"I'm beginning to know what I feel about this house. You remember what you said—that day you took me up to the waterfall—about the light and the dark in Hawaii? This house stands where those two meet. That's why it was so troubling at first."

He moved his fingers tenderly across her cheek. "I think you may be right, darling."

The next day Kaupena returned to work. But in the afternoon instead of going directly home, he felt he must go to his grandmother. From his boyhood there had been times when he was forced to puzzle out the complicated emotional structure which on occasions grew up between him and Lokalia. Because she was a grandmother, she indulged him, yet she expected everything of him. He both loved and hated her. He loved her tenderness and her pride in Hawaiian things, and he hated her anger and her stubbornness and the way she had of making him feel humble and inadequate.

He found Lokalia drowsing on a mat in the sun. The warm yellow light poured down upon her frail, transparent skin and shadowed deeply the skull structure, all too apparent with age.

He laid his hand gently on her arm and called softly, "Grandma, Grandma!"

She opened her eyes; they watered in the brilliance of the light. "Kaupena?" she asked. "It's hard to see—so bright."

"Yes, Grandma."

She yawned and stretched her arms wide, flexing her fingers. Then slowly and painfully she sat up. "The sun is good. It takes my aches away. Come in, have something to eat."

"Not now. I came to tell you we are back."

"Oh!" she exclaimed, and her face darkened. "I had almost forgotten."

"We have moved into the old house," he persisted doggedly. "And I want to take you down for dinner some evening."

"So you want me to come to dinner! With her!" Her voice was gray. "How long do you think you will be staying there? How long do you think she'll stand it? You will be moving away to please her. Going to Honolulu; going to the mainland. I can see it."

He felt her mounting excitement, and he did not know how to stem it. "Just come and meet her, Grandma. Honestly, she is not what you think. She loves Makaniloa; she had decided to live here before I asked her to marry me."

"And that house!" Lokalia continued. "You know a kahuna lived there before your mother and father. They had to have it blessed before they moved in. You are another family. If you don't . . ." she trailed off ominously.

"I do not believe in that stuff!"

"Already she has worked on you. So you do not believe any more! So you cannot remember all the people who have done what you are doing and suffered. The bad luck!"

"Well, if you are afraid to call on us there," he said, studying her face, "let me bring her here to call on you."

"Afraid!" she stormed. "You try to mock me! You will

learn. Living in that kahuna's house. I see what will happen. She will leave you for a haole man. Oh, I see it so clearly. A white man!"

He rose and staring down at her exclaimed in English, "You're one crazy old woman!"

5.

IN THE evenings when supper was over and after the dishes were clean and on their shelves, Lucia slipped from her daytime dress into one of the two old muumuus she had found laid away in a chest drawer. The muumuus were simple garments with round necks large enough to slip the head through and with loose three-quarter sleeves; their skirts hung straight and ample to the floor. When dressed she flipped her hair into a casual knot on top of her head and taking her knitting, curled up on the hikie.

Kaupena could be certain that the moment she was comfortably in the rhythm of her knitting, she would glance tenderly at him and say, "Now, darling, I want to hear more about you and Makaniloa. There's so much for me to get caught up on."

He enjoyed talking, often gesturing in vivid pantomime. He spoke of Makaniloa first in terms of his university studies, explaining to Lucia that the sociologists had called his home a racial haven.

"A racial haven!" Lucia murmured. "It sounds nice—like something hidden and sweet and safe."

He explained that it meant a place where the Hawaiians could live securely in the old ways, fishing, growing taro, practicing the ancient religions and magical beliefs. Except for working a month or two on the roads or at the ranch to earn the little bit of money they needed for clothing and tobacco and certain foods, they could avoid the shackling ways of the modern economic system, and keep the old, warm-spirited, neighborly, communal methods. The sociologists' term implied a kind of escapism, he said. Rising to stride back and forth across the room, he rejected this. He knew that the people of Makaniloa were not escapists or dreamers. They accepted life as they found it—they loved all its possibilities for happiness and gaiety and they brooded in the despair that had first come upon their race more than a century ago when missionaries and seamen had told them that their ancient way of life was primitive and degrading. They still suffered from the wound of that hour when the governing of Hawaii passed out of their hands. They planted the earth of Makaniloa, fished in its seas, listened to the stories in its wind. The old people talked on the long, warm afternoons of the future of their race.

"No," he said, "we're not escapists! We're simply making the best of the situation into which we were born." And he added that perhaps they seemed escapist because they had the ability to draw from the commonplace of human existence a heady drink that was deeply satisfying. They fished and danced, sang and prayed, ate and died, with a gusto which not all their despair could submerge.

Although Kaupena told Lucia a great deal of Makaniloa, there were some things he reserved. He could not think how to reveal to her the religious fervor that lived in many of the people, how they often practiced two faiths, one Christian and the other Hawaiian or Buddhist. In Makaniloa the supernatural was close to man. Records told that the gods had visited the island many times. Those ancient memories persisted among the people and haunted the stone walls, the curious boulders, and a few of the groves in the landscape. It was inevitable that Lucia would learn in time of this, but she must learn gradually. She would hear at a party or a picnic someone telling an "experience." Each experience would stir memories, and presently another voice would tell another tale. As the storytelling progressed, excitement would rise and the very fact of living would take on a special significance. For weren't these peole witnesses to events which proved a renewed touch with the gods?

Persons of unimpeachable character had had experiences. Old Mr. Clarke had often heard chanting and drumming when he passed the *heiau* late at night; sometimes he went out specially to hear it and refresh his touch with the past. Mrs. Wakinekona had seen repeatedly a dark dog walking down a certain path, a dog that did not exist in Makaniloa. Mrs. Kaneloa had been seated one evening on a rock wall that followed along an ancient pathway to the beach and had sensed a procession of the ghostly ones passing by. She had felt the breeze of their passage and had heard whispers and footfalls. But she had seen nothing. Kaupena himself, when he was alone one day in the forest, had seen a figure which he was sure was more than just a wind-blown drift of rain and fog moving among the trees. In lonely, remote places like Makaniloa where people are few, a man makes a companion of his gods, and the gods have ways of responding. Even Lucia, a stranger, had felt the presence of the old kahuna in the house.

Kaupena kept one other fact from her—Pohaku Lono, that rock dedicated to Lono, god of rain and the harvest. He dared not speak of it and see the corners of her mouth crease delicately in amusement, or possibly scorn at this bit of folklore taken so seriously. The rock was supposed to have been left by the god Lono during one of his visitations in the valley where Lokalia's house now stood. It was a mark of special grace. After the coming of the missionaries the stone was for many years neglected, though occasionally, furtive offerings were left by those who had prayed to no effect to the Christian God. Finally old Hoopai again openly performed the ancient rituals at Pohaku Lono. At his death he had passed this duty on to Lokalia, and she was the leader of a small group who found comfort in paying reverence to the sacred rock. When he was fourteen, Kaupena had been initiated into the simple mysteries of the ritual and had learned the beautiful chant to the God Lono. He knew that it was his grandmother's wish to pass her leadership on to him. And he wanted this leadership. In spite of the waves of skepticism, which racked him at times, he felt that there was a significance for the people of Makaniloa in the cult of Lono. The first time he had been allowed to chant before the rock alone had been a night of wind and storm; the torches had flickered low and two of them had been quenched. There had entered into him then a sense of dedication to his race, and a firm belief that in the Hawaiian ways there were qualities that should be preserved.

On the fourth evening Lucia said abruptly, "Now, my darling, I've got to know about you yourself! How did you live as a little boy?"

"I've been talking about myself all along. Haven't you had enough?"

"Don't pretend, Kaupena," she teased. "You love to do this talking."

"I warn you! I'll probably be silent for months after this binge. That's the way I work. Words suddenly cease to have meaning." He smiled to soften what he knew would be true.

"When you are silent, it will be time for silence."

Her words were calm and brave, but he thought he detected a slight tremor in her body. Was the loneliness of this place already eating into her? He moved to the hikie and put his arm about her. "My earliest memory is of something naughty I did. Grandmother says it happened when I was four. She had a chest in which she kept all her sacred things, and I was forbidden ever to touch it. Naturally I had to see what was in it. . . ."

So vivid was his recollection that he could even yet feel the tingle of his finger tips as he dipped a hand into the forbidden chest; then suddenly the giant form of his grandmother descended upon him, her eyes round and wide and wrathful, her mouth cruel with scolding. And he had fled to the woods. There he hid all the night, living in terror of ghosts and beasts. He must have fallen asleep from exhaustion, for the next memory he had was of being cradled in Lokalia's arms and comforted with her kisses and caresses.

He had early become aware that his grandmother was an unusual person, that she had a force which commanded other people's devotion and respect—and even at times, fear. Throughout his childhood he had heard the soft whispers, "Your Tutu is not like other people. She knows about the old things. She has mana." He grew up on her passionate faith in Hawaiian culture, a faith which concentrated the energies of her nature and filled her with plans for reviving the ancient pride and reshaping the old ways for modern use. If she suspected that a man held Hawaiian customs lightly or derided them in any way, she poured out a vengeful hate upon him. Side by side with this capacity for deep hatred was the natural tenderness with which she regarded people and the generosity with which she shared everything she had. If to some she seemed inconsistent, almost dual in her personality, loving one moment and hating the next, Kaupena knew that underneath there was always reason for her love and her hate. Thus he was bound to her because, from living with her most of his life, he had slowly learned to understand the pattern of her psychology. What had seemed difficult and mysterious in his boyhood had in time grown clear.

He painted for Lucia the boyhood evenings spent in isolation with Lokalia. The house was too far up the valley for him to go anywhere after dark. So he never came home after school until dusk, making with his friends long detours to the beach for opihis or swimming, or up the mountain for mountain apples or bananas. At suppertime he and Lokalia sat on the floor on a clean mat, before them a calabash of poi, a dish of fish or pork, a bowl of cold rice, some bananas or oranges or mangoes, and pilot crackers. They helped themselves with their fingers, dipping from the common dishes. If there were guests, Lokalia cooked laulaus and sweet potatoes, and made coconut pudding, and on the eating mat she would spread fresh ti leaves and hibiscus flowers. But it was very seldom that they had guests at night. People did not like walking up the valley in the dark.

After supper Lokalia would move to the cushioned softness of the hikie. From there she directed him in putting away the remains of their meal and then in gathering certain objects to be explained in the hour of instruction that always came after dinner. She had an exciting way of teaching, revealing the ancient lore as though it were a precious secret. Always she bade him light a candle for this period—not the kerosene lamp. They sat together on the old-fashioned lauhala hikie with the candlelight guttering uneasily between them, and outside the wind of Makaniloa blustering around the house. The very setting added to the tone of mystery. She taught him the sacred words of the genealogy chant and how to intone them properly. And as he learned from the chant of the exploits of his ancestors, he grew in pride and began to hold his head higher. He kept himself a little aloof from his school friends. The story sprang up that he was becoming like his grandmother, different from others. This filled him with further pride.

To Lucia he laughed and confessed, "Most of this pride was rubbed away when I went to the university. After all, what is a genealogy chant in a modern world that demands personal achievement of a man?"

On those candlelit evenings, Lokalia also taught him herb lore, showing him the leaves and fruits of different plants and making him memorize their names and their properties. She told him the secret Waiolama recipe for fish bait and stood over him as he awkwardly tried to make it. She said that with this bait he could cast his line in the midst of twenty others, and that the fish would choose to bite only at his hook. She taught him weather signs in the clouds, in the shifting winds, in the scent of the air, and the look of foliage on the trees. And she showed him the stars and pointed out those which would guide him at night on the sea or on the mountain.

On Sundays Lokalia insisted that they go to church. Only after he had gone off to the university and her legs had become filled with pain had she stopped her regular attendance. Kaupena liked to go to church because it was the center of most of the children's parties, and because he enjoyed the singing and the praying. After the service he and Lokalia invariably went to a friend's home for dinner. After dinner he and the children of the house were free to go fishing or swimming, or whatever they might choose to do. Lokalia brought to church her big lauhala basket in which she had put, along with her sewing and gifts for their hosts, his blue jeans, so that he would not ruin his good suit on these Sunday afternoon adventures.

Thus in the slow, peaceful hours of two or three evenings Kaupena spoke to Lucia of his life with his grandmother. He still left out many of the inner things. He did not tell her of that strain of withdrawal and melancholy which had troubled him all his life, making him feel that there was something abnormal about him. He enjoyed being alone for long periods of time, going up on the mountain and lying somewhere in the tall ferns, watching the clouds shift from form to form and hearing the wind's roar in the upper sky. Or he went out in his canoe and casting a line over the side, would promptly forget about it. And he would sit until he felt himself blending with everything, the extinction of his self in the blueness of sea and sky, in the sounds of wind and water.

He could not speak of the melancholy which suddenly came upon him at parties and picnics and which made him shun them often. He could never quite understand just what brought on the melancholy, but it usually struck him as sharply as a blow, forcing him to withdraw and become the watcher. His mind would dwell upon the strain of sadness running through the lives of the party makers—the illness, the death, the confusion or despair, which in one form or another had blighted the lives of each of them.

And he did not reveal to Lucia the absorption in the physical he had felt from the time he was ten until his university days. As a boy he had proudly watched his muscles grow and had exercised carefully to develop all parts of his body. In swimming and canoe paddling and hiking he could outdistance any of his friends. There was a fine exhilaration in expressing the power of his body. As adolescence progressed, this sense of power became subtly intermingled with his yearning for a girl, and for a while he was upset by what seemed a decline in his physical strength. His body felt cramped by this one restriction, and not only his dreams but also the feelings of his waking hours were turbulent.

The strain ended easily and naturally on a night after a beach picnic. He led a girl named Abigail to a hidden spot behind a rock. As she opened her dress to him, his course became excitingly clear, and he took her, exerting his strength in this final triumphant way. He had imagined in his boyishness that he now understood the fullness and the power of manhood.

Reluctantly he kept from Lucia the very core of his being— his sense of dedication to the re-endowment of his people, his conviction that the path of their future lay in the intermingling of ancient ways with the new. Although he loved Lucia because she was as she was, he loved her too for the children he wanted of her, children who with their mingled white and Hawaiian blood would know how to blend the old and the new, who would understand the subtle, complicated forces of the modern world, itself suffering from the clash of cultures. Their children would be taught to preserve Hawaiian strains. But it was too soon for Lucia to grasp this. She must understand first what living in Makaniloa meant.

Finally he said, "Well, now you know all about my boyhood."

She smiled faintly and knit her fingers together. The lamp glowed on her hair, bringing out the rich streaks of red and gold and brown. Her eyes were shadowed so that he could not see the expression which might be in them.

Finally she spoke, "Well, darling, I guess you grew up mostly in the dark part, didn't you?"

He trembled visibly. That she should say this, notwithstanding all he had kept from her!

Lucia turned over in her mind the picture Kaupena had revealed to her and the more she mused upon it, the more troubled she became by what he must have left out. For the picture seemed entirely one of background, hazed slightly with a faint smoke of romanticism. Nothing was etched strongly and firmly in the foreground; there was little of sturdy tangibility, or of conflict, or of pain, which she knew was a part of life anywhere. Perhaps Kaupena saw life in this removed fashion and that was why he had a disconcerting way of slipping through her fingers.

Consequently one afternoon when she saw Margaret's car coming up the road, she was pleased. Here was someone she could talk to.

They walked arm in arm up the stairs and sat down in the old rattan chairs. "The countryside is getting curious about you," Margaret told her. "You haven't come out often enough for them to know what you're like."

"And I'm curious about them! We've been so busy here with repairs on the house that the only people I know are Julia and her family, and of course Johnny and Joe. Dear old Joe, I'll have you know, is sewing drapes for me. He says he should be doing the painting, but as he can't do that drapes are the next best."

"Joe is a remarkable guy," Margaret said thoughtfully. "I've never known him to speak bitterly of his injury. Yet somehow I feel his songs have a great sorrow."

"I've felt that too." Lucia chose her words slowly and carefully. "It's as though an undertone of sadness somehow makes his happiness deeper."

Margaret lit a cigarette and held it in trembling fingers. "I have always seen Joe as a symbol of the Hawaiian race. With his legs gone, he cannot move forward. So he settles down and draws on the music and friendliness within him, and makes himself loved. That's what all wise Hawaiians do."

"And the unwise ones?"

Margaret shrugged her shoulders. "But I really came here to talk about you. Lucia dear, are you getting along all right? You aren't too lonely up here?"

Lucia examined Margaret's face. Why should she be concerned? There must be something hidden! She spoke directly, "I've been trying to decide what kind of a feeling I have. In many ways it's very peaceful. When I weed in the garden and feel the sun hot on my back and hear the wind in the ironwoods, I have a sense of great peace. And then when I go in the house, I feel a sense of—of waiting! And of being watched! It makes me restless. Then maybe I go over to Julia's and have a cup of coffee with her. She always fixes me up in no time."

"I suppose you are in a way—" Margaret fumbled for her thought—"waiting for all these new experiences to grow mellow."

"There's so much escaping me. Kaupena's told me a lot, yet there's so much I don't know. There's a rhythm I can't fall in with."

"These things all take time."

"Sometimes I go down by my great-grandmother's grave. I sit there, shutting my eyes very tight, and wish hard for her insight."

"Perhaps you're trying too hard. Just let Makaniloa move in and take you over. She will when the time is ripe."

"The start of my life here happened so easily, so naturally.

I knew the rhythm then. Somehow I've fallen out of step. It frightens me a little, because I never seem sure of what I do or say."

Margaret tossed her cigarette out onto the lawn. Then she rose and went to Lucia, taking her hand. "Think, Lucia, of what you are doing! Uprooting yourself from all that you have known! Give yourself time! Things are always apt to be easy at first, before one understands all the factors."

"There are roots enough here for me. Don't forget that."

"I know. . . ."

In the next two weeks while she worked on the house, she was able to forget for a while her uncertainty. The house was becoming hers, although there were still strange moments, particularly when she woke in the middle of the night and the wind was blustery, which brought back the first feeling she had had—that of trespassing. One night she told Kaupena of this, and he had become unexpectedly angry, telling her that she was worse than a superstitious kanaka wahine. It was the first time he had been harsh with her, and she was so surprised at the cause of it that his temper passed over her without hurting.

She had selected the colors for each room and had done much of the painting herself. She polished the koa furniture with oil and arranged it to her taste. With Joe's fumbling help she hung the drapes he had made for her. At last her silver, dishes, and linens arrived from home, and now she wondered how she could use such things in this Hawaiian house of hers. The dainty pattern of the Lennox china with its wreath of gold laurel leaves seemed particularly unsuited to Makaniloa. She preferred the cheap Japanese bowls and plates she had bought at the store. Her mother had also sent a few of her favorite knicknacks and books—the Chinese wooden figure which some forgotten member of the family had brought back from the Orient in whaling days, a pair of brass candlesticks which she had

had in her room as a child, and a leather box which Aunty Melissa had brought to her from Egypt and in which she had always kept her jewelry and her unanswered letters. With these and with her set of Conrad and her small collection of poetry, she began to feel truly at home.

Her garden was growing well, and already they had eaten radishes and tender leaves of lettuce from it. The nasturtiums were blooming, the ti and croton and spider lilies she had planted all around the edge of the lawn to keep back the encroaching wild grasses and shrubs were thriving. The hono hono orchid slips Julia had given her had begun to send their roots into the fern bark to which she had wired them.

They celebrated their one-month anniversary with a little supper to which they invited Joe, and Julia and her husband, and Margaret. Joe entertained them with his songs, and Julia and Kaupena danced comic hulas. Afterward when Kaupena and Lucia were preparing for bed, he said abruptly, "Luce, we've got to have a housewarming. Everyone is expecting it."

"Oh!"

"It'll have to be a luau."

"Oh, I hope I can do it right!"

He laughed heartily. "Darling, it's a science. You couldn't possibly do it. I'll get Mrs. English. She prepares the best luaus on Maui."

"How many will you invite?"

"Everyone in the community. They all expect to come. And they all will unless they're practically dying."

"I'll have a chance then to meet the people. It'll be nice."

He looked at her with a dark expression in his eyes. "You haven't really met the people as you ought to. I'm sorry."

"I haven't missed it," she replied casually, too casually, for he came and put his arm about her.

On the day of the luau Lucia cleaned the house thoroughly

and filled it with flowers. Kaupena grinned at her. "Darling, not many will come inside. You don't need to worry how it looks."

She was a little disappointed, for she had looked upon this as her share in the housewarming. She had been cut off from the rest of the work, and was troubled by a feeling of being set aside. She watched while men dug a pit and prepared the pig for the imu. And she watched as they erected a canvas shelter covering all of her front lawn, set up tables from planks and sawhorses, and put up folding chairs. Johnny came to ask her to help him cover the tables with ti leaves. As they were finishing, Julia arrived with a huge lauhala basket filled with hibiscus blossoms. "For the table," she announced. And the three of them decked the tables with the red and pink and yellow flowers.

When Lucia went to her kitchen, she found it filled with women ladling poi into cardboard bowls and arranging salt beef, and Hawaiian salt, and a variety of dark condiments she did not recognize on tiny paper plates. Joe was sitting on a stool at the stove stirring in a huge kettle that he said contained chicken and coconut milk. He looked at her, his eyes shining. "This is going to be a number-one luau. People will talk about it for years!" He winked. "I knew when I wrote your wedding song it had to be special. I still think things are special with you two."

"Oh, Joe!" she cried gratefully.

The Hawaiian women smiled, and Joe introduced her to them. Mrs. English was a tall, lean, efficient-looking woman who had reddish hair and honey-golden skin. With proper grooming she could have been a handsome person, but in her shapeless faded muumuu and with her hair streaming untidily about her face, she was typical of any harassed cateress trying to make sure that a feast for several hundred was properly prepared.

After Lucia had shaken hands with the women and admired

their work, she went into the bedroom and stood restlessly at the window. If only Kaupena had let her share in this, the housewarming luau! Then she might feel as though she were slowly working her way into the pattern of Makaniloa. She was so concentrated in emptiness and loneliness that she did not hear the music begin or the babble of voices as the guests arrived. Presently, however, she heard her name called and whirled around to see Elizabeth standing in the doorway.

"Kaupena said he thought you were dressing."

"Oh, are people here already?"

"Scads of them."

"What's the matter with me? I've got to hurry."

"I'll help," Elizabeth said, and in an instant they had Lucia in the green and white silk holoku that Julia had made for her.

After combing her hair, Lucia looped the long train of the gown over her arm. "Thanks, Elizabeth. I'm so glad you came."

Elizabeth said, sighing, "Bill and I always have to go to these things! There are several every year. Bill likes the food, I guess, but I've never learned to eat it."

"Oh," Lucia muttered. It flashed upon her that Elizabeth's whole structure of life had suddenly been laid bare. Elizabeth regarded herself as an alien, living in a Makaniloa filled with puzzling, outlandish people. To protect herself she made her home as much as possible like the Indiana one; she refused to enjoy Makaniloa food and ways, and clung tenaciously to all the customs she remembered from the past. She was willing to pay this price, for she loved Bill, who could not help having been born at the other end of the earth.

Also she had, probably unconsciously, placed Lucia in her mind with the Hawaiians. Lucia thought of the cautious letter she had had from her mother a few days ago, a letter that had tried to warn her in veiled phrases that she must not be hurt if people regarded her equivocally because she had married as she had. Everyone was contriving—her mother, Kaupena, Margaret, Elizabeth—to make her realize she had married out of her race and background.

"Lucia!" Elizabeth cried in a soft tone of shame. "I'm afraid I've said something I shouldn't have. Darling, forgive me. I really love coming for your sake."

Lucia put her arm around her friend. "It could not be a housewarming without you here. Come and see what we've done to the house."

Lucia showed her proudly through the little house, pointing out the old koa furniture, which now gleamed with her efforts, and the fresh paint that was celadon green in the living room, a pale watery green in the two bedrooms, and a white in the kitchen. "Julia showed me how to make the koa shine."

"Oh, you know Julia!" Elizabeth exclaimed. "How nice! She's my favorite of all the Hawaiians here. Always so friendly, and without the difficult, stilted moments some of them have."

"She has the most open heart I've ever known."

"Yes. She's like they always say the Hawaiians are. Actually, you know, many of them are a bit touchy and standoffish. They're generous, but they have moods."

"They're just human." Lucia had a quick intense desire to defend them—they were now her people—from even the slightest criticism.

They went out onto the lanai and Kaupena, who was at the entrance to the tent, beckoned to Lucia. She stood next to him, and he introduced her to a succession of Awais, Medeiroses, Tomitas, Yamamotos, Chongs, Chews, Kaneloas, Poepoes, Akanas, Nelsons, Johnsons. They smiled or bowed or shook hands, according to their custom, and then walked under the canvas and gathered close to their friends, arranging chairs and saving places for each other at the luau tables. Gathered here and there were little knots of women. In one group Mrs. Akana was showing off her own style of muumuu, which had three-quarter sleeves slit on the upper side to the shoulders and lined with bright yellow satin. Another small group moved among the tables, examining the food and commenting on it. Others stood near the musicians and joined in the singing and curved their hands in the symbols of the hula. The men stayed near the punch table and drank the fruit juice spiked with gin. Their faces grew ruddy and their laughter began to boom through the tent. Kaupena and Lucia had discussed the serving of liquor and Kaupena had said, "They like to get a little tight. It makes them forget."

"Forget? Forget what?"

"Oh, their troubles. If anyone gets too drunk we can have Johnny take him home."

Margaret came in just before they were ready to sit down. Lucia motioned for her to come to the host's table, and with difficulty she made her way there past the laughing, slightly drunken people, past an old woman who had risen in her place to dance. Margaret paused long enough to respond to her with a few gestures of the hula. The crowd laughed tenderly and indulgently at the give and take between a beloved tutu and the friendly Margaret.

When she reached Lucia, she swung her hand in an arch and whispered, "Now you see Makaniloa going for broke. The pressures are off."

Lucia looked at the people before her, clad in flowered shirts, muumuus, holokus; their faces were mobile with pleasure and merriment, their arms and flexible hands waved in rhythmic interpretation of their words, their voices swelled to a loud hum threatening to drown the strumming of the orchestra. Makaniloa, she thought, the people who live on this wind-swept slope or back in the dark valleys, the people who sleep and eat and make love in the little wooden shacks and who work at ranching, or fishing, or lauhala weaving, or laboring on the road, or just passing the time. These were the people her great-grandmother had loved.

She turned suddenly to Kaupena. "Darling, did your grandmother come?"

"She didn't come!"

Her heart beat rapidly at the tone in his voice, while the sound of Makaniloa wind crackled in the canvas.

6.

NOT long after the luau, an incident brought home to Lucia that a whole stratum of Kaupena's nature was hidden. He had suggested that they ride up to the crater on an afternoon, pitch a tent, and spend the night. There was in his manner a carefully curbed excitement which made her believe that this trip to the crater would be significant to him.

"Is it something special?" she asked timidly.

"For Waiolamas the crater is special ever since Tutu—" He broke off. When he continued, it was with a tinge of embarrassment. "Well, that's not really so important."

"What do you mean?"

He frowned slightly. "You may not like it up there, and in that case it's better for you not to know."

They were ready to leave, the horses waiting in the front yard, the food in the saddle bags, when Joe drove up with a group of his friends. They swarmed onto the lanai, where they strummed their ukuleles and guitars softly.

Lucia whispered, "Kaupena, what shall we do about them?"

"We'll sit a while and then go."

Joe said, "We thought you needed a little cheering up here in this lonely old valley and that maybe you had some beer in your icebox. We musicians, Lucia, are just a bunch of bums."

"There's plenty of beer!" Lucia said and went to get it.

When she returned, Joe remarked, "Well, I see you're going camping!"

"Yes, to the crater. Something I've wanted to do for a long time."

"To the crater! Aha!" Joe exclaimed and then turned to Kaupena. "You aren't such a stern old guy after all. Romance!"

Kaupena blushed and drank hastily from his beer can.

"Is it so very romantic up there?" Lucia asked.

"Very, for the Waiolamas. Don't tell me that you haven't heard of the great love story of Makaniloa?"

"No, what is it?"

"Kaupena should tell you that. How our grandmother and her lover ran off to the crater. Why, there are at least three songs about it."

"Your grandmother did that?"

"Sure. She was converted in the crater, so they say."

"Converted!"

"Yeah, to the old ways, or something. You'd better look out, Lucy dear. The bug might bite you. Maybe that's what Kaupena wants." He turned to his friends. "We'd better go now and give these guys a chance to get started. Tommy, get the crabs, yeh."

Tommy, one of the youngest of the men, brought a paper carton, and when Lucia looked in she saw three large crabs. "Oh Joe, how wonderful," she cried.

"Broil 'em tonight over your fire, and think of us."

When they were gone, Kaupena said curtly, "We aren't going."

"But why?" she burst out in amazement.

"Just accept it. We don't go. It's all been spoiled." And he went out under the mango trees. She followed him, but he would not speak a word to her.

In the slow, warm weeks that followed there were often times when he walked under the mango trees in a gray mood or sat alone on the lanai, his arms folded across his chest and his head bowed, completely withdrawn into himself. She could not learn just what action or words would set him off on these moods. But they almost always concerned Hawaiian customs or stories; it was as though he were too sensitive, hearing innuendoes of scorn or laughter when none were seriously intended, and as though the minute these things were spoken of airily, a deep hurt shot through him. Lucia shuddered at the quick sharp thought that she might lose him for lack of understanding. Her need for him was intense, beyond the union of their bodies at night, beyond the life he offered her in Makaniloa, beyond the love which glowed through all of his moodiness. He was the only person who could dispel the loneliness that had dogged her all her life—not the superficial loneliness of having few friends or of being isolated, but that deep emptiness that had persistently whispered to her that men strained and suffered pointlessly. Kaupena had filled this emptiness by involving her warmly and intimately in a struggle that meant something. It was of consequence to lay a pathway among the races, to work quietly at destroying barriers. This was her small faltering advance in the great effort toward the harmony of men.

She wanted very much to meet Kaupena's grandmother and to see the house in which he had been reared. For, she was certain, in the quality of that woman and in the tone of her house lay the solution of much in Kaupena which puzzled her. Lucia had not yet been able to feel her way toward the intimate, day-by-day aspect of his boyhood. And so one afternoon, driven by this desire to understand, she started up the mountainside in the direction of Lokalia's house. At the valley mouth, the land was rolling, open, and sunny, and she sat for several minutes on a grassy hillock, trying to picture Kaupena as a boy playing in the sun and the wind. She imagined his strong small body, brown from the sun, lithe from swimming. In this light-filled spot he could not have been anything but an average child.

She saw from her hillock that the valley narrowed quickly, and that the back of it was quite dark and shadowy. She re-

called the day Kaupena had taken her to the waterfall and had
pointed out the dark and the light of Makaniloa. Here was that
duality in the small compass of Lokalia's valley.

She rose and continued her walk, presently reaching a place
where trees arched over the trail. She realized that if she suddenly, round a curve, met Lokalia, there would be no way of
avoiding her. So she moved off to twist her way among the trees.
Wind strummed the tops of the ohias and sent a shower of pink
fuzzy blossoms to the earth. The shadow of ohia foliage was
hoary and gray on the pale grasses and shrubs of the under-
growth. She moved on into a small grove of kukui, whose dark
branches curved as intricately as a raveled fish net and whose
golden green leaves shed a warm glow on the earth. From the
kukui she went into a deep-shadowed cluster of mango trees,
where the air quivered with a dank acrid scent rising from the
decaying mat of leaves.

Soon she saw the corner of a house. Cautiously she stepped
closer, making certain that she was kept from view by foliage
or tree trunks. The windows of the house stared darkly, and an
irrepressible sensation trembled in her that someone must be
looking out of each of them. The house was simply built; the
roof pitched steeply, and changed abruptly to a gentler angle
over the lanai. Elaborate jigsaw scrollwork decorated the eaves,
the lanai balustrade, and even ran in a broken, weathered strip
across the roof peak. It looked very strange up there, as though
a child had forgotten it in play. The house had once been
painted red but now it was the softest of gray pinks. One half
of the lanai, which extended all across the front, was enclosed
with a finely meshed latticework over which crawled a lilikoi
vine, the passion fruit. A heavy, many-hued foliage of red and
shell ginger, of pink and green and red ti, and of spindly bronze
and yellow crotons, banked the house up to the level of the
windows.

Clinging to the protection of the woods, Lucia skirted the

house to a point where she could see the back. She realized then that it had been built much as her own, even to the kitchen ell which in both must have been added later. She was sensitive to a quality of muted twilight in the house and woods and imagined that there must be long days of rain when the lamps would have to be lighted for any work to be done. Here in loneliness and darkness Kaupena had grown up. What strange companions of the imagination he must have had to make life bearable!

She continued through the woods toward the back of the valley until she felt secure from the view of the house, and then she returned to the trail. The path seemed to be well used, and in places someone had laid flat rocks across muddy patches. She was now in a grove of pandanus; the spidery fronds were massed so that the light filtered down in silver-green shadows. The triangular forms of the roots and the spiral motif of the foliage created a curiously rhythmic pattern of abstract design. As she went on, the roar of water grew louder, thrusting into the background the rattle of the wind in the pandanus. She caught glimpses of the dark green-clad cliffs that were slowly closing in upon her, and she was oppressed by their closeness. There were moments along the way when she imagined it was difficult to breathe.

With startling suddenness she stepped from the seclusion of the woods into the narrow cul-de-sac which was the back of the valley. The waterfall glowed in a milky mist against the darkness of the cliff, and the pool into which it fell had an unnatural, still brownness. On the edge of the pool rose a pillar of rock in the crevices of which grew small clumps of fern, giving the rock a slightly shaggy appearance. Although the falls had caught her eyes first, she saw that the stone pillar held them. Each time she glanced around, she found her vision returning to the rock. It was a guardian, a watcher—a god, perhaps. It was beautifully, harmoniously formed and stood out sharply against the whiteness of the falls. Slowly she walked toward it and laid a hand on its mossy wet flank. Then she looked up the length of it until her eyes rested upon its crest, dark against the limpid blue sky. Abruptly she jerked her hand away. Something had seemed to move under it, not a small motion like an insect crawling, but rather large and shuddering as though the whole pillar had stirred. She backed away and then saw lying at the base of the rock a brown and withered plumeria lei. She bent over to pick it up and found underneath a rotting orange. Her guess had been right; this was a god. She dropped the lei and gazed with penetration at the rock. A moment of pure silence seemed to descend as though the falls had ceased and the wind had dropped. She turned suddenly and ran through the woods, stumbling among the stones and roots and the soft beds of slimy leaves.

For many days afterward, the trip to Lokalia's valley lingered vividly in her imagination; she even dreamed of it. The rock moving under her finger tips, the moment of silence—it was as though something were trying to emerge from the ancient locked force of the primeval. She longed to tell Kaupena of it, but she dared not.

On a morning less than a week after this adventure, and before she had had time to let it drift quietly into the subconscious of her experience, Kaupena announced at breakfast that he would be away for the next few days. He was going with Johnny up to a pasture near the gap to treat some sick cattle.

"Are you going today?" she asked.

"Sure, why not!"

"But it's so sudden!" Her breathing had grown difficult.

"No more sudden than anything else. You aren't scared to stay alone?"

"No!" she said emphatically. "Did you know yesterday?"

"Yeah, I knew."

"I wish you'd told me then."

"Why?" He seemed surprised.

"Just to give me a little time to prepare."

"There's nothing. I've done everything. The food's all packed. I have an extra change of clothing."

She rose from the table and moved to the window. "Kaupena, I'm always on the outside. How can I get in?"

He pushed back his chair. "What's the matter now?" There was an undertone of impatient concern in his words.

"Well," she laughed self-consciously, "I guess there's nothing the matter really."

"You're always imagining things, Luce! I can't keep up with you."

She went to him. "I'm sorry! Awfully sorry! It's my old habits lingering on, I guess."

"You know, darling, we aren't formal here. Things happen, and we adjust ourselves. Whatever happens, we just take. You can't ever tell about the future. Maybe I'll get up to the office and discover I'm not to go at all."

"Yes," she said musingly, "I guess that's so. I have to begin to think in new ways, casual ones."

"You don't have to think at all! Just feel it out—respond! That's all! Just respond! That's what Makaniloa people want."

"Oh Kaupena, be patient with me!"

He put his arms around her. "If you're too lonely, go to Julia's. Or come with us, if you want. Johnny won't mind."

She reflected a moment and then said she would go to Julia's.

He kissed her mouth, her neck, her hair. She strained against him and whispered in his ear, "I want the most profoundest harmony between us—the harmony which is so basic."

He took her by the shoulders and rocked her gently back and forth. "You are the funniest little person. Don't worry about harmony and all that." He kissed her again, long and tenderly. "This is our harmony. Miss me a little—not too much, though. And look up at night and think of me."

He broke away and went out. At the edge of the lawn he turned and waved. "Three or four days at the most!" he called.

She waved, her fingers growing listless as he disappeared. She went into the house and washed the breakfast dishes. Her mind ached with a rush of morbid imaginings: he might be thrown from his horse, or stumble into a crevice, or catch pneumonia in the cold wind of the gap; he might come back changed toward her; for some unfathomed reason she might never see him again. Presently she closed her mind to such ideas.

After the dishes were dried she made the bed. It was then that time seemed suddenly to weigh upon her with its endlessness. What did other people do with great chunks of time that were unplanned and uncharted such as she had before her. With Kaupena gone there would be no significance to the hours. Julia was lucky to have so many children, animals, and people constantly coming and going. For her there was always the wash to get out, the meals to cook, the floors to be swept, friends to talk to. Even Elizabeth had her reading, knitting, gardening, riding, and the constant entertaining of house guests. And Margaret, of course, had her painting; she too was a lucky one.

Lucia went to the door and leaned against the frame, gazing over the treetops to the sea. The water was a brilliant oily blue. Dark against it was the steeple of the Protestant Church. And her great-grandmother, she mused, what of her time? Every moment of it must have been filled until at night when she had fallen exhausted on her bed. Lucia went to the little table where the journal lay. Above it on the wall she had hung Margaret's watercolor of Makaniloa, a wedding present.

She took the journal out into the sun on the lanai steps and read at random. On an April third, Lucia Appleton had fitted a new dress for Charity from material that had come in the last box from home. On April twenty-fifth she had baked bread and then had gone up the valley to nurse a child down with a fever. On May seventeenth she had harvested a crop of sweet potatoes, mended the thatch where the rain had come in, and started a new Bible class for women. On June tenth she had spent the day watching by Willy's cradle after the doctor, who had come all the way from Wailuku, had told her the baby was sure to die. But as it turned out, he didn't die. She smoothed the fine wet hair back from his forehead, held his tiny hand in hers, and he opened his eyes and looked at her. She knew then that he would recover, for soon his skin was cool and his eyes clear. . . .

There was significance in what other people had to do, and so little in what she did. She closed the journal and sat on the steps for some time, feeling only the sun hot on her hair and hearing the wind roaring down the flank of the mountain. Then she stood up and moved so that she might see the gap. She wondered if Kaupena had really wanted her to go along today. But she could do nothing to help him there, and here, too, there was nothing she could do.

She climbed the stairs into the house and laid the journal back on its table. Then she found herself moving out of the door again, down the lanai steps and across the lawn toward the path to Julia's. The woods closed in about her briefly and opened at the clearing around the Kaneloa house.

"Hello!" Lucia called, seeing that Julia was seated on the floor at the open doorway. She was sewing together pieces for a quilt.

"Come in!" Julia said. "I'm alone today. The kids have gone fishing; Georgie is with my mother-in-law visiting in Hana."

"I'm alone too. Kaupena's gone up to one of the gap pastures to treat some sick cattle."

"Yeah, I heard. I hope the sickness isn't too bad. Sit down."

"May I help?"

"Sure. All these pieces gotta be sewed together. Just like this, see?"

"When I was a little girl I helped my grandmother sew a

quilt. I'm sure when I was asleep she ripped everything out and did it over."

"Yeah, funny how kids like to help when they're really a lot of trouble. You've gotta let 'em, though."

Lucia sat on the floor and picking up pieces of red and white calico began sewing them together to form stylized lehua blossoms.

"Do you ever get lonely living up here, Julia?"

"There're plenty kids around all the time. If I get lonely, I just go down and visit somebody."

"I suppose you know everybody."

"Oh sure! After a while you get to know them all. They're kind of scared because you're haole. And then Kaupena's kind of standoffish."

"I wish they wouldn't be scared." Lucia was beginning to imitate unconsciously the pidgin intonation Julia used.

"Kaupena oughta take you around more. Like Momi did Paul."

"Momi and Paul?"

"Ritten. I told you about them once. I don't think they were at the luau. They've been in Honolulu for a couple of months while Paul learns about some new kind of machine for the ranch. He's an engineer. He came down during the war and was stationed at the big camp that wasn't far from the Catholic Church. He liked Makaniloa, said there was no place else to live. That he couldn't imagine going back to the mainland. So he came back after the war was over and married Momi. They've got three kids."

"And he's really fitted in?"

"Yeah. Plenty good for a stranger. Momi is one pretty, lively girl; she took him around so people could know him. Of course there were some things tough on her at first, his wanting her to keep house just like haoles—all that fuss about furniture being just so and meals being on time. But she got used to it."

"And do you think he's happy?"

"Seems to be. He won't even go back for a trip. He says if his relatives want to see him and the kids, they'll have to come here."

That's a boast, Lucia surmised, for he's afraid to go back. She hoped she could meet this man who was making much the same experiment she was.

Her fingers were tired with sewing, and she paused to stretch her back and arms and to gaze around the room. It was spotlessly clean; the mat and the floor were worn with the scrubbings they had had in strong soap and water. A low table covered with a starched white cloth held the photographs of all the family, as well as a bouquet of cannas. The only other furniture in the room were two chairs, a small hikie or couch, and a bookcase in which were only half a dozen books, the rest of the shelf space being used for shells, glass floats for fishing nets, a piece of lava rock curiously shaped like an animal, a broken vase, and a large ugly figure of a cat of the type made in Japan. On the walls there were only two pictures, one a color photograph of a Hawaiian landscape and the other a lithograph of the Sacred Heart.

Lucia began to sew again. "Are you a Catholic, Julia?"

"No. If you mean that picture, my third daughter got it. She went to the Catholic Church for a while. She said it would bring good luck, so we hung it up."

"Do you go to church?"

"Sure. Almost everybody in Makaniloa goes to church." She laughed. "There's nothing else to do."

"Do you believe in God?" Lucia was startled at the boldness of her own question. Julia had a way of drawing out these hidden questions.

"Sure, why not?"

"I wish I could." She hesitated briefly. "I don't seem to believe in anything—except maybe a little in life itself."

"You think too much."

Lucia laughed. "That's what Kaupena always says."

"You sound just like my sister in Honolulu. There things get kind of complicated and hard to understand, and she's always fussing. But out here in the country it's easy. There's always things to be done, and if there aren't, you can just sit around and nobody cares."

"But don't you ever think about the world—how so many people are starving and unhappy now?"

"Yeah, sometimes I think. I feel sorry for the little kids." She sighed with a strange melancholy contentment. "Even with us here it isn't always happy. Some of our people say the Hawaiians are done for. Some of us are so poor that we just have to go back to fishing and growing taro. We can't seem to get along like in the old days. Why, there are kids right here in Makaniloa who don't get enough to eat."

"I know!"

"Their papas get drunk and spend the little bit of money they have. Or else they are sick and can't work. Some of them just sort of get into moods and won't do anything. It's hard on the keikis."

Julia was comfortably started now, and her words rolled out effortlessly. "Yeah, there's a kind of despair in some of us. And with it there's a kind of wild hope that comes out in funny ways." She laid her sewing in her lap and gazed thoughtfully out of the doorway. "There was an old man who lived here. . . . He's been dead a long time. One night he had a dream that an island would come sailing into Makaniloa and anchor just off where the Protestant Church is. He called it the "Kane huna moku," the hidden island of Kane. Of course that's an old Hawaiian idea, sort of like heaven, a beautiful place to live belonging to the gods. Well, this old man dreamed that everybody should get ready with all their pigs and their chickens, and white clothes enough to last them for the rest of their lives, and that they should get on that island and sail away to a beautiful warm place in the sea. He had a day all picked out when this island was going to arrive. And lots of people, not only from Makaniloa, but from all over this island and from the other islands, gathered to wait. They knew because it had got in the papers. On the night before Kane huna moku was to arrive, they all went to a big house there used to be down near the beach and prayed all night. Well, of course, the next day no island came."

"What did they do?"

"They just went back home. And the old man went back to his taro patch."

"Weren't they upset?"

"I guess they musta been. But it was a funny thing. Most of them didn't say anything about it. I was a kid. My mother believed, and I remember her dressing me in a new white dress. After nothing came, she cried. She told me later that only one or two people called the old man names. The others were too disappointed and ashamed."

"I see."

"That's how the despair comes out in us, though. We're always hoping something wonderful will happen."

She picked up her sewing again, and they worked together silently. Presently she said, "I think you better stay here while Kaupena's up the mountain. Then you won't get so lonesome."

"Thank you, Julia."

"I'll get Paul and Momi Ritten to come over for supper and you can meet them."

Kaupena and Johnny had built a fire in the lee of a huge boulder, and over the coals their coffee was coming to a boil. The steam was fragrant in the cold sharp wind that came down from the summit. They were just a few hundred yards below the gap, near enough to see the crests of two purplish cinder cones and the opposite side of the crater wall tinted in pinks and reds and mauves. Johnny opened a tin box of pilot crackers and Kaupena untied a calabash of poi. They sat on the grass and ate silently, washing down the food with draughts of strong coffee. When they were finished, Johnny took out his ukulele and strummed. The sound was faint in the blast of wind from the gap.

"Lonely as hell up here," he said, gazing at the giant mountain slope sprawling to the sea below them.

"Yeah, it is." Kaupena sang a few words of the song Johnny was playing and moved his hands casually in the hula gestures. "My first night without her since the wedding." He sighed, feeling a deep letting-go in all his being. She was not easy to be with all the time. There was a strained quality in her, and a curious obtuseness to his feelings about things Hawaiian.

Johnny laughed at Kaupena's remark and made a lewd gesture.

Kaupena ruffled. "Don't get smart!"

"O.K., O.K., so you miss her. I don't blame you."

"You oughta get married, Johnny."

"Nah, waste time. I like plenty wahines, not just one."

"I used to feel that way. But somehow . . . Oh hell!"

"Eh, you know that Kapahokea girl? Well, the other night . . ." and he launched into a long, salacious story.

Kaupena did not listen. He had heard too many others like it from Johnny. He took a bottle of whisky from his knapsack and, unscrewing the top, drank from it. When Johnny had finished his story, he handed the bottle to him. "I feel like getting drunk."

"There's no one to stop us." Johnny took two deep gulps.

Kaupena drank again and wiped his mouth with the back of his hand. "Women are funny. The only way you can get away from them is to get drunk. I used to drink gin every time my grandmother got burned up. God, what a temper! These wahines are queer. They always want things just so."

"That's one reason I don't get hitched. You can go to bed with them without all that."

There was a long silence, during which they drank often from the bottle. "Most women are easy," Kaupena muttered. His voice was beginning to thicken. "I love that wahine O.K. But everything's so damned serious with her. She's always wanting to discuss things. Waste time!" He gulped at the whisky. "I tell her it's better to go to bed and make love."

"Wahines always want to talk, talk, talk. Where do they get all those ideas?"

Kaupena felt the whisky hot in his veins, and his vision swam. A fine lighthearted mood came upon him, and he remembered the first time he had taken Lucia in the kamani grove. In some respects it had been the best time. They had lain together on the leaves, moving to the rhythm of the sea and the wind. He had been perfectly happy, not only with the pleasure of his body but with a sense of the unification of all life—Lucia, his grandmother, Makaniloa—all were in that moment closely knit and harmonious. He must take her there again, teach her the utter simplicity of the act, for she had a tenseness in her appetite for love. There must be no hesitancy from thinking or remembering; there should be just the two of them, moving in the rhythm of the water, their limbs pressed close together.

His body was feverish with longing, and he turned to lie face down, pushing himself tight upon the grass. Yes, he must teach her the simplicity of things, the goodness of eating and talking with friends and fishing and making love. Life didn't have to be strained and difficult. In Makaniloa it was meant to be plain like pilot crackers and poi. She was always trying to relate it to other places, other lives. In Makaniloa it should go along in the same old stream it had for centuries—hard work, hunger, love, ease, birth, death—a flowing of Hawaiian children out of Hawaiian wombs, living restless Hawaiian lives, searching for a peace of heart in the ancient, simple, instinctive ways. The Hawaiians had a belief in the goodness of life itself: the wind and sun and sea on their naked bodies, the poi in their mouths, their legs close locked and warm with love, the deep-laid stir which hinted to them of things significant, mystifying, powerful, beyond the grasp of mind or sense.

His head swam in its drunken lyricism until presently he was asleep.

As evening drew near, an agitation grew in Lucia at the thought of meeting Paul Ritten. She had regarded Makaniloa as peculiarly her own. The people who were born here could claim it as she never could. But it remained her discovery, it had nourished her ancestors, and she had recognized it instinctively and immediately as hers. Paul Ritten, though he had come first, was an intruder; he was a poacher upon her domain. Yet she was curious about him.

She stood at her kitchen window looking up at the gap; the light draining swiftly from the sky cast a greenish haze over the landscape. She wondered where on that great mountain slope Kaupena and Johnny would camp that night. She wished suddenly that she had gone with them.

She moved from the kitchen window to the bedroom, and taking her nightgown from the closet, tied it with her toothbrush in a scarf. She turned the key in the front door and started down the pathway to Julia's. Walking slowly and scuffling through the matted leaves, she wondered if Kaupena might look for a lighted window and be disappointed. She hesitated, thinking of turning back, and then abruptly scolded herself for continuing to be the sentimental fool she had been all her life. It was her old fault, this spinning of frail fantastic sentiments which no one but herself would ever dream of. Now that she had thrown her lot in with a simple, passionate people, she must give over these middle-class instincts of hers.

She mounted the stairs of Julia's house and, as Georgie lunged forward to greet her, caught him up in her arms. He fastened his hands at the back of her neck and she pressed her cheek close to his soft warm one. Then she leaned against the frame of the door and said hello to those within. Julia was sitting on the floor smoking a cigarette and petting a puppy that was curled up in her lap. Two of the older boys were mending a fishnet, and Lei, the oldest daughter, was sewing on a new dress. A smaller girl was lying on the hikie, strumming an ukulele. Through an open doorway Lucia could see Mrs. Kaneloa moving about the stove, absorbed in supper preparations. The big table in the kitchen had been covered with a white cloth and set with odds and ends of forks and spoons and jelly glasses.

"I hope you don't mind sleeping with Lei tonight," Julia said, "we don't have any extra beds. I'm sorry."

"If Lei doesn't mind me. . . ."

"Oh she usually has Susie and sometimes even Georgie. But Susie's gone to sleep with Aunty for a few nights. And Georgie will come in with us."

George indicated by kicking his feet that he wanted to get down, and Lucia put him on the floor. Then she moved into the house and sat down on the floor next to Julia.

"Want a cigarette?"

"Yes, thanks." It was a gesture of companionship to smoke with Julia.

Julia pulled gently at the puppy's ears while she told the latest gossip. When Paul and Momi arrived, she brushed the puppy from her lap and heaved herself up. Lucia followed and was introduced to the Rittens.

After greeting her Paul Ritten said, "So you're throwing your stakes in with Makaniloa too!"

"Yes," Lucia said weakly. She saw a tall blond man, his eyes a soft gray-blue, inclined to be dreamy and yet with a stern look occasionally sharpening them. His skin was so deeply tanned that his hair appeared to be silvery.

Momi was a part-Hawaiian girl, daintily formed, with small slender hands and feet and with large melancholy eyes dominating a delicate, pointed face. Lucia imagined that they must have handsome children.

Mrs. Kaneloa called them to dinner, and they all flocked to the kitchen. Tom Kaneloa, Julia's husband, was serving laulaus onto the plates. He sat at the head of the table. His bald brown head shone in the glow of the kerosene lantern as he leaned over his plate and deftly peeled down the smoking leaves of the laulau to get at the steamed pork and fish inside.

Paul sat next to Lucia. She opened her laulau silently and took a mouthful of poi from the bowl in front of her.

Abruptly she asked, "How did you happen to pick on Makaniloa?"

"I was stationed here for a while during the war. And after I left, the place haunted me. I began thinking about it and realized that the life I saw here was better in its simplicity, its goodness—even its badness—than any I had seen anywhere else in the world. I couldn't bear the thought of going back to Pittsburgh and that stale life—the office, the golf course, the club. So I came here."

"And you like it?"

"Of course. I never want to go back, even to visit! I've burned all my bridges." His voice had a tone of defiance as though he suspected she might not believe him. So she smiled. He asked softly, "But you? How did you happen to do it?"

She explained her case to him simply.

"You make me feel more than ever that I'm right. You've felt what I felt."

As he said this, they were suddenly friends. She looked at him and smiled, feeling a warmth within her. He responded, pressing the fingers of her hand that lay close to his. "We're damned lucky," he said.

Later when she was lying quietly in bed beside Lei, she wondered if she had been drawn to Paul by his personal charm or simply because he was the only other person of her race present. The race issue took many subtle forms, she was learning. She thought of Paul's fierce assurance that he had done the right thing. He had found a kind of peace in Makaniloa, but there must have been thin, persistent strains of doubt; he had been so obviously delighted that she shared his discovery. He had dared to cut across the tight barriers of race and class, to mingle his blood and his life with simple, direct people. There must have been times when he had yearned for companionship in his daring. It is a fearful thing to stand alone.

The wind rattled the windows and twanged upon the tin roof. Makaniloa, the place of the long wind, she thought; Makaniloa somehow blended differences, tensions. She moved closer to Lei, feeling the girl's warmth, and her throat choked suddenly with the long-awaited sense of belonging that took possession of her.

7.

WHEN Lucia awoke the next morning she found that Lei had already arisen; the muffled noise of Kaneloas moving through the house, calling to each other, plucking an ukulele, came to her ears. Outside the dogs barked and Georgie was crying. A scent of coffee was in the air. She dressed hurriedly and went to apologize for being late for breakfast. Julia said they all ate breakfast whenever they pleased; there was no sitting down at table.

She pointed to the kitchen. "There's some coffee out there, and mush. Help yourself."

Morning sun warmed the kitchen and picked out in brilliance the shabby stove, the scarred table, and the chipped sink. She took a handleless cup from a shelf and poured it full of strong coffee. She stepped to the doorway and sipped her coffee, gazing into the yard. Mrs. Kaneloa and Georgie were feeding the chickens, which clustered around them, jumping to snatch the grain from the small fat hand of the little boy. Julia came and stood next to her. Her body was relaxed and warm, and smelled of soap and coconut oil. Lucia envied the calm in her, and the way she went about life directly and naturally, accepting the free flow of friendship. Julia slipped her arm around Lucia's waist as they stood together in the morning sun.

Presently through the wind noise and the sea noise they heard a low sustained sound, half chant and half wail. Julia stiffened, listening. It continued, and she exclaimed, "The fish are running! It's the fish caller." She took Lucia's hand and said, "Come on! You haven't seen a hukilau. Plenty fun!" She shouted the news to the rest of the family, and they scrambled to the car.

"The kids in the back!" Julia cried. And she directed Lucia to get in front along with Mrs. Kaneloa and Georgie. She cranked the engine, and the car shook violently, but the motor settled down to a staccato throb. They bumped their way down the road to the beach. The children shouted and the dogs barked all the way, and Lucia felt in both young and old a wild sense of holiday.

A boat was already out past the surf, and the men in it were carefully lowering the net. On a promontory above the beach was the lone figure of a man, his hands cupped about his mouth. When Julia had shut off the engine they heard his voice clear and loud through the hum of wind and sea.

"When they pull in the net, we'll help," Julia said.

Lucia pointed at other boats setting out to sea and asked about them.

"They'll fish by line from those boats. When the fish are running good in Makaniloa, everything stops—the school, the store, even people from the ranch come down. A good haul will mean a lot to some of these families."

"That fish caller has a wonderful voice."

"Yeah. His father was one too."

"Kaupena'll be sorry to miss this!"

"Uh huh. He likes fishing all right. But he likes to go out in an outrigger all alone. He has one down the coast a way with an outboard motor on it. Everybody laughed when he got the motor. But now two or three others have. They can go pretty far out to sea with those motors."

"I didn't know he had an outrigger!"

Julia flashed a sharp glance at her and then muttered softly,

"Yeah, he has one. Paul has one too. They had a contest once to see who could go out the farthest. Kaupena won because Paul had motor trouble. Say, look! Ther're the Rittens with their kids."

Lucia saw Paul and Momi with three little boys trailing after them. Julia honked the horn and got out of the car. Paul waved and he and Momi started toward them.

When they were near, Paul cried out laughing, "Lucia, you don't look right here!"

"What do you mean?" Her heart pounded at this strange remark.

"Your blond hair blowing among all this dark hair."

"Oh!" she exclaimed, troubled by his insistence on her difference from the people of Makaniloa. "And what about your own blond hair?"

He grinned. "At least my skin is brown. You don't give yours much of a chance, hiding up the mountain all the time."

"Yeah," Julia said. "I was telling her only yesterday she ought to get out more. Kaupena ought to take her out the way Momi did you—get her acquainted."

"It's those Waiolamas!" Momi teased. "They always think they're special people—sitting up there with their ghosts."

Lucia blushed. For all of Momi's light tone, she felt a sting suggesting jealousy or dislike. She replied softly, "I haven't discovered they're very special yet. Except, of course, Joe."

"Oh yes, Joe!" Momi said warmly. Her voice shifted. "But what about Lokalia?"

"I haven't met her!" said Lucia bravely.

"Oh, I see." She paused as though understanding something for the first time. "So you haven't met her!" Then she put her arm in Julia's. "Let's go down to the beach!" They went ahead, the boys following their mother.

"I'm sorry about Momi," Paul apologized. "She isn't always —well—tactful."

"Oh, she didn't mean anything. . . . What about Lokalia Waiolama? She must be quite a person."

"She's a magnificent, stubborn, sinister old lady, and she's no bigger than a minute." He pointed suddenly. "Look! There she is up the cliff. I thought it was about time for her to be here."

For a moment Lucia could not look. When she did turn her eyes, she saw standing next to the fish caller a tiny dark figure in a muumuu and a broad-brimmed hat.

Paul went on, "She's here to make certain they put back part of the catch for the gods. She keeps these old customs alive and tries to make the people proud instead of ashamed of them."

Lucia stared at Lokalia, but the distance was such that her figure might have been that of any old Hawaiian woman. There was nothing to distinguish her except possibly an unusually supple grace in the movement of her hands as she gestured.

"Let's sit down," Paul suggested. "It'll be some time yet before we can help. Look, you can see the fish in the waves!"

Lucia saw only flashing blues and greens and silvers. "I can't see a thing but water."

"Watch as the waves rise. You'll see darkish silver streaks."

"Darkish silver," she repeated, gazing steadily into the waves.

"After a while you'll be able to tell the different kinds of fish from just such glances as this."

"I think I do see!" she cried. "Oh, I want so much to learn all that sort of thing! I have so much to get caught up on in Makaniloa."

"It's a wonderful life in its way. And not so simple as you might think."

"Yes, I've guessed. Kaupena says there's a dark side."

"That's a good way to put it." He faced her, his eyes warmly upon her. "You know, I'm glad you're here, making the same experiment."

She was troubled by the intimate emphasis, but glad that he had said those very words. It made her feel at home in a way neither Julia nor Joe had been able to do.

He continued, "I hadn't realized how isolated—no, that isn't the word—" He broke off with a little frown. Then he smiled. "Well, anyhow we can share certain things these people wouldn't understand."

She thought a moment. "Wouldn't that in a way defeat our purpose? We don't want to be set apart."

"We shall be anyhow. Oh, not obviously! But subtly. They'll think of us together. You watch."

She pulled a branch of naupaka and twisted it in her fingers. Then she was aware that Momi had returned and was staring blankly down at them. Momi said pointedly, "You two seem to have a lot to talk about."

"Sit down with us, darling. We're talking about Makaniloa. You know more about it than either of us."

She remained standing. "Lokalia's up there," she said to Lucia. "I tried to get her to come down and meet you. But she wouldn't."

"Why?"

"Oh, she's busy now," Momi said, with the clear innuendo that she didn't care to give the full reason.

Paul rose and took his wife's hand, and Lucia was grateful to him. Momi for all her beauty and sprightliness had the sharp blundering ways of a girl unsure of herself. Lucia could see that she guarded Paul jealously; the fear of losing him seemed always with her.

"It's time to help now," Paul said. And he started quickly toward the beach where two groups of people pulled rhythmically on the net, slowly hauling it in to the shore. Lucia and Momi followed him closely.

"Look at Julia!" Lucia cried. She was at the head of one of the lines, tugging at the heavy net and shouting merrily.

Paul seized Lucia's hand and led her to an open spot on the ropes and cried, "Pull with the rest." The rope was wet and harsh, but she grasped it firmly, putting all of her strength into the tug. The rhythm was easy to fall in with and presently she found herself laughing from the pure joy of moving in the sway of the successive pulls.

When the net was finally in, she ran with the others to examine the catch. Fish, large and small, shining with pinks and blues and greens and silvers, writhed against the confining brown mesh. Men and women pushed ahead of her to gather the fish into piles, and she moved away, walking alone up the beach. Her eyes caught the vision of two figures standing at the back of the sandy area. Lokalia and Momi, she was certain! They leaned together in the intimate way of plotters and talked in each other's ears. Lucia whirled about and hurried to the safety and anonymity of the Makaniloa fishermen.

At noon the next day, Kaupena came home unexpectedly. He walked through Julia's ever open doorway and called out, "Lucia!"

She ran to him, stricken that she had not been at home to welcome him. "Oh, I'm so sorry!" she cried.

"Sorry? What about?" He was surprised.

"That I wasn't home."

"I didn't expect to find you there." He took her in his arms and kissed her with all the ardor that two nights away from her had stored up in him.

"Oh, these brides and grooms!" Julia said laughing, and shook her head until the bun came loose and her hair cascaded down her back.

Kaupena went to her and wrapped her in a vigorous embrace. "You're jealous," he teased. Then he went back and took Lucia's hand.

There was something in his manner that made Lucia's nerves tighten, shedding the calmness she had absorbed from Julia. She recognized then that there was tenseness in living with him. He was unpredictable, giving to her abundantly and also taking away. The vision of Momi and Lokalia leaning together like conspirators came into her mind. She wondered if Momi had once been in love with Kaupena.

"Julia, we're going home now," he said. "Thanks a lot for taking care of Luce."

"Ah, we love her here."

Kaupena and Lucia walked slowly down the stairs and waved their way across the lawn and into the little pathway.

When they were in the woods, Kaupena took her again in his arms. "I missed you. I came home because I couldn't stand it." His voice was sharp with the fullness of his emotion.

"I'm glad you came," she whispered.

He pressed his mouth tightly upon hers, and she moved so that her body lay close against his.

"Come, darling," he said and pulled her toward the deeper woodland.

"Wait until we get home!"

"It's better outside."

"Someone might come."

"Not where I'll take you."

He led her through the woods to a close-tangled clump of hau trees. The foliage seemed dense and impenetrable, but Kaupena went directly to a little tunnel that gave access to a small grassy plot within. "This was our secret hideout when we were kids."

It was shadowy and clean and fragrant. "How lucky you were as a child," she said.

He pulled her down beside him and encircled her waist. "Listen to the wind, darling. The Makaniloa. You can even hear the sea if you listen carefully." Slowly and tenderly he unfastened her clothing.

She listened to the wind and the sea until the motion of these sounds seemed to be humming within her body. She swayed slightly, and he laid her gently down upon the grass. "This is our rhythm," he whispered. And she received him in deep harmony.

When they were back in their own house, Kaupena announced that he had the rest of the day off. "After lunch, darling, I'll go up in the woods and get some of those fern stumps you've been wanting."

She smiled, still feeling the warmth and contentment of their embrace in the woods. "Thanks, dear."

She heated canned soup and made tuna-fish sandwiches, and they sat down at the kitchen table. A soft wind blew in upon them, carrying the scent of the upper valley. They watched a flock of plovers skitter across the back lawn and disappear into the woods. The great red hibiscus blossoms of the bush by the tank bounced clumsily on their stems, and banana leaves clashed in the gusts.

Kaupena broke the long, comfortable silence. "Are you happy with me, Lucia? Isn't it fun to be together!" His voice had a pinprick of worry.

"I'm terribly happy."

"I've always been a kind of lone wolf. Not mixing with people quite so much as the others. I hope you don't get lonely."

"Only when I stop to think how few people I see. It's silly, I know."

"I must help you to get to know more people. Thank God for Julia, anyhow."

"Don't worry about me. I'm really happy. . . . Tell me, what did you do up the mountain? Anything exciting?"

"We mostly worked. But a funny thing. Early this morning I met Grandma up near the gap. She was on her way home with a few mountain apples. I don't know how that feeble old lady possibly walked so far."

"Especially as she walked down here yesterday." Lucia's heart was beating rapidly.

"Oh?"

"For the hukilau."

"Did you see her?"

"Yes."

"To speak to?"

"No. She didn't want to speak to me. Momi asked her to."

"That gal should know enough to keep her hands off!" he said sharply.

"I was sorry she didn't want to speak to me. And a little hurt." Lucia's voice was unpleasantly constricted in her throat.

He flushed and said uneasily, "Oh, she's queer."

"I wonder why she went all the way up to the gap for mountain apples? There are some much closer."

"It probably wasn't for mountain apples that she went. She's kind of pupule, you know. She has crazy ideas and believes in some of the old gods and all that." His tone now had an undercurrent of irritation.

The old gods! Lucia saw the rock with the withered plumeria lei. She felt again the movement under her hand and the strange silence. Her heart beat wildly, and she continued impulsively with her probing. "Oh Kaupena, can't I meet her? Why does she avoid me? Why does she hate me? For she must hate me to stay away like this!"

"Hate you!" Kaupena was angry. "Whatever gives you that idea? She's just a crazy old woman. She doesn't know how to behave."

Lucia forced her voice into a taut calmness. "It's not natural the way she keeps away from us."

His face was red and his fingers trembled. "Can't you understand she's just a little crazy?"

"Others have told me she's a wonderful person. . . . What would happen if I went up to see her?"

"Let's forget about it!"

"But Kaupena darling, she's your closest relative. She's the person who reared you. I really want to know her." Her tone was shriller than she had meant it to be, and she felt the tension growing in her. Now was surely the moment. She would get to the bottom of this.

"Leave it alone, Lucia," Kaupena said curtly and rose from the table.

"Why don't you ask her to call?" Lucia persisted, with the clear insight that she was starting a quarrel and that she would bitterly regret this scene.

"It's that damned kahuna working in this house!"

"What do you mean? A kahuna working in the house! Oh Kaupena, why won't you clear up these mysteries for me?"

"Oh, for God's sake, Lucia! You're just like any other haole woman! Can't you let us alone?" He strode from her, out of the house and down toward the main road.

Her heart pounded violently; she felt her nails bite into her palms. The silence became unbearable, and she cried aloud, "Kaupena, why won't you help me? Why are you so stubborn?" And she went in and threw herself on the bed.

Kaupena walked straight to the ranch and saddled Panini. He mounted and rode up the slope toward his grandmother's house. At the valley's mouth, he paused to look back at the bit of roof he could see jutting above the foliage, the roof that sheltered Lucia in her misery. He both hated and loved her in this moment.

Although it was only three in the afternoon, dusk had already settled into the valley. The green of the foliage was dull, the leaves drooped strangely, and the grass seemed limp. The heavy, sweetish odor of tropical decay hung in the air. He noticed suddenly that the wind had dropped completely, a curious thing for this land of continual blowing. He brought Panini to a stop and dismounted.

He lit a cigarette and squatted on his heels. As the smoke curled pleasantly around his face, filling his nostrils and clouding his vision, he wondered how he could convince his grandmother that she must meet Lucia. He cast back over the days of his boyhood. Once he had been able to get anything from her— by threat. He had used a great variety of threats: to run away, to refuse to learn the ancient things, to kill himself. Then one day when he was fifteen he had realized the cowardliness of this method, and had abandoned it. He still despised the way of threat, but it seemed the only means left. He crushed his cigarette in the grass, then rose and stretched, spitting the bitter taste from his mouth.

At the house, he saw old Mr. Clarke coming down the stairs. That meant something—another of those treks to the rock for ceremonies and incantations. This would play into his hands. He greeted the old man.

"Hello!"

"Hello, Boy. We hope you'll be with us tonight."

"Something on?"

"Yes. At Pohaku Lono."

"Well, I don't know if . . ."

"We need young people. The old things are disappearing too fast."

He saw the tender, watery-weak eyes of the aged man. His

face was symbolic of the passing Hawaiian ways. The old, worn gauntness was there, with its strength, its mysticism, its primitiveness. And over it hung the darkness of time. These men who had grown up when the old ways were still practiced had a quality in them that no young Hawaiian had. Their sturdy racial pride had been undercut with a doubt created by the new civilization being forced upon them. They had accepted of the new those things that could be fitted into the pattern of the past. Out of complexity they had devised a simple morality and justice. The young scoffed at this, plunging into the new, willfully forgetting the old. And so they had torn up their roots and found themselves thrashing aimlessly, uncomfortably, in a world that greeted them either with scorn, or with a sugary condescension. He, Kaupena, had determined long ago never to give up his roots. Lucia would have to learn that his living with her did not mean that he was abandoning his heritage.

"Sure, I'll be there," he burst out at Mr. Clarke. "I'll come up tonight."

In the house he found his grandmother reading the genealogy chant. He sat down and waited for her to finish. Her old voice moved proudly among the rhythms of the poem, and her body had now some of the resilience of youth.

When she had finished, he said, "I saw Mr. Clarke outside. He asked me to come up tonight."

"I hope you will." Her eyes rested upon him in devotion and despair. "We need you. You are part of our way into the future."

His eyes became wary. "Perhaps I should say I will come, if you will do something for me."

"What?" Her voice was clipped and suspicious.

"You know what it is, Tutu." He forced his tone to be gentle and tender.

A long silence remained between them. She sighed. When

she spoke it was with insight. "Now you bargain with me. You tell me that you will come tonight if I will go and visit your wife and kiss her and call her my child. You tell me that never again will you share in our ritual unless I do this thing you want me to do." Her Hawaiian became more rhythmic and sonorous as she continued. "Don't you know, Kaupena, that you must either live completely in the Hawaiian way or completely out of it? There is no half way."

"I don't agree with that. And you don't either. You sent me to the university. You said I had to train my mind. And I trained it in the American way. That doesn't prevent me from keeping my roots firmly in our own past."

"But this woman! She is different!"

"Why do you hate someone you've never seen?"

"She takes your mana, your power, away from you. She will desert you for a haole man. You will see. They all do in the end. That is how she robs you, by filling your spirit with hurt. She will give you a wound from which you will never recover."

"If she leaves me it will be because we both agree to part. But right now we are in love. And you are causing misunderstanding between us. This very moment she is sitting in our house thinking bitterly of me."

"And casting her eyes in the direction of Paul Ritten."

"Already!" he said acidly.

"I saw Momi! She said Julia had them to dinner. And Paul and your wife talked to each other the whole time. They were attracted. It is inevitable. You are keeping her here to disrupt Makaniloa."

He rose impatiently and said in English. "What goddam minds you all have!" His voice hardened. "Take it or leave it. If you will call on her I'll stay tonight. I'll come often to help. If you don't I'll never come here again."

Lokalia responded with dignity. She rose and regarded him

thoughtfully. "I have no choice, Kaupena." She left the room.

She had stature, he thought. For all her humble background, she had the manner of a chiefess. She had a wisdom and a passion that drew people to her.

When at dusk Kaupena had not yet returned, Lucia got into her yellow coupe and drove to the ranch. Johnny had not seen Kaupena since they had come down the mountain. She met Margaret in the driveway. "You haven't seen Kaupena?"

"No, is he lost?"

"We had a quarrel after lunch, and he went off."

"Have you gone up to his grandmother's?"

"No, she won't see me." Lucia's voice was curt.

Margaret searched her face. "She's a stubborn old woman."

"Why does she hate me?"

"She hates anyone who she thinks is taking Kaupena away from her. Her whole plan of the future is centered in him. He is the only surviving heir of the Waiolama tradition. The Waiolamas have been quite a family, you know."

"I know, and I'm proud of being one. Just as proud as she is."

"Marrying a Waiolama made her the wonderful old creature she is. She came from a poor and low-born family, and you'd think she was born to the *alii*."

"Somehow she has stood between us from the beginning."

"Don't press it too much. This is a matter between Hawaiians. I've noticed that when these Hawaiian children are reared by their grandparents, the tie is closer than with the parents."

"Do you think Kaupena is up at Lokalia's now?"

"Probably, if you quarreled about her."

"That's all we ever quarrel about."

"If I were you I'd just go home and wait. He'll be back when he's settled things with her."

"It's strange. With Julia and her family everything is so easy and natural. With Kaupena there is so much mystery and tension."

"I've known all kinds of Hawaiians, but I've never known one with quite the sensitivity and acuteness that Kaupena has. He is deeply responsive to all that goes on about him, yet he'll stand aloof. He turned down fine chances in Honolulu to come back to Makaniloa. And I've always admired him for the pride he has in his heritage. So many Hawaiians hide this pride with an uneasy or apologetic manner." She took Lucia's hand. "Go home now. Don't worry. He'll figure this problem out some way. You'll just have to wait."

"I'd like to help him."

"He's got to do it alone. Remember that there are some things which can be done only alone."

Back in her little house, Lucia lighted the lamps. The wind had grown to a gale's strength, and the whole house seemed to shake under its impact. The coldness that came with the wind made her hungry, and she took a piece of cooked steak from the icebox. She boiled water for tea and spread a piece of bread with butter. Then she stood at the window and ate.

When she had finished, she went to bed. The sheets were cold. Curling herself into a ball, she listened for the beat of Panini's hoofs on the road or of Kaupena's footsteps on the lanai.

When she finally did hear him, she pretended sleep. She could not face him now in this turmoil of loneliness and anxiety. She would say cruel things she did not intend.

He undressed in the dark and then stood a few moments beside the bed. She felt her eyelids quiver and was in an agony lest he should discover her wakefulness. Then he went to the other side of the bed and cautiously crawled under the covers. He stayed carefully on his side, holding his body tense, as though afraid of touching her. He sighed deeply.

She waited, hoping he would move to her, take her tenderly

in his arms. She felt that through an embrace understanding would come. All the mystery of his secret life would vanish in the strength and intimacy of their union. But he lay rigidly, and soon she knew from the huskiness of his breathing that he was asleep. She felt in that moment completely desolate, and the painful rhythm of dry sobs contorted her body.

8.

AFTER the rites at Pohaku Lono, Lokalia sat in her rocker, gathering in her mind the loose strands of events of the past few days: Momi and her jealousy of Lucia, embittered by the old love she had had for Kaupena; the glimpse she had had of Lucia and Paul talking together. Her mind turned most, however, to Kaupena and his restlessness and tension. The woman, Lucia, by the passion she aroused in him and the alien ways she brought to his daily living, was destroying his calm. It was she who had driven him to his means of winning a victory over his grandmother, the threat which had hurt Lokalia more than anything he had done or said in many years.

Lokalia sighed a woman's sigh of acceptance. Men crudely and ruthlessly plundered their way toward their desires. Her mother had warned her of that. "Yield," she had said, "it is easier." But her mother had been a simple woman, content to yield. Lokalia had battled with anger and passion against all her men. She had lost this outward battle with Kaupena. Now she must be subtler, she must win Lucia to Hawaiian living. It would be a difficult task, she imagined.

Paul Ritten was, she saw, the real danger; she understood the strong magnetism in time of loneliness or trouble between those of like races. She had seen it over and over again, Japanese clinging to Japanese, Hawaiians clinging to Hawaiians, haoles clinging to haoles. Paul was a handsome young man with much personal charm, and Momi was so afraid of losing him that she did and said foolish things. Already she had confided her fear of Lucia to too many people. And Kaupena, giving way to that melancholy streak in him, might push Lucia to arm's length. . . .

Again she sighed. It was late and she was tired. She rocked slowly back and forth, back and forth, searching for peace in the gentle rhythmic movement. As her nerves relaxed and drowsiness came upon her, memories seeped from the past. Memories came easily these days, so easily that she was afraid. They made death seem close, for when the past was more real than the present, the time had come to die.

She was seeing now the face of her mother at that moment when she had confided to her that she wanted to marry Joseph Waiolama; at first her mother's mouth had been curved in a broad smile of pleasure, but this rapidly faded to an arch of dismay. Her mother had given a quick despairing glance around the shabby wooden house, at the hungry dirty baby lying on a mat in the sun, at the two thin children playing out in the dust of the yard. "No," she had said reluctantly, "it cannot be."

Lokalia's family came of common stock, and it was not fitting for such to unite with the chiefly Waiolamas. Her father had a piece of arid ground on which he tried to raise taro and sugar cane, but his family grew lean on his efforts. At twelve Lokalia had gone into a missionary home to be half servant girl and half scholar. In the comparative plenty of the mission home she had spent two years longing for her family. The Reverend Mr. and Mrs. Johnson had finally sent her back, for instead of growing plump and happy as they had hoped, she continued thin, and notwithstanding the fact that she was an apt student, she grew morose and nervous at her studies. On her return home, she had clung to her tenderhearted, easygoing mother, not letting her out of her sight for days. In the next two years, with the coming of maturity and surrounded by the love of her family, she had found new strength and vitality flooding into her. In the period from fourteen to sixteen she had changed from a gentle, melancholy child to a young woman of determination and rich feeling.

Two months before her seventeenth birthday, Queen Liliuokalani had come to the village for a brief stay. The people organized one of the biggest luaus ever known, and Hawaiians from all over the island came to see the Queen and to share in the three days of feasting. They came even from remote Makaniloa, and among them was Joseph Waiolama. The Waiolama family had hoped that the Queen would take to the young man and offer him a position at court. His blood was chiefly, and he was a tall handsome youth who might very well attract a queen.

Joseph, however, met Lokalia, and he thrust aside his worldly hopes as easily as he might toe a stone out of his path. They danced together and kissed on the first night. On the second they went together to a secluded spot on the beach. On the third night they made plans to marry.

When both families protested, they plotted a wild escape to the crater of the mountain, an adventure that had turned out to be one of the grave, far-reaching influences in her life. Joseph went home in seeming obedience to his parents. But he built in the following week the little grass house near the crater spring where he and Lokalia were to live until their families gave in to them.

The night that Lokalia left her home was still one of the most vivid in all her life. She had arisen at three, stealing carefully from the side of her younger sister. The darkness was heavy inside the house, sour with the odor of sleeping bodies, dust, and fermenting poi. She breathed deeply of this odor, for it meant home to her. Stealing her mother's finest koa wood calabash, she packed her few clothes in it, wrapped it in a piece of fishnet, and tied it for comfortable carrying. The calabash, she mused, would be the only dowry she could bring her husband. Kneeling above her mother, she tried to pierce the darkness to see the soft round lines of the gentle face. In her simplicity and tenderness, her mother was, she reflected, a great woman. Presently Lokalia rose and moved silently out of the house. A faint, glimmering paleness in the east forecast the dawn; a few roosters crowed, and the pigs stirred as they sensed her presence. She tore a banana from the bunch leaning against the stone outdoor oven, and ate it. Wind rustled in the starchy cane leaves and brought the stench of the pigs to her.

She walked swiftly down the path to the sea. At the beach she undressed and bathed herself. The night water was cold and harsh against her skin. She could feel the sting of salt in scratches she had on her legs. She rubbed her body with an old piece of towel and massaged her hips and legs briefly. A fountain of energy welled up in her, and she wanted to run down the beach singing. But quietly she dressed and set out on her way to the crater gap and her meeting with Joseph Waiolama. . . .

Lokalia rose from her rocker and shuffled into the bedroom. She ached more than usual tonight; the wind at Pohaku Lono had been sharp and bitter, blowing through the frailness of her aged flesh and penetrating to the core of her brittle bones. She lay down fully clothed on her bed and pulled a crocheted afghan over her.

Kaupena had been fine tonight, his voice resounding in the ancient Hawaiian way. She knew that Mr. Clarke and the others had recognized his excellence, for they had smiled with pleasure even in the midst of the solemn ceremony.

She must have slept, for when she opened her eyes she saw that a faint light had entered the room. The dawn had come too quickly. She rose and removing her wrinkled clothes, slipped into a favorite muumuu which had a design of breadfruit leaves appliquéd around the bottom. She pulled a wool shawl around her shoulders and fastened it with a cameo brooch. In the mottled mirror she saw that her hair was disheveled, and she took down the knot, removing the pins and holding them in her mouth. Then she brushed her hair with a few gentle strokes; her scalp was sensitive this morning and the bristles hurt slightly. She started to do her hair up, but the pins hurt too. So she left it hanging, although she fastened it behind each ear with small tortoise-shell combs.

She walked to the lanai to examine the morning and was startled to see coming up the path a woman and a little girl. "Mrs. Poepoe," she muttered aloud, "and Mele."

The child walked listlessly, bending her little shoulders in a stoop. She was thin, her elbows jutting out like sharp points, her face gaunt, her stomach protruding unnaturally in contrast to the sticklike quality of the small body. Lokalia's eyes suddenly burned with tears in pity and love for these two.

After greetings, Mrs. Poepoe said, "We need your help." She pointed to the little girl, who stood gazing placidly from the balustrade. "She gets worse. The teacher says she pays no attention."

Lokalia knew that the child suffered from lack of food. No kahunaism was necessary to tell her that, and no kahunaism was necessary for the cure. For two generations the Poepoes had not had enough to eat. Their babies had died off like little sick animals, and of those who lived, half suffered from tuberculosis. They lived at the beach in a wooden shack that had once been a canoe shelter and had only three sides to it. Mrs. Poepoe fished and grew sweet potatoes to supply food for the household. Her children had grown up on this diet, often skimpy when the fish were not running or when a blight had struck the sweet potatoes. Then she would tramp back into the valleys, hunting the wild bananas, the thimble berries, the few stands of taro surviving from the old days. But in spite of her efforts, her children starved. She herself had never known what it was to have enough to eat.

Finally Lokalia spoke. "Let me take Mele for a while. Perhaps if she lives with me she will get better. I cannot cure her in an hour."

Mrs. Poepoe looked sadly at her child, and Mele, who had turned to listen, began to weep. She lunged into her mother's arms. "No, no, no!" she cried.

Mrs. Poepoe shook the child roughly and spanked her. "Shut up, Mele! Mrs. Waiolama knows best. You stay here." Her harshness masked fear. She knew that if a kahuna asked for a child, the child must be given. Horrible things might befall the family who refused.

Gently and tenderly Lokalia said, "Come, Mele, let's go get a piece of cake. A friend brought it to me yesterday. I'll give you a piece."

The child left off clinging to her mother and turned to Lokalia. "Real cake?"

"Yes, come into the kitchen."

Slowly Mele followed her. Lokalia cut a piece of the white cake heaped with fudge frosting and handed it to the little girl. Mele took a bite and chewed thoughtfully. Then her face broke into a broad smile. "Look, Ma. Real cake. With frosting!"

Mrs. Poepoe was weeping. "Yes, dear," she muttered. "Now you'll be a good girl and stay with Tutu Waiolama."

"Tutu!" the child exclaimed. "Tutu gives me cake!"

Lokalia smiled at Mrs. Poepoe, who slipped out of the kitchen and away from the house. Then she gazed at the bony child and sighed. She was so different from the little boy, Kaupena. But she already had a plan for this child.

The morning after their quarrel, Lucia did not mention to Kaupena his long absence. She made coffee and toast and set them on the table. Then she fried an egg for him.

He watched her closely but he too did not speak of his disappearance. When she sat down across the table from him, he said cautiously, "It's good to be home."

Tears started hotly into her eyes, and she turned away to gaze out of the window. "I'm glad," she muttered.

"Is there anything I can get today?"

"No. I think I'll go down to the store myself. I need to get out a little."

"Yeah, I guess so. Say! What about driving to Hana for the movies tonight?" His voice was eager, anxious. She knew he wanted her to face him.

So composing herself, she turned to him. "That might be fun."

He reached across the table and squeezed her hand. But this did not make up for the anguish he had caused her yesterday, and she turned from him, masking her gesture by rising to pour him another cup of coffee.

When he had gone, she would not allow herself to wonder why he had made no explanation. Hurriedly she took her basket and her purse. She wouldn't drive, she decided suddenly. She would walk. It would take more time, and it was a lovely golden day.

At the store she handed Mr. Oshiro her list. He gathered the things from the shelves and set them on the counter, talking the whole time about his son who was graduating from Oberlin in June. When he had finished, he totaled the amounts on an abacus and handed the slip to her. She paid the money and began to fit the items into her basket.

"How did your son happen to pick on Oberlin?"

"He had one friend who went there."

"Have any of your other children gone to college?"

"My oldest daughter went to Iowa. She's teaching in Honolulu. My third son is at the University of Hawaii now and the second at Kent in Ohio."

"You're going to have an educated family!"

"It's important now. If more of these Hawaiians went on to school it'd be more better. Old Lokalia's right!"

Again Lokalia! Her spirit haunted Makaniloa. Lucia sighed and asked, "What does she believe?"

"She made Kaupena go to the university. She's one smart old lady." He interrupted himself. "Hello, Mr. Ritten!"

"Hello, Oshiro. I want half a dozen cans of milk."

Lucia turned to Paul. "Hello. How are you today?"

"Oh, I didn't see you when I came in."

The storekeeper put the tinned milk in a sack and handed it to Paul. "Thanks, Oshiro, how are your kids?"

"Fine, Mr. Ritten."

"That's good. Lucia, can't I carry that basket home for you? It looks pretty heavy."

"Oh, I can manage," she said quickly.

But he took it from her and led the way out of the store. The wind had shifted and was no longer blowing from the cold purity of the crater but rather from the sea. There was a fragrance of warm seaweed and salt and fish in it, and a softer, moister quality in its touch. Lucia found herself expanding under the gentleness of it and under the easy friendliness of Paul's presence. He talked for a while of Oshiro, the storekeeper. "I'm not sure I'm so ambitious for my boys. It's pretty hard on the poor kids. And yet those children have responded; they're all fine young people, alert and intelligent. Either he was lucky in his kids or his system works."

She acknowledged Paul's words softly from time to time with indistinct murmurs, enough to satisfy him of her attention. She carefully matched her stride to his and enjoyed the little extra effort it was to take the longer steps.

He spoke of Makaniloa in the lyrical fashion of one who is in love with the spot in which he lives. He spoke of its beauty, of the shifting of weather and color and mood. Then he spoke of its quietude, and of the richness of day-to-day experience. "We don't have many doubts in Makaniloa, because values are simple and straightforward."

She interrupted for the first time. "Yet is it so simple? You yourself said it wasn't the other day."

"Not with the simplicity of childhood, no. But with the simplicity which comes from a people loving their land—a people fairly well able to cope with the tragedy of being born into the ebb tide of a race and culture. They have resolved life into the terms of every-day living—of fishing and singing, loving and hating, and—" he paused to laugh lightly—"most important of all, gossiping. Out of all these little bits of daily experience comes a sense of the wholeness of living."

"The wholeness of living," she mused softly.

He stopped to shift her basket to the other hand. "Man belongs here. He's not set apart from the course of nature. He's part of it. It's a healthier way, I'm sure."

"I think I used to feel that a little when I was a child on the farm."

They rounded a curve and she could see the green of her lawn and a corner of the lanai of the house. She was sorry it was coming so quickly, for she had never heard a person speak so thoughtfully of the life he had chosen for himself. It was an exciting experience.

He went on, "What we have forgotten back home is the peace and sense of importance that can come from a daily life fully realized. It can be like poetry. And that's what these people know instinctively. They can eat and be glad they're eating. They can sit on the lanai and quietly absorb the life around them if it be nothing but the wind in the grass or a procession of people passing the gate."

They had reached the house now, and she asked him in for a cup of coffee. He refused, saying that he must get up to the ranch. She thanked him for helping her and for the interesting talk. "You're an amazing person, Paul," she said.

He gazed at her silently, and she heard the wind thrashing the trees. Suddenly he laid her basket on a step. "God, why did you ever have to come here!" he said curtly and strode across the lawn to the road.

9.

PAUL'S words had been a blow strong enough to unsteady Lucia's balance for a moment. She grasped the railing and leaned against it. Then slowly she mounted the stairs, pulling herself up by the bannister. When she reached the top she saw her basket where he had laid it in that final gesture. Abruptly the vision came to her of Lokalia and Momi whispering together. Momi, with quick penetrating intuition, had early foreseen the darkness ahead. Lucia broke away from these thoughts and ran down the stairs to fetch the basket.

In the kitchen her eyes turned to the two coffee cups on the table—her own with a slight stain of lipstick on it and still half full, as she had left it when she rose to pour Kaupena another cup, and his full and shoved slightly to one side. It was significant that he had not drunk it; he was aware then that she had avoided him.

She stared into the deep green of the mango trees. Paul, it was clear, felt himself falling in love with her. It was a troubling, confusing thing to know; but more troubling than that was the thin vein of happiness which stirred within her at this knowledge and the conjecture as to what his love might mean as a refuge in the difficult twilight of her relation with Kaupena. For Kaupena had hurt her this time with a sting that lingered, one that evoked in her a faint rebellion, a slight hate. Would he never be open with her? Would there always be this dark turning-in at just that point when light and openness were most needed? Was he too much haunted by the dark of Makaniloa?

In the days that followed, an undefined and masked restraint grew up between them, and she found herself curbing any effort to lay bare the shifting ground of emotion. He sat often in the evening, as she sewed or knitted, and stared at her. Once she ventured, "A penny for your thoughts." He had merely sighed and smiled faintly at her. She had the disturbing sense that he was looking upon her as one lost to him, and in the loneliness within her she let her thoughts turn to Paul. She could, if it were ever necessary, go to him; he would understand her problems, for he too must have faced them.

Each night after these evenings of silence Kaupena took her with what seemed a progressively mounting passion. In the moments of their union and afterward, as they lay close, she would feel that their problem had been resolved. But then again at breakfast the restraint would come upon them, and it was as though they were strangers.

One sunny morning when the wind traveled in sharp gusts, she surprised herself by asking abruptly, "Kaupena, what is this growing between us?"

"Between us?" He stared in astonishment. "Is there something between us?"

"I have thought so."

His brows knitted and he said quite seriously, "You've felt that kahuna all along. Funny I haven't."

She said lightly, "It's no kahuna. It's what makes it impossible for you and me to share our days in that close intimate way husbands and wives should."

He let a long silence pass between them. Then he said, "You really do feel something, don't you? I wonder if I do. Or is it your troublesome little mind that's always got to analyze?"

"It isn't thinking that does this. It's feeling."

He lighted a cigarette and blew the smoke in a thin line from his mouth. "Darling," he said, "in Makaniloa we just live. We eat and work and make love. Sometimes we listen a little to the old gods, but that we keep mostly to ourselves. You never can tell these days who believes in the old gods. A man doesn't want to be laughed at. Maybe I don't want to be laughed at, so I keep my mouth shut." With that he rose and, after kissing her on the top of her head, he went out to the ranch and his work.

She felt a sudden tenderness for him. He was, in his way, afraid of her! And he must be infected with the despair Julia had talked of, that despair roused first in his people by the ancient disdain of missionaries and seamen. He was aware deep within his mind that she, Lucia, was of the same blood as those who had first stripped the dignity from the Hawaiians. She lay her head in her arms on the table and thought of the long difficult years of hurt endured by so many.

In the afternoon, she went down to the Protestant Church, a jaunt that was simply an excuse to walk in the sun and the wind. She felt a great need for the healing power of the sun and the cleansing force of the wind. At the churchyard she sat in the hot grass near the white marble headstone of her great-grandmother. Clasping her hands together and bowing her head, she pushed out all thought and emotion. Wind hummed and the sea sounded in hollow reverberation on the lava. Clouds moved from the crater, shutting off the sun for brief, chill moments. Presently her muscles slackened deliciously, and she lay down in the protecting grass for a nap.

The clouds had quite filled the sky when she started home again, and trudging up the hillside she became aware of the undercurrent of darkness in Makaniloa. It was visible in the somber grasses, in the black lava and the gloom-blue cliffs, and in the thick tree foliage that daily caused a premature dusk in the valleys. Kaupena was right when he said there was a dark spot in the spirit of people who lived in such a place. It made them sensitive to the inexplicable; it kept them on the alert for the actions of the gods. Long ago they had decided that the meaning of certain events lay beyond the present grasp of man. This awareness of mystery and of god-given protection was probably the real spell of Makaniloa, she thought. But it was this very darkness she feared, for in it she was utterly alien.

On the slope she met a boy who was playing an ukulele and humming as he walked.

"Hello," she said and smiled in friendliness.

"Hi," he responded. His grin reminded her of Joe Waiolama, and the music too, for he was playing one of Joe's songs.

It came to her that she should ask Joe to stay with them for a while. He would bring people and music to the house; he would banish the darkness and relieve some of the tensions between her and Kaupena. Joe with his happiness and his songs might very well be their salvation! She began to run in eagerness to tell Kaupena of the idea. Growing careless, she stumbled against one of the rocks along the trail. With the stab of pain in her ankle came a flash that perhaps this meeting with the boy who looked like Joe had not been entirely a coincidence. She stopped, her heart pounding. Was the darkness of Makaniloa engulfing her too?

Kaupena had seen Lucia in the cemetery and had considered going down to sit with her. But so much strangeness had grown up between them that he was never certain she enjoyed being with him. So instead he had gone again to Lokalia to urge her to call on Lucia soon. Lokalia said that she had a plan to develop first, and then she would come.

As he returned, he saw Lucia pause to speak to the boy. Kaupena hurried so that he might be at the door to greet her.

She came to the lanai steps and breathlessly exclaimed that she wanted Joe to visit them.

"But darling, Joe has to be closer to the village! He's crippled and can't—"

"I know. But I've already thought of that. Any time he has to go somewhere I'll drive him and pick him up again."

"Why do you want this, Lucia?" His tone was grave and probing.

She suddenly began to cry. It was the soft kind of weeping in which the tears swam into the eyes and then slowly rolled down the cheeks. "Oh, I don't know." She hid her face in shame at her weakness.

He put his arm around her. "Makaniloa has not been good to you. Are you so terribly lonely?"

"No . . . It's just that I can go only so far. Then I'm up against a stone wall."

"The first day we came to this house, you said you felt a presence here. You felt you were trespassing. Do you still feel it?"

She was quiet now and though he tried to turn her face to him, she avoided his eyes. "Sometimes," she mused. "I wonder why I do."

"It's because years and years ago a kahuna lived here." Her eyes were now upon him, brilliant with moisture and sharply penetrating. "He was not the healing kind, but the avenging kind, and he filled this house with fear and hate and death. The Hawaiians believe such things linger on in a house unless they are properly driven out. My grandmother moved into the house for a while years ago to break this spell. She had a bigger kahuna than the man who lived here."

"Your grandmother is a kahuna?"

"As much as one can be now. People go to her to be cured of sickness and to solve family problems."

"If she comes here, she might take the fear and hate away again?"

"I saw her this afternoon. She said she was coming soon."

"I'm glad," Lucia sighed. "And she can take away this unhappiness. A kahuna! His evil living on."

"Lucia, you don't really believe in that!"

"One almost can in Makaniloa." She paused and then went on. "Such things are true because people want them to be true. It's amazing how men can force the supernatural. Why, one night not too long ago I talked to my dead great-grandmother. She came and stood at the foot of our bed, and we talked about Makaniloa. It doesn't make any difference whether or not this vision was real. It was psychologically true for me."

She moved close to him and laid her hand upon his arm. "If you or I believe there is confusion in this house, there is. If we believe she can dispel it, she will. That's the simple magic of the mind—far greater than any physical magic."

"Lucia, sometimes your thinking frightens me. It makes you a stranger."

A flush of astonishment crossed her face. "You think me a stranger and I've thought that of you. You evade me, and I evade you."

Anger was beginning to mount in him; she was perplexing him and giving him a sense of his own inadequacy. He mocked, "It's the simple magic of your mind."

"You won't face things, will you?" she said softly. "Your escape is into moodiness or anger. We've got to face things together, not isolated as we have been. That's why I want Joe. He can be our norm. When we go off we can look at him and know it. Living here alone we never will straighten things out."

"You want to hide behind Joe!" The anger was thick in him.

"If that's what you want to call it." She spoke coolly.

"What can I do, for God's sake? I try to give you every tenderness. I've quarreled with my grandmother about you. I'll bring Joe up here if you want. I knew there would be difficulties about our marriage, but I've tried to help. What can I do that's right?"

"You can make yourself known to me."

His wrath had become corrosive, and he said something he

had sworn he would never say to her. "I can see I should have married a Hawaiian. Perhaps my grandmother was right."

Her first impulse was to cry out at him, "I wish you had!" But deep within her flashed a warning. This was not a moment to give him up. What she said now might determine the future, and she was not ready to turn one way or the other. So she simply gazed at him, her eyes wide, her lips parted. This was a moment that could not be forgotten; these were words that would leave their mark deep within each of them. As she stared at Kaupena, her eyes judged him. And presently he looked away, his face pale and his pupils dark with that inward gaze. Slowly she turned and walked from him. Her feet led her out of the house and into the path through the woods. Ahead of her in Julia's house was the noisy, easygoing tranquillity in which she could rest. She ate supper at Julia's, picking at the bowl of rice and stew feigning, unsuccessfully, an appetite. She held Georgie on her lap as Kaneloa family life frothed about her, including her casually in its talk and activity, and bringing to her a peace of spirit.

An hour after supper, however, a restlessness came upon her and she rose to go. Even before she reached the edge of her garden, she heard music and knew that Joe had come.

She ran up the stairway of the lanai. Joe was seated on the hikie, cushions heaped up around him. Across his lap was a steel guitar. Two men sat near him at his left, strumming ukuleles, while a bass-viol player stood at his right.

Joe beckoned for her to come in, and introducing her to the orchestra, explained that they were practicing for the church bazaar. "I've written a couple of new songs the boys are learning." He winked at her. "They're not too bright, you know. It takes them plenty long."

She smiled, and the men grinned. Seeing the shyness which had come upon them in her presence, she tried as best she could to use the pidgin intonation in her speech. That, she had learned, put people at their ease more quickly than anything else. But she had to be careful not to overdo it or they would think she was talking down to them.

"Have you seen Kaupena, yeah?" she asked.

"I think he went out in back," Joe replied.

"Oh! He didn't say anything?"

"That guy doesn't talk much, you know. He said I was to stay with you people for a while. Then he walked through the house, looking for you, I guess. Then he went out."

"Will you stay, Joe?"

"Are you sure you want me?"

"Yes, we do! Very much!"

"I have a lot of noisy friends, and I don't like to butt in on your peace."

"We want you—do you really think he was looking for me?"

"He didn't say. I just had that feeling."

"I see. May I listen to your rehearsal?"

"Sure, we love an audience."

They played with enjoyment, grinning little secret messages to each other as they missed a note or added a special flourish. They played with the same casual, warm ease with which Julia drifted through the days and weeks. Why, Lucia wondered, was this fine quality of repose missing in Kaupena? What in the chemistry of his nature made it impossible for him? And yet, it was not wholly missing, for at times there was a glorious contentment in him, which expanded into her life and gave them days on end of happiness. Then suddenly the darkness would descend, destroying this happiness in a moment.

After an hour she rose and slipped to the kitchen where she put on a coffeepot and made sandwiches. She opened a can of olives and a jar of nuts and placed them on a tray with the sandwiches and coffee, and carried it in to the musicians. "How about some kaukau?"

They stopped playing abruptly and smiled their pleasure. She placed the tray on the big koa table, and the bass-viol player helped Joe walk with his wooden legs and cane to join them. While they ate, they teased each other. "Jees! The way that Charlie slaps the bass, you'd think it was his favorite girl." "And Tiny's ukulele! Plenty sour! That guy can't hear nothing." "And Joe! What kind pilau songs he writes! And he expects us to play them." They laughed and munched and told her how good everything was.

After she had carried the dishes back to the kitchen and washed them, she did not rejoin the men but went into the bedroom. She would sit by the window and read; then perhaps Kaupena might see her and come in from where he was hiding. She lighted the lamp and sat with a book in her lap. She stared for a while at the blurred pages; then she began to shift her glance abstractedly here and there about the room. She became aware of a dark shadow on the bed, a shadow that could not possibly be a part of the quilt design. She rose and moved toward the bed in a strange spasm of fear. Abruptly she recognized what the object was: long strands of sweet-scented maile leaves. She knelt and gathered the lei into her arms. The maile was fresh and damp from the woods. She twisted it about her neck and smoothing her hair went out the back door into the night. She whistled softly as Kaupena had taught her to do when she wanted him. Soon his answering whistle came. She moved across the lawn and waited at the edge of the trees.

He was breathless. "I waited for your call."

"Oh, Kaupena!" She put her arms around his neck, and he drew her close to him. She thought of their love as a candle flame in a window; in the stillness it burned steadily, richly, but at a gust of wind it was nearly quenched.

Joe insisted on taking Lucia to the bazaar. "You sit around this house too much," he said. "You ought to get out and meet people. Don't be stuffy because Kaupena is."

Kaupena said that he never got enough poi at such affairs and that the laulaus were always skimpy. "Take good care of her," he admonished Joe. He kissed Lucia. "I'll miss you. So don't stay too late. But have a good time."

The parish house was festooned with ferns and strands of maile gathered from the mountains; ironwood branches and palm fronds were clustered in the corners. The bazaar tables were arranged neatly around the big room, leaving the center area clear at one end for dancing and at the other for the tables and benches for the poi supper. Behind the tables displaying needlework hung four Hawaiian quilts in pink, mauve, blue, and red designs on white. In back of the tables that exhibited crocheting and tatting was a rattan screen against which hung some children's dresses and muumuus.

The other tables were laden with lauhala work and jams, jellies, and cakes. A palm bower was set aside for the musicians. The supper tables were decorated with ferns and hibiscus, and young girls, dressed in their brightest muumuus, stood waiting to help with the serving.

As Joe and Lucia entered he said, "I'm afraid I won't be much of a help. I'll have to play most of the evening. But you will see here what Makaniloa really is, and you can sit with Julia or Paul. Momi, of course, will be singing with us."

"Oh, does Momi sing with your orchestra?"

"Sure. She's the best singer in Makaniloa."

Lucia wished that she hadn't come. Listening to Joe's enthusiasm she had forgotten that he could not be with her throughout the evening. And she hadn't known about Momi.

Joe steered her toward the supper tables. "We'd better eat now," he said. "They'll be after me to start the music. I see the other boys have already eaten."

Lucia helped Joe settle in a place at the tables, and then she went to get their supper. As she crossed the floor she felt eyes turned obliquely upon her, some shyly, some with curiosity, some even with a sort of compassion. It was the first time that she had been to a church bazaar, and she guessed that they were wondering where Kaupena was. Back at the table she directed her full attention to the poi and lomi salmon and laulau in an effort to hide the self-consciousness which blurred her mind. At her side Joe ate and laughed and talked to passers-by.

He turned to her. "You eat as though you're awfully hungry." He took her fingers and smiled warmly. "Everybody's friendly here. Don't feel so shy. Look! Paul and Momi just came in. Let's have them eat with us."

"Maybe they have friends . . ."

"No one better than us. Besides, while Momi's with the orchestra, you can dance with Paul."

She said impulsively, "Maybe when we're through eating, I'd better go home to Kaupena."

Joe looked at her in amazement. Then he grinned. "You've been living too long with that guy. You're getting to be just like him. Relax, Lucy dear. Have a good time. That's what life is for."

Joe waved for the Rittens to join them, and when they had filled their trays, they came to the table. Paul sat next to Lucia.

Momi exclaimed, "Well, a surprise to see you here!"

"It's Joe's fault," Lucia responded. "He invited me. But the minute we arrived he told me he was going to desert me."

"Well, I always desert Paul too. Now you two can hold hands." Momi's voice was delicately sharp.

"I'd much rather dance," Lucia said lightly.

"Are you a good dancer?" Paul joked.

"The best. And I'm getting better. Joe's friends are teaching me the hula."

"Yeah, Joe," Momi put in. "I hear you're living up with them."

Her voice was probing, and her eyes slid a glance from Joe to Lucia and back again.

Joe brushed aside her remark. "Come on, Momi baby, we've got to go and start the music. Everyone's waiting."

When they had gone, Paul—as though freed from some vague restraint—began to talk. It was a drifting desultory monologue, that of a person who is with someone he is certain will understand all his nuances. There was nothing to hide now, no words to stifle, no accent to disguise, no instinct to curb. They were two persons alike in blood and culture. And there was no hint of the mood of his exclamation on the day he had carried home her grocery basket. She was glad, now, that he was with her, and she listened contentedly. The music grew loud, and she swayed slightly to its rhythm.

She found that her attention could be easily divided between him and what was around her, and she gazed at the throng. Most had satisfied their curiosity about her, and she could look at them without their being aware of her examination. When she did meet with an appraising glance, there was always from the Hawaiian a quick friendly smile.

The people were brightly dressed, their faces active with the flash of expressions, their bodies rhythmic and graceful, their voices humming in a low resonant tone. They stood out as individuals: an old woman with a feather lei on her head and an old-fashioned high-necked holoku, a large woman in a flowered muumuu the sleeves of which were lined with scarlet, a man in blue jeans and red shirt, an old man in a dark blue suit, with a heavy gold watch chain dangling from his trouser pocket. Each expressed a distinct personality, and yet each blended with the others. And as she sat there, listening to Paul, catching the smiles of friendliness and responding to the nods of greeting, she felt that at last they were beginning to accept her as one of them.

"Do you think," she broke in upon his talk, "that such experiments as we make are possible?" She wanted affirmation of the confidence that had settled over her.

He seemed surprised. "Why Lucia, hundreds, even thousands have done it in these islands." He took her arm. "Come on, let's dance. We've talked enough."

She was comfortable in his arms, moving to Joe's music. And she was happy. Paul was going to let her have the peace of his friendliness and of that mutual sharing they enjoyed of thought and feeling, untroubled by those words of two weeks ago. That moment must have been forgotten; it had been on his part a false impulse. She smiled in her pleasure, and presently other men were dancing with her. She laughed and talked with them as though she too had grown up in Makaniloa.

10.

AFTER the bazaar, Lucia's life broadened. She took Joe here and there, stopping to sit on lanais and listen to conversations which moved lazily from mood to mood and topic to topic. Often the background of these hours of warm association was the wind scraping in the spiny pandanus or crackling like a sudden squall in the coconut fronds. This wind-noise had a way of blending the most desultory bits of talk until they glowed with the significance of the peacefulness and the warm communion of human spirit among the people of Makaniloa. With Joe, she found herself at ease among them.

"They like you," he said, "and they wonder why Kaupena's kept you so hidden. I tell them to remember that Kaupena keeps his own self hidden."

She said, "I wish we could help Kaupena come out of himself."

"Oh no! That isn't the way for him. Some of us Hawaiians have to do the thinking and the brooding for the rest of us. He was chosen almost from birth for that—what with Lokalia taking him."

Joe had quickly become a member of their little family. He took Lucia not only out of the house, but out of the brooding to which she had given too much time. Thus Lucia quickly grew to love Joe and found herself often seeking his company. An ukulele was seldom far from his reach, and he spent what little free time he had away from people and social engagements, composing and writing lyrics. Often he would go through a tune for Lucia and ask how she liked it. She helped him on occasion, for she had a natural way of jingling rhymes together. "We ought to collaborate," he said. "I can see it on a printed sheet, Waiolama and Waiolama."

"It's strange," she said, "that you've never had anything published, yet I hear your songs on the radio."

"I teach songs to people, and they go back to Honolulu and teach them to someone else. Pretty soon a lot of people know them. That's the way it was done in the old days."

"But you ought to sell them! Publish them with your name!"

"Most of those who make any difference know what I write. And as for money!" He slapped a wooden leg soundly. "Uncle Sam takes good care of me."

"I suppose so." Her face flushed a soft pink in enthusiasm. "I like working with you on the lyrics! It's something new for me."

He responded obliquely. "It's kind of lonely for you, up here in the woods! You'd better hurry and have some kids. Don't let Kaupena keep on making a hermit of you."

"I'll never be a hermit. It isn't my way." Her eyes misted. "Do you think Kaupena's getting more hermitlike? At the ranch before we were married he never seemed especially so."

"Well . . ." He knocked his cane in a little tattoo against a leg. "Kaupena has always sort of gone in cycles. Sometimes he's worse and sometimes he's better. You know he lived with Tutu. Poor kid, up there in that ghostly valley! Everyone says it wasn't too good for him. He wasn't like the other children— kind of aloof and queer. We were a little scared of him. He knew so many things. And then he pretended to be a kahuna. I guess we didn't like him very much." He grinned. "You know how kids are. . . . But then, of course, he grew up to be the best one of the lot of us."

"Tell me," she asked, "do you feel there is a dark side to Makaniloa?"

"A dark side," he mused. "I'm not sure I know exactly what you mean. But anyhow Makaniloa is not an easy place. People have starved here. The winds or the floods sometimes wipe out all the gardens. Then there's only fish, and you can't always get them. Also it was a place in the old days for gods and ghosts. There must be something dark in the atmosphere of a place like this."

"Some days I can feel the darkness. It's in the landscape and in the people. As though they were haunted. Even Julia, sunny as she is, has moods."

"Don't let it bother you. Besides, the ghosts left Makaniloa long ago. And it's not isolated like it used to be. Cars and airplanes can bring in food if a flood comes. I suppose you've heard that Mr. Perkins is going to make a small landing field down by the church. He's bought a little plane."

"How grown up that makes Makaniloa, for Bill to do that!"

It came over her that she had not thought of Elizabeth and Bill for weeks. Kaupena no longer went to their cocktail parties, and Elizabeth had stopped inviting them to dinner after the first month of their marriage. Those few dinners had been awkward occasions; Elizabeth, who had come to regard Lucia as a person of exotic behavior, constantly probed her with irritating little questions about how she was getting along, what she was feeling, and did she miss her family and old friends. Bill would discover his wife at this and send her off to get him a drink or a bowl of olives; then in her place he would thrust Margaret. Lucia had not missed her contact with the Perkinses, and even in her moments of deepest loneliness she had not once considered them as a possible haven.

"Yes," Joe commented. "Makaniloa is finally growing up. Soon there won't be any lost places in all these islands. That will be too bad."

No more lost places, it occurred to her, might mean no more dark places for the Hawaiians.

"Oh Joe!" she cried, "there's so much here to be learned, to be felt. There's so much which can be understood only slowly and softly, step by step, day by day!"

He grinned at her. "You're O.K., Lucia. You'll come out on top."

It was an unusual day of fog and great stillness. In the afternoon Lucia sat in the big rocker by the front window and knitted on a sweater for Joe. He had been complaining of the cold and had said with a smile, "When you're only half a man it's harder to keep warm." From the window she watched the fog-shapes in the trees, the sudden rents in the mist, which gave vistas of the sea and shore or of the gray-dark Protestant Church. Once as the fog parted, she thought she glimpsed a figure far down the road. When the fog lifted again, she saw that there was in actuality an old woman coming toward the house. Lokalia, it flashed upon her. Her heart pounded, and she hurriedly stuffed her knitting into the bag. She sat breathless, her fingers twisted together. She had tried to prepare herself for this moment, but here she was meeting it with all the fear she had sworn to stifle. She rose and went to the doorway to greet the old woman.

Lokalia's appearance did not help to calm her. She seemed, as she moved across the room, the very epitome of the darkness of Makaniloa. She sat down in the big koa chair next to the table with the bouquet of orange croton leaves, and the warm glow of this foliage only emphasized her darkness. She wore a black holoku and around her shoulders a yellow feather lei. The holoku was of the old-fashioned type with a high neck and long sleeves. Her face was set in stern lines, her eyes sharp and dark, and her lips although full and capable of great tenderness, were pulled into an arch of disapproval. Her hair was not worn in the loose up-swept effect of many elderly Hawaiians, but was brushed back severely and done in a tight, crabbed little bun. Her gnarled fingers were clenched in her lap.

She looked slowly around the room, her back straight as a pillar and only her head turning. Lucia remembered a faded photograph she had seen of an old chiefess seated stiffly, behind her in shadowy darkness the faint outlines of kahilis—the royal feather standards. The photograph, poor as it was, had had about it an aura of power and melancholy and mystery, and Lokalia in her chair, with the croton for the kahili, created just that effect.

"You have changed it," she said, drawing out the full richness of the vowels and emphasizing the rhythm of the words, as many Hawaiians do.

"I hope you like the changes," Lucia responded timidly.

"It's like you, not like him."

"We did it together. He said he liked it."

"You're changing him." Then with challenge, "When are you going to take him away?"

"Take him away? What do you mean?"

"Take him to Honolulu, or California, or wherever!" Her eyes flashed like cold wet rocks.

"I'm not going to do that. I love Makaniloa."

"Perhaps instead, you are going to run off with Paul Ritten!" The words were spoken as though they had been calculated long in advance.

Lucia was at a loss to reply. "I know Paul Ritten only a little," she muttered. Then as the full import of Lokalia's words unfolded in her, a wave of anger surged up and gave her courage. She rose and walked toward Lokalia. "Why do you dislike me? I've wanted desperately to be friendly with you."

"Haven't you done enough for me to dislike you? Marrying Kaupena and taking his power away from him?"

"I've taken nothing from him!"

Lokalia stood up to face Lucia. Notwithstanding the frailty

of her figure, she seemed large and overpowering. "You have taken his power, I say! How can I forgive you for that?"

"What do you mean, power?"

The old woman spoke proudly. "Thank God, we have some secrets left! People like you have taken everything else away from us."

Then something gave way in her forcefulness, and she sank back into the chair. Her voice took on a tone of sorrow and defiance. "Yes, you have stripped us. The land wasn't of supreme importance. But the dignity was. Can such damage ever be repaired? I've wondered, I've tried . . ."

Lucia stared at her. What did this chameleon behavior mean? Then slowly it came over her that this was the old Hawaiian despair of which Julia loved to talk so easily and loquaciously. "I'm sorry for such things," she whispered.

On a sudden impulse she sat at Lokalia's feet. "My great-grandmother didn't steal your dignity. She loved you. . . . She lived and died here and she is buried down by the sea. I've yearned since my childhood to come here."

"Who? Who is she?" There was a huskiness in the old woman's voice.

"Lucia Appleton. I carry her name."

"Mrs. Appleton!" Lokalia's hands quivered, and she gazed with penetration at Lucia.

"My maiden name was Appleton."

"Lucia Appleton!" She nodded her head and continued softly, "My husband's aunt lived with her as a foster child. We have always thought of the Appletons as part of the Waiolama family." Lokalia bent slowly down and laid her arms across Lucia's shoulders. "You are one of our family. Why didn't Kaupena tell me?"

Lucia suggested gently, "Perhaps you wouldn't let him."

"No, of course I wouldn't." She took Lucia's hand. "Child, I am a very stubborn old woman. Sometimes I think I love my people too much. I'm always afraid for them. What little we have left is so precious."

Lucia felt the weight of Lokalia's sorrow. "That's true!"

"A people who have suffered as we have find it easy to go to pieces. After a while there's nothing solid to hold onto. Finally we don't care, and then we destroy ourselves."

"But that's true for all of us now! There's nothing solid to hold onto. We are all destroying ourselves. Look at the world!"

The old woman remained calm in the face of Lucia's excitement. "Hawaiians fortunately have some saving qualities. We have friendliness—no one has been able to destroy that in us— and an ability to enjoy things. We don't let worry about the future spoil our happiness too much."

"No, but I feel—that there is a shading in the happiness."

Lokalia sighed. "There is. There's always trouble whenever nature is not followed. That's what the old Hawaiians knew— to live contentedly with nature."

Lucia rose to her knees. "Now that I'm one of you, let me share in everything—happiness and unhappiness."

"Yes," she murmured. "Yes, of course you must now. It is what I plan."

Lokalia got up from her chair and walked slowly through the house. Lucia followed.

"But you are lonely here!"

"A little."

"I'll bring you a child to keep you company."

"A child?"

"Yes, a sweet little girl." She held a hand up to Lucia's mouth. "Don't refuse her. No Hawaiian would."

Lokalia turned and without speaking again left the house. Lucia stared after her. She knew that Hawaiians sometimes traded their children in a way that would seem heartless on the mainland. But she knew also that foster children were always as much loved as natural ones. A little girl to join Kaupena and

Joe in her household—the days would be less empty. Her rooms were slowly filling until soon the air in the house would be alive with the clatter of many people going in and out of the doors and calling from room to room. A full household . . . As her mind began to accept this child, she felt herself entering irrevocably—without any possibility of escape—and intimately into the life she had chosen.

In an hour Lokalia returned bringing with her a small, timid girl. "This is Mele Poepoe."

"Hello, Mele." Lucia held out her hand.

"Mele is seven. And she needs lots of good food. She's been sick."

Lucia put her arms around the thin frame of the child and felt her shrink away.

"Don't be shy, Mele," said Lokalia. "This is your new mother for a while." Then to Lucia, "She's not used to haoles. She'll be all right in a few days. Kaupena and Joe will help."

"I'll try to feed her well. She's so thin!"

"She's been almost starved. Her family's so poor— Be a good girl, Mele, and do what your new mamma tells you to."

When Lokalia was gone, Lucia took Mele to the small back bedroom. "This is yours, dear, to have all to yourself."

"Thank you."

"Shall we hang your clothes in the closet?"

Mele silently held out the small bundle she carried. Lucia untied and took from it one faded worn dress, a pair of blue jeans, a palaka shirt, and two pairs of panties. Silently she hung the dress and shirt in the closet and laid away the jeans and panties in a drawer. Mele watched her closely.

"Would you like a bouquet of flowers in your room?"

"Thank you."

"Let's go out, then. You may pick them."

Cautiously Mele tore a few African daisies from their stems, and two nasturtiums. "Pretty," she whispered.

Lucia took her into the kitchen and showed her where the vases were kept. "Pick out the one you want."

She chose a chipped pink bowl left by Kaupena's mother and arranged her flowers in it. "Are you sure this room is mine?" she asked, her voice high and quivering.

"Only for you, dear." Lucia struggled to keep tears from her eyes.

Mele slipped across to the bed and peeked under the covers. "Sheets!" Her slender fingers caressed the fabric. "For me?"

"Yes."

"They're so soft. Better than army blankets." She moved to the window. "And curtains. With ruffly edges. Just like Maria's house."

"Yes, dear." Lucia could bear this examination no longer. "Would you like a sandwich now and a glass of milk?"

"Thank you."

Lucia cautiously put her arm around the child's shoulders as they walked to the kitchen. While Mele was eating, Kaupena came in. When Mele saw him she flew into his arms.

"Why Mele Poepoe!" he exclaimed. "What are you doing here?"

"Tutu Waiolama brought me. She says I'm to live here for awhile."

"Good!" He squeezed her and kissed her lightly on the head. He sat down and she climbed on his knee.

"And I have a room of my own! And a bed with sheets on it! And a bouquet of flowers! Oh, Kaupena, I'm so happy."

Kaupena grinned over the child's head at Lucia. Lucia smiled in return, but she felt estrangement chilling her. Mele had fled to the man of her own race. And Lucia was still alone in her household.

"Lokalia came today?" he asked.

"Uh huh."

"Everything go O.K.?"

"Not at first. Better after she found out about my great-grandmother."

"Oh, of course. . . . And she brought Mele?"

Mele broke into their conversation. "Kaupena, may I stay here forever? It was so lonely up at Tutu's. Here there's you and Joe."

"Yes, baby," he muttered, and the child continued to chatter gaily to him.

Lucia left the two of them and went into the living room. She stood hesitantly near the koa table. The nasturtiums she had picked in the morning were reflected like a flame in the polished surface. Joe's ukulele was resting on top of her great-grandmother's journal on the little table in the corner.

Voices continued happily in the kitchen. Joe, she remembered, was with the boys for the afternoon and evening. She went firmly down the steps and into the path through the woods.

At Julia's she announced, "I've got a child now."

"Who?"

"Mele Poepoe. Lokalia brought her to me."

"Yeah, I heard she was going to do that. But I didn't believe."

"You heard!"

Julia laughed. "Nothing's a secret here. Not even your inmost thoughts."

"She probably knew everything then, even about my great-grandmother."

"Of course she knew. Everybody knows."

"She is an amazing old woman, a wonderful actress."

"You should have seen her in the old days when she used to dance at the political luaus, and do take-offs on the politicians. She was plenty good."

Lucia shifted her ground. "Julia, how can I win Mele?"

"Just feed her and love her and she'll be yours. These Hawaiian kids are like little puppies."

Lucia sat on the floor drinking Julia's coffee, absorbing the calm of her presence, and thinking that for the first time since she had left the farm she had a real family in Kaupena and Joe and Mele. She would bind them to her in the ancient ways women have of holding their families.

Lucia found a true ease growing in her spirit. With Mele's welfare and Joe's needs to be considered, Kaupena's moods no longer loomed in their fearful significance. Balance and variety had come into her days, giving her perspective and quietude. Subtly the family gathered about her, weaving itself through the fabric of her emotion, stretching out its tendrils to link her with the community, establishing the sense of belonging for which she had yearned. She was a parent now, and the school expected her to be active in its program; Joe's friends shared their parties and picnics with her whether or not Kaupena went. The community looked for a response which she gladly but timidly gave.

She cooked special things each day for Mele, stuffing her with good rich food. She displayed her love, caressing the child, tucking her in bed at night and rousing her in the morning with a kiss. She watched her grow plump and sleek and happy. She let Mele and Joe roughhouse in wild pillow-throwing games; Joe would be ensconced on the hikie behind a bulwark of cushions, and the game was for Mele to throw a pillow and hit him in the head before he could duck. Often Mele invited her friends to the house after school for cookies and milk, and their mothers occasionally came to sit and gossip. Joe's orchestra rehearsed weekly at the house, and together Mele and Lucia learned the songs and hulas. Kaupena joined in, teaching them the ancient chants and hulas he had learned from Lokalia.

Julia came more and more often to spend the afternoons. It

was then that Lucia felt that the ghost in the house must surely be dispelled, for Julia, who liked to stay comfortably on her own mat, daily took the path through the woods.

The most enjoyable part of each day was that quiet period after supper when Mele was put to bed. She always ate her dinner in her flannel pajamas and then went out to romp briefly in the grass. After her hands and feet were re-washed she climbed into bed. The wind by then had usually died down for that brief diurnal period of stillness which hovered among the trees and penetrated the dusk. The sky carried faint pink tones mingled with the green and blue of the coming night, and the sharp fragrances of the dark had already scented the air. Mynah birds gathered in the giant mango outside the kitchen window and chattered their evening gossip, their sharp tones echoing strangely in the silence.

It was Mele's task to choose each evening what she wanted before going to bed: a song from Joe, a story in pantomime from Kaupena, or a story read by Lucia. Mele remained rigidly impartial, going the rounds so that each could count on a performance every third night, but she always pretended that she had a tremendous decision to make. And they all carried out her pretense with sober demeanors and when the choice was made, with a shout of enthusiasm.

This gathering in the evening became the quiet focal point of the family. Kaupena never let his anger or his melancholy interfere. Mele, the child, was the center, the symbol of what each of them was seeking. She completed the family, and the sense that she was not truly theirs intensified their love and the sense of protection they had for her. Lucia wondered if she were beginning to understand something of the kind of love Lokalia had for Kaupena, that love which is never quite within your grasp, and is consequently most precious. Joe often said to Lucia, "You are so good to let me live here. I never expected to have this!" But the tie that was closest was that between Mele and

Kaupena. They understood each other instinctively, and their moods and responses were often the same. Mele did not have the anger of Kaupena, for she was a gentle child, but she did seem to have the attacks of melancholy.

Lokalia came once a week, always bringing a present: a cake, a lei of rare mountain blossoms, an ancient calabash, a stone she said would bring good luck, a bowl of chicken stewed in coconut milk, or a muumuu she had made for Lucia. When once she found Lucia wearing the muumuu, she was pleased. "You are becoming a real Hawaiian," she said, "eating our food, wearing our clothes, learning our songs." She laid her hand on Mele's dark head: "And you have been a good foster mother to Mele. She loves you now. And you have been a good sister-in-law to Joe. He loves you too."

Lucia turned to the window to hide her emotion.

On an afternoon some six weeks after Lokalia's first visit, Lucia went up the valley on one of her frequent calls. The weather broke suddenly into storm. A squall crashed through the woods, thundering on the tin roof and swelling the falls with water until they roared so that the noise could be heard above the clatter on the tin. "The falls are loud," Lucia said.

Lokalia, excited by the storm, did not respond. She stood stiffly at the window, listening and watching. The house had grown dark, and outside gray light flickered and shimmered, streaked with silver jets of rain. The noise of water was portentous, and wind quivered along the thin split boards of the house.

Lucia sat rigidly on a corner of the hikie. Her heart throbbed, robbing her of even breath, and her eyes stared round and wide. She had never before felt as she did at this moment, as though she might somehow slip into the dark rhythm of the storm. A current in her body responded to the wind and the rain, yearned toward them; but she was afraid. It was as though she were turning back on the clear, firm path that her hard-thinking, hard-working forebears had laid out in the jungle of primitive human experience. She was not yet ready to yield to the spell of the ancient gods.

Lokalia turned abruptly from the window. "It is the moment," she announced, "for you to know of this."

She walked with dignified, measured steps to the chest and after carefully removing two or three quilts took out some yellowed sheets of paper. "When I die, these are Kaupena's. When Kaupena dies, they will go to his son." She stood commandingly.

The papers quivered in the old hands. Lucia was drawn slowly toward her.

"This is the genealogy chant of the Waiolamas." She held it out. "You will not understand. It is in Hawaiian."

Lucia took the papers softly. She knew that a genealogy was one of the most cherished of family secrets, that Lokalia in showing it to her was accepting her completely. She read a few lines, whispering them aloud. She had learned how to read Hawaiian from the songs Joe had taught her, and although she did not understand, she spoke with a good Hawaiian accent.

"You read the words well. Let me show you the rhythm of the chant." Lokalia's voice became young and strong in the resonances of the verses.

When she paused, Lucia said, "It's very beautiful. Even not understanding, one has a feeling . . ."

"Yes, it's possible."

"Tutu, won't you teach me Hawaiian?"

"Do you really want to learn?"

"Oh yes! One can't live in Makaniloa and not want to."

"So!" she muttered. And then brightly, "From now on we will speak together only in Hawaiian. That is the easiest way. However, you must be sure to teach your children from the beginning."

Lucia laughed self-consciously. "I will if I have children. But perhaps I won't. I didn't in my first marriage."

Lokalia's eyes grew round and concentrated. "You will have a child. Not for a year or more. You will have three children of your own."

Turning away, she lay the genealogy sheets carefully in their place, put back the quilts, and closed and locked the chest.

Lucia stood as though in a spell, filled with a curious assurance that she would have those three children, that there was no doubt at all. It was as though in that moment they had already been born to her, and she knew the first sharp pleasure of motherhood.

II.

NOTWITHSTANDING the new fullness of Lucia's life, there was a gap of foreboding, an awareness that all was not yet settled with Kaupena. One evening when this unhappiness lay on the surface of her mind, she accepted Joe's invitation to stay at the rehearsal, which was being held at the Rittens. She told Kaupena that she would listen to the music for a while and talk with Paul. He cast a bright sliding glance at her. Was there, after all, a kind of jealousy in him? Or was it the subtle struggle of race appearing? He knew perfectly well that since Mele's coming she seldom saw Paul. She kissed Kaupena good-by, lingering a little with sensitive regard for the reaction she had felt in him.

When she and Joe reached the Rittens, Momi rushed out crying that one of her boys had come down with the measles and that the rehearsal would have to be moved. "We're going to the Parish House," she said. "Lucia, don't worry about Joe. I'll bring him home. Why don't you stay and have a drink with Paul? He doesn't much like baby sitting."

She demurred slightly, but both Momi and Joe urged her to cheer up Paul.

She went into the house and told him that Momi had sent her in to have a drink with him.

"Good!" he responded. "What would you like?"

Lucia laughed. "I've almost forgotten what people drink. It seems so long ago."

"I have a good Scotch right now."

"Fine," she said.

He fixed the drinks and they sat together silently for a while. He sipped from his glass and gazed at her. She felt in his look a sharp probing coupled with tenderness, and his old disturbing words flooded her mind. She guessed that they must be in his too, and was sorry now that she had come to unsettle the ease they had established at the bazaar. Presently however, drinking the Scotch, she became conscious of warm fingers of pleasure reaching through her veins. She leaned against the cushions of the hikie and curled her feet under her. She felt at last a need for talk, and she asked him the question she was putting to so many people. "Do you feel there is a dark side to Makaniloa?"

He did not answer immediately. He refilled his glass and hers too. She waited without impatience.

"Yes," he said finally. "There is a dark side. A little of it may be in the quality of the landscape, but most of it is of their own making."

"Of their own making? What do you mean?"

"I mean the long building up of legend and superstition. Isolated here, knowing everyone from birth to death, they've had to do something to bolster the importance of life—its sacredness. So they keep secrets such as old prayers and genealogy chants, their recipes for fish bait, and the location of holy places; they visit kahunas and preserve stones as talismans for good luck; they watch for strange happenings. All of this creates excitement and speculation. And so then when the winds tear down from the gap or the floods come, it seems quite naturally the act of a god. Certain curious events occur, and after them birth or death. These events become omens, and they are put into story and song."

He paused to light a cigarette.

"I see my own children developing these instincts, these superstitions. At first I tried to stop it. Then I said to myself, why do that? They are growing up here in Makaniloa. It is in their blood. And these things are no worse for a person than the superstitions of snobbery and middle-class morality in which I grew up in Pittsburgh. Less so. Because these rise out of the relationship of earth and man—I think a much sturdier one than that of man and man. At least it's not so easily corrupted."

The Scotch hummed in her head, and her words came without her being too sharply aware of what they were. "But don't you think there's something we can never understand in this darkness, something that makes Makaniloa half an enemy?"

"Maybe that's true. I think the part we can't understand is the division. How can these people be two things—simple and happy and easygoing on one side, and on the other, they are proud." He paused, gathering his thoughts. "They are filled with a kind of dismay at what is happening to them. Look at what they've been through in little more than a century—their native ways degraded, their country taken away, an alien civilization forced upon them. If they had not been Polynesians, they could not have taken it as gracefully as they did."

"But the dark places," she repeated. "They have grown deeper and more bitter."

"Yes, but there is a new hope for them; the part-Hawaiians are going into all the activities of island life. It is a kind of rebirth. Even some of the old people feel it."

"I know the despair in Kaupena," she persisted intensely. "There are times when we cannot meet. It's that dark background which he hides from me." She was no longer relaxed and was growing excited.

"Remember, Lucia, he doesn't understand your background either. He has only your word for what it is. He has never known anything like it."

"I know. But it isn't the same. Mine is American. He learned about such things in school. But his—"

He interrupted, "You're typical of people like us. Our rules apply to everyone but ourselves." His voice was acid. "We are the normal! Everyone else—" He shrugged his shoulders.

She jumped up from the hikie. "You're right, Paul!" Slowly she moved toward him. "But still, can't you feel something, something inexplicable?" She could not choose her words properly.

"Yes," he replied and rose to his feet. There was a subtle change in his manner. She moved back slightly. "I can feel the inevitable attraction between you and me," he continued gravely, tenderly. "We are alike. They are different. It is the old story, and we can't help it."

He took her in his arms and kissed her. For a moment she responded, aware of a warm tendril of security twisting into her brain. Here was the familiar, the understandable, the precious rapport of people with the same background, of the same race.

Then abruptly she pushed him away. "This is not the way to fight our battle. We shall have lost at the outset."

He spoke bitterly, "Unfortunately I love you."

"Oh no!"

"Oh yes!" he mocked.

"Paul, what can I say?" She laid a hand on his arm. "I'll go home now."

"I warn you. I'll teach you to love me. I'll do everything I can. Kaupena is no person for you."

She bridled. "Perhaps I'm the judge of that." And she went swiftly from the house.

Kaupena had often reflected on the Hawaiian secret societies, and at the university had come to the opinion that they only confused his people with vague aspirations toward a greatness they could not have in the modern world. Their ceremonies created the illusion that there was something left of the old alii power and that those who shared in it had a greater significance in the territorial scheme of things than was actually true. He had argued heatedly with Joe. "You only fool yourselves," he cried. "And you know that hocus-pocus doesn't mean a damned thing. Waste time!"

"That's no waste time," Joe responded. "What you call hocus-pocus means plenty for these people. It isn't really the hocus-pocus that counts, anyhow. It's what a man brings to it. His hopes and dreams and his need for self-confidence."

"Can't you people stand up by yourselves?"

"No, frankly! Not many men can. And what right have you to make fun of us?"

Kaupena had not answered this. He never wanted to make fun of his people. His wish was to perserve them—and himself—from the hurt of disenchantment. Joe, who was easygoing and skeptical about many things, took the Hui seriously.

But after the coming of Mele, Kaupena's attitude slowly changed, and when she had been with them seven months, he decided to join the Hui. He could not understand all that brought about this reversal. He suspected that it had something to do with that portent of disaster which was growing in him. He recognized he was utterly unprepared for adversity and he had become doubtful that he could keep his equilibrium in the face of it. The Hui would give him the fellowship of others and link him with hidden forces through its ritual. Then too, its activities were in part affiliated with the ceremony at Pohaku Lono, which now at Lokalia's insistence he practiced more frequently.

But most of all, he surmised, the change was because of Mele. She had developed in him a sense of continuance even though she was not of his blood. Already in her he could see his mannerisms, his habits, and he recognized the influence he had on her flexible nature. He wanted to give her the Hawaiian attitude toward life. The Hui stressed that; it emphasized benevolence and sharing, and through the ancient ritual based on the memories of a priest who had been seventy years old in 1862, it fostered that precious sense of history so important to the dignity of any group. The Hui was rich in racial memory and feeling. And it encouraged that pride of which the Hawaiians had been nearly bereft by the turmoil of the past century. He could learn these things and pass them on to Mele.

He kept his decision a secret from Lucia, even as he did his activities at Pohaku Lono. He did not think she was ready to know of such things, and he could not bear her laughter or her thinly veiled skepticism.

One night at Pohaku Lono he let it be known to Mr. Clarke that he was interested in the Hui. A few days later the elaborate, formal printed invitation came for him. He wrote his acceptance and waited for instructions.

Joe spoke to him on an afternoon when Lucia was at the church guild. "You've got to learn some ritual, you know."

"Sure, I know."

"I wish I knew what's come over you."

"It's not as sudden as it looks. It's been coming for months. But say, don't tell Lucia, yeah?"

"O.K. But she'll find out sooner or later, from those women down at the church."

"Yeah. Funny thing, that. All of a sudden going to church and joining with those women. I had expected her to go at the beginning—what with her great-grandmother and all. But she didn't. Not until Mele came."

"She doesn't do things unless she can do them honestly."

"You think Lucia's number one, don't you?"

"You're lucky, Kaupena, and you don't know it."

"Things are better for her now that Lokalia isn't so stubborn. But what a goddam time I had for a while with those two wahines."

"Uh huh." Joe said with a shrug. "You made it worse. Keeping everything so secret. I never could understand you that way. It's growing up with that old woman, I guess."

Kaupena was ruffled. "Oh for God's sake don't start in on me now."

"O.K. O.K. No offense. But some day try to learn to relax a little. Life isn't so serious as you make it. I hope you'll learn a thing or two in the Hui."

"Yeah," Kaupena said musingly. "I hope."

On the night of the initiation, he told Lucia he had to go to the ranch office to do some work and that he would drop Joe at the Hui meeting on the way and bring him home again afterward. He saw her comfortably settled in a chair with a book. "Good-by, darling," she said. "I'll wait up for you two. We can have some coffee and sandwiches."

In the car Joe said, "I have a present for you."

"Oh?"

"Yeah, for tonight. You'll have to wear it."

"The cape?"

"Yeah."

"Thanks, Joe." He knew it was customary for the capes worn by Hui members to be presented to them by relatives or friends.

"It's really from Lokalia. Our grandfather wore it. Lokalia gave it to me, saying you must have it when you finally joined the Hui."

"I hate to take it away from you."

"I've just been borrowing it these years. Mrs. Kaneloa made one for me. I have it for tonight."

The Hui met in an old building at the back of the Mahoe property. Because it had been unused for years the guava had grown thickly around it and scraped loudly against the walls; the back was partially engulfed in a thicket of bamboo. When it rained the building seemed to be sodden with water like a sponge, and the interior was constantly musty with the odor of lizard droppings and rotting wood. Kaupena paused on the threshold; the room was obscure in the smoky orange light of four torches, and kahilis threw enormous blots of shadow on the walls. Tabu sticks glimmered darkly in the uncertain glow. The members of the Hui, dressed in black suits and wearing over their shoulders capes of chicken feathers clipped and dyed brilliant yellow in imitation of those worn by the chiefs and warriors of old, stood in a solemn row.

Joe guided Kaupena to a spot in front of the group. "You stand here alone, facing them," he whispered.

Kaupena glanced at the members before him. They looked like children, standing there gravely self-conscious and holding their lips firmly in a serious expression. Kaupena wanted suddenly to laugh. He yearned for a cloak of invisibility instead of the faded feather one that had belonged to his grandfather. But there was nothing to do but clench his teeth and bear the process passively.

A youth clad only in a red malo, his body glowing like dark brass in the flame light, walked slowly down the aisle of kahilis. His steps were graceful and dignified. At the end of the room he turned and blew on the conch shell that he carried. The deep sound reverberated against the walls with a rough sea noise. Following like an echo, a blast of wind beat against the windows, and the torch flames flickered. The young man blew the conch again, and Kaupena felt the sharp tones penetrating the very flesh of his body. He blinked at the men before him. They seemed to have grown in dignity; in the dim, fluctuating light their shadows were like vast pillars of darkness across the floor. For the third time the boy blew the conch; it sounded long and tremulously as though his breath were nearing exhaustion. The rain now flooded against the windows, blending its tones with those of the conch. Mr. Clarke began to chant in a high, clear tone.

These ancient, primitive sounds echoed deep in Kaupena's blood. The conch! For centuries Waiolamas had listened to its call and had responded. The conch! A prelude to the wind of Makaniloa, to the swift dipping of the paddles of war canoes, to the sustained chant of the priests in the heiau! He recognized suddenly that for too long he had paid attention to the haole scorn for Hawaiian ways. And as the ritual proceeded he watched intently, throwing his spirit into it. Presently he felt himself gathered into the historic rhythm of his people.

12.

ONE late afternoon Lucia was fitting a new dress for Mele. Joe was in his favorite spot on the hikie, picking out chords on the ukulele for a new song. Kaupena had not yet come home from the ranch. The day, which had been rainy and gusty, had grown quiet, a quiet that bred restlessness rather than peace.

Joe threw the ukulele aside saying, "I don't think this new tune's very good! I'd like to go fishing. How about it, Luce? Mind driving me down to the Point."

"Not at all," she responded and lay down her sewing. "Come on, Mele."

They left a note for Kaupena and drove to the Point. Lucia helped Joe across the lava and settled him comfortably on a rock that rose just a few feet above the wind-swollen water. Mele proudly carried the pole and bait. "Uncle Joe, is the tide coming in or going out?" she asked.

"It's coming in." He saw the flash of worry on Lucia's face. "But I'll be O.K. I used to fish off this rock when I was a kid. It's seldom reached by the waves. Only in unusual tides."

"Why don't Mele and I wait for you?"

"Lucia, you are good to be worried about me. But these rocks are my old friends. The sea is my old friend. They won't harm me."

She knelt and kissed him. "Just watch the water, then, and take care of yourself. I'll send Kaupena for you when supper is ready."

161

Some time later as Kaupena was driving down the rocky road to the Point, he glanced at the fading colors of the sky. There was never a real sunset in Makaniloa; the mountain shut off the west with its huge dark bulk. But faint pinks and beiges sometimes tinted the upper reaches, and sharp greens often lay along the horizon. This evening a few fluffy clouds caught pomegranate rays and were brilliant in the heavy steely colors of sky and sea. He noticed that the waves frothed up unusually high on the rocks, the foam reflecting the faintest of pinks. Reaching the end of the road, he parked the car and strolled leisurely out to that part of the shore where Lucia and Mele said they had left Joe. Already the pomegranate had gone from the sky and darkness was falling like a series of gauze curtains.

"Joe!" he shouted into the wind. He could not see the figure of his brother anywhere. The rocks were wet and even now the water washed over the favorite perch of the fishermen. "Joe!" he shouted again. Damn it! Why did he have to wander off in the darkness with those wooden legs.

Kaupena ran along the top of the cliff calling, "Joe, Joe, Joe!" There was no answer. For ten minutes he called and searched, but he found no trace of his brother. Then slowly and clearly in his mind the thought formed. The high tide. Joe on that rock. He had tried to move back, but his wooden legs were not swift enough for that. Or perhaps one of them had caught in a hole in the lava. The wave had taken him. He might even now be washing about offshore. Kaupena ran back to the car and raced up to the store for the searchlight kept for such emergencies.

The alarm went through Makaniloa and reached even to Kipahulu and Hana, and all that night the people took turns in searching for Joe. Those not engaged in the hunt gathered in little silent huddles along the beach, or went excitedly from house to house speculating and wondering. Women made coffee and sandwiches and took them down to the shore; Bill Perkins and Paul came to stand with Lucia and Mele; Lokalia remained aloof, searching the sea intently for some time and then abruptly turning to disappear into the night. Lucia heard the soft whisper, "kahuna," among the people standing nearby as the old woman hurried up toward the road.

Certain small groups tried their schemes. The Japanese wrote a Buddhist prayer on a slip of paper and corked it tightly in a bottle. They put the bottle into the sea near the rock where Joe had been fishing, and when the bottle began to whirl in one place, they sent their divers down at that spot. But the divers found nothing. The Filipinos tried their method—sprinkling dry leaves on the waves. When finally a mass of the leaves gathered together and spun in the froth, they sent down divers. But again nothing was found. A group of Portuguese women knelt at the edge of the cliff and recited a rosary for Joe, and an old man wailed for him. Throughout all this, Mr. Oshiro of the store swept the sea with his searchlight, and Kaupena and Johnny continued in an outrigger to comb the waters for any trace. Many of the Hawaiians launched their canoes and joined in the hunt on the sea. They kept up the search all night, and along the shore people continued to come and go.

At midnight Lucia took the sleepy Mele home and put her to bed. Then she went to the hikie where Joe's ukulele still lay as he had left it. She picked it up and played the chords he had been practicing over and over throughout the afternoon. It was not yet real to her that he was dead. She felt little emotion except that of loneliness and emptiness, and she lay down finally, holding the ukulele close to her.

Kaupena's slamming of the door at dawn awakened her. She looked questioningly at him.

"Nothing so far! I'm going to bed for a while."

She helped him undress and pulled the covers over him. He was at once asleep, and she kissed his forehead and sat for some time watching him. His face in the repose of sleep was marked with sorrow. His hair stiffened with salt was like a dark undulation of seaweed against the pillow.

Mele crept in and stood at her side. "Mamma," she whispered, "I'm hungry."

Lucia rose and went to the kitchen. She cooked oatmeal and placed a bowl of it on the table, and made coffee for herself.

"Didn't you put on your nightie all night?" Mele asked.

"No, darling."

Then in a hushed, frightened, child's voice, "Is Uncle Joe really dead?"

"I'm afraid so, dear." It was at that moment that his death became real, and the tears started down her cheeks. She had loved him so, and she would miss his songs, his easygoing, happy ways. Why had she not insisted that she and Mele remain with him? They might have saved him, and he'd still be here, laughing over the breakfast table, teasing Mele, arguing with Kaupena.

"Have they found him?" Mele had finished her cereal, and her voice was calm and curious.

"Not yet, dear."

"Sometimes it's days," she said matter-of-factly. "When they finally found Mr. Luahine there was only a part of him. The sharks had eaten the rest."

"Oh Mele, you mustn't say that!"

"Why not? It's true."

"We just don't say such horrible things." Lucia saw the surprise on Mele's face and realized that the child had merely been stating a thing that had happened on occasions for generations in Makaniloa. Fishermen had been drowned, and the sea had given back only fragments of their bodies—sometimes nothing at all. It was a historical, ancestral fact, not one to shudder at politely and push out of the mind, but an item in the sum total of experience.

"You must dress for school now," Lucia said.

When she had gone, Lucia sat numbly at the kitchen table, sipping her cold coffee, and staring into the woods.

At ten Julia came in softly. "Is Kaupena awake?"

"Not yet."

"I think we'd better awaken him?"

"Is there any news?"

"Of a kind."

Lucia went into the bedroom and called his name softly. Slowly he awoke, stretched, blinked his eyes. He yawned and took her hand. Then suddenly he sat up in bed. "Any news?"

"Julia is here. She says she has something to tell you."

He dressed hurriedly and went out. "What is it?"

"Your grandmother asked me to go down to Mrs. Kanakanui's with her and ask about Joe. She told us that the Japanese girl who took care of Joe was jealous when he came up here to live. She was in love with him and was jealous because you people took all his time. Her jealousy kahunaed him and caused his death. Mrs. Kanakanui said that the sharks had already got him. But that in a few days something would be found."

Kaupena held his head in his hands. "Poor old Joe," he said. Then abruptly he rose. "We must start searching again."

The days drifted on, light fogging into darkness, then the dark glimmering into the brilliance of windy, sunny days, and still they found no trace of Joe. A tension was growing in Kaupena; he seldom spoke now, and his waking hours were all spent in the search. At home he slept and ate lightly. Once at breakfast he said, "It's a horrible thing to think of Joe out there. At the mercy of the sea and the sharks. I dream of it. It's horrible, horrible! Wasn't Iwo Jima enough for him?"

On the morning of the sixth day, Kaupena was up early. He wrapped one of Joe's shirts in a piece of tissue paper and then commanded, "Come on, Lucia. We're going to Kahului."

"Oh."

"Yes, to visit a woman there. She can tell us about Joe."

"But how?"

He looked straight at her, his eyes flashing anger. "You won't believe. Maybe I don't. But I can't stand this uncertainty. Just come with me. That's all I ask."

She drove the car, and all the sixty miles to Kahului he said nothing, sitting with his hands folded loosely about the tissue-wrapped parcel. His face was set in a mask of sadness, and occasionally one finger drummed lightly on the tissue.

In Kahului after he had directed her to the proper street, she said softly, "We're going to miss Joe terribly."

His flood of speech surprised her. "He was always somehow just what I wanted to be. He lived so wholeheartedly, so easily. He lived as Hawaiians ought to live. I want him buried in the old cemetery at the abandoned village. He belongs down there with the others like him. That's why we must find him."

She stopped at the house Kaupena pointed out to her, and they went together up the walk. The house was a small one, the green stain badly weathered so that in some places it was streaked yellowish and in others bluish. From the ceiling of the lanai hung six round baskets of lawai fern, which swayed dizzily in the wind. The space immediately in front of the lanai was thickly planted with croton, ti, and spider lily, giving the illusion that the house had been set down in the midst of a thicket of bright foliage. Blowing out of the unscreened windows were pink organdy curtains.

Kaupena rang the bell. Lucia's heart beat heavily; this was to be her first experience with the practices of a kahuna. The woman who answered the door was plump and elderly. She had on a white dress so simply designed and well starched that it might have been a nurse's uniform. Her hair, white and wavy, was pulled back in a neat bun. She seemed motherly and sympathetic, a handsome type of Portuguese-Hawaiian woman.

"Mrs. Rodrigues," Kaupena started, "I'm Kaupena Waiolama. This is my wife. You've probably read about my brother."

"Oh yes! Won't you come in." They entered an immaculate room furnished with rattan, upholstered in pinks and blues. The pictures on the walls were all religious, the largest and most dominating being of the Virgin Mary. There was a small shrine to the Virgin in one corner with a lighted votive lamp before it. "Please sit down . . . You would like some help, Mr. Waiolama?"

"I've heard that you can help. I've brought a shirt of my brother's."

She took the parcel and reverently unwrapped it. Her long flexible fingers caressed the shirt briefly before she put it aside. "Excuse me a moment." She left the room.

"Who is she?" Lucia whispered.

"I suppose you'd say she was a kahuna."

"I know. But all of these religious things! I mean Christian things."

He was impatient. "Kahunas nowdays use Christian prayers mixed with Hawaiian ones. After all, they're just people trying in their own strange way to get help from God. What's wrong with that?"

Mrs. Rodrigues re-entered with a glass of water and a small vial of an oily liquid. In the vial was a medicine dropper. She took a table from a nest in the corner and placed it in front of her. Then she put the shirt, the glass, and the vial on it.

She went to a shelf on which were rocks of different sizes and shapes. They were all dark porous lava rock. She selected one and laid it on the shirt. "This stone is from Makaniloa."

She sat before the table, clasped her hands, closed her eyes, and began to pray. She asked God for insight to help these grieving people, and she prayed to the Virgin to protect the unhappy man who still lay in the waters of the sea. She continued for about ten minutes with prayers, obviously of her own composition, although drawing strongly from the Missal and the Psalms. She closed with a brief prayer in Hawaiian. Her tone was resonant and melodious as it mingled with the soft sounds of the wind in the foliage outside. The woman had some of the powers of an actress. She commanded her audience by a simple dignity, a personal magnetism, and sincerity.

At the close of her prayers she drew the glass close to her and dropped into it half the contents of the vial. The water immediately leapt and churned in the glass. She watched it with the dreamy, calculating eyes of those who read from tea leaves or a crystal. As the churning quieted, she spoke in half a chant, "A wave took him. It washed violently over the rock, and he clung with his hands but he was not strong enough." She shuddered slightly. "The sharks have already been at him. But do not worry. Tomorrow a portion of his body will be at the beach near the Protestant Church. Look at dawn tomorrow."

She relaxed suddenly and smiled at them. "I hope I have brought you comfort. Remember God cares for those who remain alone upon the sea."

Kaupena rose, and Mrs. Rodrigues handed him the shirt.

Lucia followed them to the door. She saw him put a five dollar bill in an empty calabash.

When they were in the car, he took the wheel. "I'll drive back. We'll stop at the store on the way and stock up on a few things we can't get in Makaniloa."

After their shopping, he seemed more normal than at any moment since Joe's death. She asked, "Darling, what did you think of Mrs. Rodrigues?"

"She's a handsome woman, a good woman."

"Ye-e-es. I mean what she said and all that."

"I know . . ." he said hesitantly, and then continued firmly, "when I think of her logically and in the light of American views, I know she's a fake. But in another way she's got a lot on the ball. She carries off the thing well. She believes herself. Why shouldn't *I* believe her? I bet we'll find Joe tomorrow morning."

"She convinced you!"

"She knows that if the sea is going to give up the dead, it will usually do it within a week. Tomorrow is the seventh day. She knows also that those who are lost off the rocks almost always come back. It's those who are lost in boats who seldom return."

"But you know this! Then why did you go to her?"

"Because I wanted to," he said gruffly. "I want to do everything possible for old Joe."

That night as she lay in bed Lucia realized that the days would mount in suspense and tension until Joe was found. Time seemed to enlarge the anguish rather than to allay it. There had been such a concentration on the fact of his death by everyone, so much open show of grief and sorrow, that Makaniloa was reaching a semihysterical, primitive state. She preferred the dignified way her own people approached death, a simple swift funeral and then a quiet submerging of the grief for expression only in private moments—or better still, not at all. Lokalia and Julia and Momi talked about Joe constantly, repeating the story of his tragedy, expressing themselves richly and vigorously in grief. It seemed to her almost as though they enjoyed the excitement; their thoughts were constantly directed to the mystery of death. They were planning the funeral ceremonies and feast. Already the pig was butchered for the imu, and the Poepoe children had been set to work husking coconuts. Lucia felt a flood of bitterness in her mouth; this brooding emphasis was oppressive, morbid. Finally she buried her head in the pillow and tried, by shutting out all the sounds of the night, to find sleep.

Just before dawn, Kaupena rose and set out for the beach. She had suggested that she go along, but he had answered with an impatient no. The sky was a pale luminous green against which the trees loomed black. There was little wind, but the surf was loud and portentous. As she watched him go off down the road, it came over her that he still remained a stranger, perhaps more so than ever, going constantly on mysterious errands.

She turned back into the house and sat limply on the hikie. Her mind in its weariness thrust aside the present and turned to the Connecticut farm with yearning. She remembered the gentle squeak of her mother's rocker on the verandah as she passed a summer afternoon crocheting and talking quietly to a neighbor, the spicy scents on a hot day of garden pinks and the drawn-out twang of the cicada, the window seat in winter where she could sit and watch the drifts forming and smell from the kitchen the sweet rich aroma of beans and the hot fragrance of johnnycake. She wanted to escape into her girlhood room with its red mahogany furniture, the quilt on the bed, the rag rugs on the floor, the blue flounced curtains at the window. In all her life there had never been a spot so secure, so beloved as that room. In it she had had her own close-meshed little world, entered only by her mother and father, her few friends, and all the wavering thoughts and emotions of her growth into womanhood. Here were her dolls and her books and her collection of shells made on summer trips to the sea. Here in her college days she had come home on vacations to compose poems expressing the fullness of her feeling, to write careful love letters, to read philosophy and sociology and history. To this bedroom she had come after her breakdown. She had found in its quietness her strength and composure. . . . And now! How troubling it was to be in the midst of such strangeness, of exotic things and people and attitudes! She would like one hour in her room to breathe its sweet cleanness and to feel the profound well-being which had come upon her in it.

She rose. It was time to awaken Mele, and a warm rush of feeling drove out her nostalgia. The child had become as her own, and whenever she folded the soft brown body in her arms and stroked the fragrant black hair, she knew a peace that shut away all of the tension and the sorrow.

When three hours later Lucia saw the procession coming up the road, she moved behind the draperies to watch it unobserved. It was like a medieval cortège, she thought.

The procession was led by Lokalia and Kaupena. The old woman chanted softly in Hawaiian, occasionally raising her arms, and Kaupena walked with his head bowed and his hands hanging limply at his side. Behind them four solemn, self-conscious boys bore the casket that was festooned with leis, and in their wake moved a small group of people carrying flowers and branches.

Lucia shrank into the darkest corner of the room as they entered. She watched intently while they put the casket on the hikie and heaped it with flowers. Kaupena brought the brass candlesticks from the bedroom and placing them on a small table near the head of the casket, lighted the candles. From that moment until twenty-four hours later when Joe was buried in the ancient cemetery, Lucia existed in a dark Polynesian dream. The house was filled with a restless coming and going of people who sat with Joe a while and then went into the kitchen to have some of the roast pig and other delicacies that Kaupena had been careful to provide. The living room was festooned with leis and bouquets of flowers, the scent of which mingled with the tallow smoke and the salty smell of humid flesh. Occasionally one of the older visitors broke into a low wail or chant; many sat and stared into the candle flames for long periods of time.

After the casket had been lowered into the shallow grave dug out of the lava, Lucia found herself drifting to Paul's side. It was the first time she had allowed herself to be alone with him since the night he had proclaimed his love. But at this moment his presence gave her comfort. "Will this display go on much longer?" she whispered. "I can't stand much more." Her whisper had a sharp, hysterical edge to it.

He took her by the arm and pulled her into the shelter of a

clump of puhala trees. Then he shook her gently. "Don't be a little fool!"

"They make death so horrible!"

"Not at all! You don't understand."

"It goes on so long!"

His voice was metallic. "You and I were brought up to be cowards about death—because it's unpleasant. These people recognize it for what it is—a part of life. It's a reality. Joe was swept out by the waves, his body was torn by sharks; his family and friends loved him and are horrified at his untimely end. They grieve openly; they cry their sorrow to the world."

"It's so unnatural!"

"No, it is we who are unnatural. Death is always with us; it's embedded deeply in life. They face that squarely. They see that in the full expression of grief comes an eventual peace."

"Peace," she murmured. She smoothed her wind-ruffled hair nervously. "Perhaps you and they are right. The calm after the storm."

"That's it!"

She gazed directly at him. "Oh Paul, you've helped!"

His voice was low and passionate. "I want to help. You can't do without me in Makaniloa. That's what I'm going to teach you. Lucia, I'm waiting. Even when you think you know everything about them, there'll be strangeness and darkness. When you learn that, you'll come to me."

"No," she said solemnly, "I'll not come if I can help it."

For Kaupena a kind of peace came when he saw the lava rocks heaped over Joe's casket. Here under the sun and wind and rain, close to the sea, Joe could live out his unfinished life. On Iwo Jima he had learned what death could be in life. This experience he had confided to Kaupena. "I thought I heard music like an ancient chant. And it was a wonderful feeling not to be confined in a body any more. But I was glad later to get back to life." Now perhaps in this ancient, man-haunted spot Joe could learn what life was in death.

Kaupena felt that somehow in returning Joe to the ancestral place, he was returning him to the old Hawaiian stream. That was where he should be. He had the warmth, the friendliness, and the deep interest in the community, and hidden in him was that sensitive rapport with the basic tide of life, which was the great gift of all the nobler Hawaiians.

But as Kaupena turned away from the grave, he saw something which filled him with trembling. Paul was talking earnestly to Lucia under the puhala. Mele stood alone, bewildered, frightened. It was like the flash of a symbol, and his mind clouded with a difficult and choking emotion. He ran and clasped Mele in his arms.

13.

ON THE third night after Joe was buried, Mele awoke screaming, and Lucia and Kaupena rushed to her. Kaupena sat on the bed and took the child in his arms, pressing her tightly against him, one hand at her waist and the other holding her head. Her little fingers clutched excitedly at him. "What is it, baby dear?" he asked.

"Uncle Joe!" she screamed hysterically. "It was Uncle Joe!"

"Uncle Joe!" Kaupena's face went white, and he let her slip back onto the bed. Her small body lurched anxiously toward him and he took her again.

Lucia said quietly, "But it couldn't be Uncle Joe, Mele. You know that." She laid her hand on Mele's forehead and brushed the damp hair back.

"He looked in through the window at me. His face was all torn."

"Darling, it was only a dream," Lucia said firmly.

"No, Mamma, I was awake. I sat up in bed. I saw him." She broke out afresh in tears. Lucia picked her up and carried her to the window. The night wind was strong, and the light through the window revealed the thrashing tree branches and the darting arrowy tips of shining leaves. Almost any image might have been detected in that turmoil of movement. But Lucia said, "Look, darling, there is no one there."

Mele burrowed her face in Lucia's shoulder. "I don't want to look. His face was torn."

Lucia gently but firmly turned the child's head until she

faced the window. Mele stiffened. "He's there! I see him again! Look!"

Kaupena moved from the bed to the window. He peered into the dark, his breath coming stertorously. "Joe, Joe!" he cried. "Where are you?"

"Kaupena sees him!" Mele screamed. She was now hysterical, arching her body and flailing her arms.

Lucia spoke sharply to her husband, "You're only making her worse. You know there's no one there."

"I'm not sure," he said, passing his fingers across his eyes. "One can never be sure."

"My God, Kaupena, help me with this child!" Lucia cried, struggling alone.

His muscles twitched about his mouth as he took the kicking, screaming child in his arms and carried her to the bed.

"Lay her down!" Lucia commanded. "Hold her!" Then she slapped Mele's face sharply once, twice, three times. Mele recoiled, gasped slightly, and remained quiet, although she breathed heavily. Kaupena watched until the little girl seemed quite normal, and then without a word he left the room. Lucia lay down by Mele's side. "I'll stay with you, darling. And there won't be any bad dreams."

This nightmare was the first of a series that Mele dreamed for more than a month. She would awaken screaming that she saw Joe outside her window. As the month wore on, her story grew. Joe was trying to get in; he tapped on the window. Finally one night she said Joe had come into the room and was trying to pull her out of bed. She became more difficult to quiet, and her little body began to grow thin again. Her eyes, always dark and pensive, took on a strangely adult look. She became grave in demeanor and seldom spoke, and the vision seemed presently to move with her, sleeping or waking. Her friends no longer came to play, and Lucia had to reply to many an oblique inquiry about the child. Each time she told as clearly and frankly as she could, that Mele had been so upset by Joe's death that she was having nightmares.

When one evening Lucia tried to talk to Kaupena about the little girl, he said, "She is seeing something, but you won't believe her."

"It's only a dream. There's nothing there."

"It was you, if you remember, who talked about the magic of the mind. It was you who claimed to see your grandmother at the foot of our bed."

"I know. But Mele is a child. We've got to teach her there's nothing there that will hurt her."

He seemed not to have heard her words and continued softly, wonderingly, "She sees Joe. I can't see him. I've put leis on his grave at dusk, but I have never seen him."

Lucia burst out impatiently. "It's that mood in you which encourages her!"

He looked at her darkly. "No, of course you can't understand. It isn't in your blood. You are like all the others about such things. But I'm learning how wrong you all are."

Swiftly Lucia changed and spoke more gently. "Mele's just a little girl. And she's terribly frightened."

"When she learns that Joe has come back because he loves her, she'll be all right." His voice was low and reflective, and he spoke with deep seriousness.

Lucia went to Julia. "Poor kid," Julia said. "Let her come sleep my house. With the other kids. By-and-by she forget her dreams." So Lucia took Mele through the woods to the Kaneloas.

"You can play with Georgie!"

Mele smiled with real pleasure, and Lucia thought it augured well.

In a week Julia sent Mele home cured of her nightmares. Lucia exclaimed over how quickly it had been done, and Julia replied somberly, "It was Kaupena's fault she was that way. He filled that kid with stories. No wonder she couldn't get over it at your house."

"Kaupena!"

"Yeah. Funny kind talk he make to her. I don't believe all this kind stuff. Maybe there are old ghosts, but not any new ones. Kaupena, he's one funny man these days."

The joining of the Hui and Joe's death had focused Kaupena's mind completely on the ancient channels. And the passion grew in him to soak himself in the old lore. The compromise between the old and the new he had been trying to frame seemed suddenly thin and futile. At his death what would he have from a lifetime of being neither one thing nor the other?

He began to devote his spare time to fishing. But he did not give up the modern motor he had attached to his canoe. It lent him the added strength to go alone, as his ancestors had, far enough out so that the islands were only a breath of bluish haze and the faintest scent of earth and foliage. When he was at sea, he summoned the picture of the men voyaging from Tahiti across the hot, windy blue wastes of the Pacific. No wonder their passion was poured upon the land, so precious were the little spots of it in all the welter of water: islands, green, soft, inviting, out of whose soil grew the breadfruit and coconut and pandanus; islands whose mountain peaks gathered the clouds and fostered the rain and hid the gods; islands flat, jewel-like, and peaceful with a brooding sense of remoteness and a constant wind in coconut fronds; islands with fire in their wombs, thrusting up to peaks, breeding turbulence along with beauty.

He loved the going out, the sense of swiftness created by the waves rushing toward him, the lonely thrill of the possibility of a sudden squall and a swamped canoe. He occasionally glanced back longingly at the land, but each wave whispering against the canoe sides lured him on, and the clouds forming a pathway to the south beckoned. He loved too the coming back; it was like a voyage of discovery, watching the growing island, at first only a shadow of blue, then slowly gathering the form and substance of a mountain with dark shores and a white-edged sea lashing it. Then the vegetation: coconut palms, grasses, pandanus; and the dark syrupy spills of lava flows. And at last, suddenly and nostalgically, the sharp scent of earth overwhelming the salt fragrance of the sea.

Lucia watched, in growing bewilderment, the change come over Kaupena. It was first evident in his growing desire for Hawaiian food. One day about four months after Joe's death he said he would eat nothing but a very limited diet of fish and poi, fruit and pork and sweet potatoes. Also he insisted upon certain customs he had once regarded as superstitious and which she knew many others in Makaniloa observed carefully. To keep from bringing bad luck he would not allow her to sweep the dust out at night, and he uprooted all of the red ti which she had planted near the front door. He kept a number of tabus regarding his fishing; he would not eat bananas before going, and if she asked him if he were going fishing, he would not go.

She noticed that he was slowly withdrawing from her as though she too were one of the tabus. She did nothing to bring him closer to her, for she was afraid to act—she understood so little of what was happening to him now. One afternoon she admitted quite bitterly to herself that it seemed as though this marriage too was on its way to failure. And she tried to feel her way back to just why she had consented to it. The simple life! The direct life! The life close to the earth and without barriers. She laughed. It was all wrapped up in the darkness, in death and fantastic beliefs and fears. For the Hawaiian sitting on his lanai, seemingly so calm, so relaxed, the very air was filled with evil spirits; his neighbor, the kahuna, augured evil; his life was hedged with ridiculous tabus.

The thought of leaving Kaupena entered timidly into her mind. But she did not accept it gladly. There was much to bind her—Mele and Lokalia and Makaniloa itself. She loved Mele as though she were her own, and it seemed to her that Mele was drawing closer to her as Kaupena moved away. Lokalia too she loved. The weekly lessons in Hawaiian had turned out to be not only lessons in a language but also in a culture.

Lokalia seemed at times to be a reshaping in modern Hawaiian terms of her great-grandmother. They had the same passionate approach to life, the same romantic attitude, the same deep desire for communion with God. And thus because of these two women, Lucia was establishing for herself a life in Makaniloa which was deep-rooted and which might or might not include Kaupena. This mountain slope was already in many ways truly her home.

The most significant reason, however, why she could not leave Kaupena was that she still loved him. Notwithstanding all the hurt and bewilderment he had caused her, whenever he entered the house she was instantly aware of a trembling, excited response. There was that in him which intensified life for her. And he had only to smile and flop in the big koa chair, his shoulders hooked over the chair arms, his fingers tapping little rhythms on the floor, for her to know a settledness, a sense that in his house was where she belonged. Her one deep concern was whether or not he would come out from the present darkness with his love for her still intact. Her only course was to live quietly and unobtrusively, devoting her time to Mele—and to him, when he would let her.

Perhaps she should stand up to him, face him with the facts as they were. But she knew she could never do this. There was too much unexplained feeling in the currents which moved between them, too much of a reciprocal sense of pleasure even during their unhappiest days. So often in the night, he moved from where he had lain primly on his side of the bed to hers, and she felt the warmth and tenderness of his body as it sought her in a state numbed with sleep. In those moments when consciousness was clouded they often reached a directness of relationship that in waking moments was shadowed by the darkness in him. She regretted often that she had been reared in an atmosphere where distinctions had become too fine and too precious. She recognized with shame that she had never felt as poignantly as she knew Kaupena sometimes felt—as poignantly even as Julia or many of the others. She had never given herself, as they had, completely to an emotion.

She remembered Paul's suggestion that they could share the experience of Makaniloa in harmony because they started with the same equipment. He was, unfortunately, too close to the truth.

She wished that she could talk with Paul about this turning of Kaupena to his ancestral ways. She guessed that Kaupena's behavior had arisen from a deep need within him brought to the surface by Joe's death. Probably he had always wanted to find out just what it meant to be Hawaiian in the ancient sense. Only by complete immersion could he know.

As though Paul had made his way into her thought and read it, he came one late afternoon with a bag of lichees as an excuse. He sat down before she had invited him to with the manner of one who wished to talk. "Momi sent me up with these," he said. "It's a special tree that her father planted." He hesitated. "I was a little worried about you."

"Don't worry about me," she said.

He was in the rocker by the window and the light fell harshly on his face. She saw dark sharp lines of fatigue about his eyes and a hint of sorrow in his mouth.

"But there is some trouble with you."

He fingered his chin. "Yes, there is. Our second son, Jackie. He's ill, incurably."

"I'm sorry!" She moved her hands in a gesture of compassion.

"We've had him to the doctor in Wailuku. It's *petit mal,* they say. Some day it'll probably be epilepsy."

"Oh Paul, how terrible!"

"I don't quite know what to do about him. He's a bright little boy and already talks of going on to the university. He's fascinated with chemistry. But it's too dangerous. What if in the middle of an experiment. . . The poor kid."

He took out a cigarette and lit it. The match flame flared against his face with a brief rosy glow. His voice was low and tired when he continued. "And then Momi! She can't reconcile herself to it! She's gone all to pieces. She weeps and clings to Jackie as though he were about to die. She gathers all the neighbors in, and they lament in a sort of wild chorus on the lanai. The other two boys already regard their brother as someone strange and to be treated circumspectly." He waved his arm impatiently. "Oh I've seen this kind of thing happen before. This wave of emotion which grips them—lamentations and headshakings and whisperings. Sometimes I think I can't bear —" He stopped abruptly, and hid his head in his hands.

Lucia whispered softly, "Is there some way I can help?"

He seemed not to hear her words. "Momi has taken him to Lokalia."

"To Lokalia!" Lucia gasped.

"Yes, she's a kahuna, you know."

"I know."

"She's a shrewd old woman, though. She told Momi the boy would never be cured. But she gave her a stick of wood that she said was a sacred piece. When Jackie has an attack Momi is to put this wood in his mouth and sit quietly by him. That will make his attacks easier. She also scolded Momi and said she was making him worse by all of her carrying on in front of him. Momi, of course, didn't like what she said and went to another old lady who prayed over Jackie and said the reason he had this affliction was because Momi was jealous of another woman who had a little girl just a few days before Jackie was born. Momi wanted a girl and was disappointed to have Jackie."

He began to rock quietly back and forth.

"You see, Lucia, how these people struggle blindly to account for all the subtle effects of jealousy, love, or hatred. They know; it is in their racial experience that these emotions have long arms and can cause illness and unhappiness. We simply look at the child and see that he has epilepsy. And we try to plan a satisfactory life for him. They must have explanations, compensations. If he had been born to them a couple of centuries ago—who knows? He might have been called a seer; they might have mistaken his attacks for trances in which he communed with the gods."

She saw some of the fatigue passing from his face; his mouth had relaxed its stiff sorrowful thin line, and a faint flush had come into his cheeks.

"I can't say all these things to Momi. She would be hurt. That's what makes things so difficult, not being able to talk frankly." He shrugged his shoulders. "There're some things they just can't seem to understand."

It flashed upon Lucia for the first time that he considered himself superior—that Momi was like a child to him, a person from a race of children. And he was the superior white man! She fingered attentively a button on her blouse so as not to betray by her expression what she had read from him.

"Oh Lucia!" he appealed. "What am I to do with the child?"

She did not answer immediately. Finally she sighed and said softly, "I'd keep him here. This is his home; these people will love and accept him in their ancient way of friendliness. Here he'll have the quiet such people need. Teach him to love the quiet, to love Makaniloa, so that he'll never want to leave."

"You may be right. I had somehow thought . . . Oh, I don't know what I thought." He suddenly seemed weary of the topic. "I hear Kaupena has joined the Hui. It quite bowled them over. He's been so scornful about it."

"Yes, I've heard. He's never told me though."

"No?"

"No. Joe's death, I think, is still bothering him."

"Yeah, I heard that too. Death is real here; it isn't a cutting-off as it is for us. The person gone has a strange extension of life for quite a while. People talk about him, lament him, and often even see him walking in his old haunts." His voice was thick with distaste.

"Mele had nightmares," she continued softly, watching him; "She saw Joe at the window. We had a terrible time for a while."

"Yes, I can imagine." He lifted a hand, palm toward her. "Who knows? She might really have seen him!" His voice had an unpleasant mocking tone.

"Oh, Paul!" she cried and got up from her chair. "Don't be so contemptuous of them."

He was at her side. "Darling, I'm sorry! Can't you see what's at the bottom of everything I think and say? We're the same. Kaupena is a stranger to you, and Momi is a stranger to me."

"And your sons? Your little Jackie?"

"I really think they'd be happier without me. I only jam them up with things that would never enter their heads. And now that Jackie . . . You yourself say he belongs with his own people. And his people aren't really us. That's what hurts so when you've got kids in a situation like this. They aren't really yours."

Lucia thought how much Mele was hers, and she pitied Paul. He set himself too irrevocably apart. "They can be," she whispered.

He took her hand and kissed it. "Darling, you can't know yet. I hope you never will have the pain." He turned and without speaking again went out of the door. The kiss tingled on her palm for long after he had left.

After this, she thought often of Paul. He must be lonely in confronting the problem of his son. She saw that all along he must have been lonely. For he had had an ideal in his head, a simple back-to-nature theory. The people he chose to live with were for him a simple people. Because he could never lose himself in them he would always be lonely. He was the watcher and observer, finding their life better than the one he came from but at the same time being repelled by their superstitions. She could perhaps, she thought, help him more than he could help her. And from that day she made little occasions for seeing him from time to time.

The morning had been inclined to wind and squalls, but after the Hawaiian lesson, Lokalia asked Lucia if she would go with her to a place in the woods. There was a tautness in her manner as though she were suppressing a strong and pleasant emotion. Her eyes glistened. "The time has come," she said, "to show you something beautiful and lonely and wonderful."

Without another word Lokalia took her arm and led her down the valley path to the waiting car. Not until they were inside did she speak again. "Go down to the highway, and then turn right. At the third clump of ironwood trees we turn right again up a narrow dirt road."

Lucia laughed and said, "You're so mysterious!"

"That's my trade!" Lokalia said jokingly.

Lucia was surprised at this sort of humor coming from the old woman. But after all, she did not know every facet to Lokalia's character.

The road was deeply rutted and rocky and Lucia had to drive slowly. As they bumped along, Lokalia spoke in Hawaiian, telling of the families who had once lived in this district, sketching brief little stories of loneliness and despair and yearning for the glittering things of American life. The old satisfying ways had gone for them; the new was confusing, and they struggled unhappily in between. "They went away," she said gravely, "and like many of the others they were bitterly fooled." Then her voice brightened. "But, I think things are getting better for such people now."

They drove for more than forty minutes through the ruts and rocks until Lokalia said, "Around the next curve is the end of the road."

"Did people really live this far out?" Lucia asked.

"About fifteen years ago a family used to live here. There's an old rotting house back in the brush. Only last summer one of the daughters came back with her children to stay in the house for a while. She told me she just couldn't forget the place. Makaniloa is in the bones of these people."

Lucia left the car standing in the road as Lokalia directed her. "No one ever comes here!" she exclaimed.

Lucia had not realized how much they had climbed. The morning mists of the higher slope were frothing just a short distance beyond them. The air was cold and brisk, and the acrid scent of the mountain permeated it.

Lokalia led the way through a thicket of stunted lehua trees. Within a few hundred yards they reached an open terrain which ended abruptly in a mist-filled abyss. Lucia ran to the edge, crying, "Where is this?" She could not penetrate the clouds which surged milkily and obscured the valley that must lie below. She gazed up to the right where the crater seemed almost within walking distance, and then to the left where at the bottom of the vast slope lay the sea glittering with a deep hard blue. Mauna Loa and Mauna Kea hovered across the channel like great wind-filled mauve sails.

"The clouds," Lokalia cried. "We'll have to wait." She made

herself comfortable on a clump of ferns and motioned to Lucia to join her. Then she took a crumpled package of cigarettes from her bag and offered one.

"The wind!" Lucia shouted. "I'll never get it lighted."

Lokalia put the pack away.

Neither spoke against the buffeting of the wind. Occasionally in the abyss the clouds parted sufficiently for Lucia to see a precipitous slope green with vegetation and once in the distance she spotted a waterfall. She gave herself over to the magnificence and the wildness of the place, feeling with all her senses the power of the landscape; as the emotion rolled in upon her, her throat became swollen, her eyes swam with tears.

Just as she was beginning to feel the coldness of the wind penetrating to her bones, the clouds abruptly cleared away. Lokalia rose and pointed, "There!"

Lucia saw below her a boat-shaped valley enclosed by green perpendicular cliffs, over which, at intervals, waterfalls plunged into leaf-hidden pools or rocky basins. The back of the valley was enclosed with a tangle of kukui, hala, and hau foliage, impenetrable and brooding, yet sparkling with the yellowish cast of the kukui leaves. Two tall boulders rose above the trees in one spot—gods, they might be, or guardians. In the center of the valley was a large coconut grove, its plumes thrashing languorously and voluptuously in the wind. In front of the grove was an area of close-cropped green marked with patches of black crumbling lava walls; two spindly coconut palms rose from the lawn, suggesting that once a man might have planted them there, close to his house. The stream fed by the falls flowed along the opposite cliff, and just back of the beach it broadened into a lagoon shaded by a few clustering puhala trees on the banks. The lagoon waters were an iridescent bronze, flecked in green and blue; in spite of the wind, they seemed placid and mirrorlike. The beach was a great heaping up of black sand and stones on which the sea pulsed in sparkling white. Over all the valley was a faint haze of blue that lent it a kind of enchantment and the spell of remoteness.

With the passing of the clouds, the wind had abated somewhat, and it was no longer necessary to shout. Lucia said, "It's beautiful! Beyond belief!"

"It can be reached only by sea. These cliffs are too steep."

"I didn't dream it existed."

"It keeps itself well hidden from prying eyes. I'm glad it's difficult to reach."

"I'm glad too," Lucia said impulsively. "I hope there are dozens of such places through all the islands."

"Not dozens. But one or two on each island, at least."

"What a beautiful life must have been lived here!"

Lokalia turned her back on the valley. "You have understood what I came to show you. You know, Lucia, people of your kind have allowed us little dignity. We once had great dignity; we still have much, but we use it sparingly now. The West prefers in us the clown or the child. But men must be allowed dignity. Then they know that life is sacred. Without that they go to pieces."

"I know you are right," Lucia muttered.

Lokalia painted a picture of the life that had been lived in the valley. She told of the people who grew taro, sweet potatoes, banana, sugar cane, wauke; how the taro growers terraced their wet fields, trampling the earth to make it waterproof, strengthening it with rocks. She told of fishing, of the men going out in canoes with nets or trolling hooks, the women casting at the shore, and at night the spear fishing by torchlight. She described the canoe building and the tapa pounding and how the valley constantly echoed to the beat of the tapa makers. She told of the poetry and music and hula loved by the people. She spoke of the religious celebrations and feasts, and of the intimacy of the old gods; in those days power could be achieved through prayer and incantation, and through the hula and the ministration of the priests. These valley people had lived in harmony and health; the warm air, the sea, and the mountains gave them strength and ease and good nature. They knew the security granted by their valley.

She concluded, "Now perhaps you may understand why some of us dream of the old. Of course we can't have it; we have to compromise with today."

She paused, and Lucia watched in silence as the clouds began to move down, shrouding the valley.

Lokalia sighed deeply. "Sometimes it's hard to compromise. It seems almost dishonest." She took Lucia's arm. "And so some of us have to try the bitter lesson of going back to the old before we can learn how to compromise. The trouble is, of course, we don't know exactly what the old was, and we fall into confusion."

She pressed her fingers tenderly around Lucia's wrist and held them there for some time. Slowly it came to Lucia that this trip had been, in its way, a special plea for lenience to Kaupena.

14.

UPON their return from the valley, Lucia left Lokalia at the pathway leading to her cottage. She took Lokalia's hand. "Thank you, Tutu, for today. You certainly showed me something beautiful and lonely and wonderful." She smiled and squeezed gently the gnarled old fingers. "And I understand!"

Lokalia watched as Lucia drove away. Kaupena had chosen well. But he was making it difficult! Lokalia sighed. She could only hope that the two young people would come through this crisis safely. If Lucia could endure. . . . And if Kaupena could hurry through his testing. . . .

She turned and made her way up the valley. Now that Lucia was gone, she felt a slow yielding of her strength. It seemed a long way across the hot, hard stones and she was glad when the boughs arched over the trail and shaded her from the moist yellow light. Even in the shadow, though, heat clung stickily to her. Her ears began to ring with fatigue and the breath to rasp in her throat, and it was with a great flooding of relief that at last she saw the house ahead of her.

The stairs up to the lanai looked unusually long and steep, and she paused to catch her breath at the bottom. Then slowly and with some pain she began to mount them. On the fifth step she stumbled from dizziness and a sharp pain in her temple. She lost her balance and rolled to the bottom, knocking her head on a flagstone. There she lay unconscious for more than half an hour. The winds of Makaniloa passed over her, graying her aged flesh with chill and ruffling the folds of her skirt. A dried mango leaf drifted down and settled on the palm of one of her hands. Lizards scurried from the grass and gazed curiously at her; one ventured onto her chest and rested there briefly in a patch of sun that filtered through the leaves.

As she was returning to consciousness she had a vision of her husband when he was only twenty-five. He bent over her, and the old tenderness was in his eyes, and his hands reached out for her in the way she had known so well. She felt a surge of youthful passion, and her body trembled. At the moment that consciousness was fully returned, her vision fled. Slowly she grasped her situation and a fear entered her. She wondered how long she had lain there; it was as though she had been dead for an unknown period. Wasn't her flesh still gray and cold, weren't her limbs stiff, the juices of her body sluggish? With difficulty, she rose and climbed into the house. Her left leg was numb.

She put water on to boil for tea and then went into the bedroom for her comfortable old gray sweater, the wool of which had come originally from Scotland. It had been knitted and unraveled and knitted and unraveled three times and had come from Kaupena's mother who was part Scotch and had had it from her father. Lokalia buttoned the sweater tight around her and returned to the kitchen. There she closed the windows, poured out her tea, and huddled herself in the wooden rocker. The teacup was hot enough to burn her palms and finger tips when she wrapped her hands about it, and she enjoyed this sensation because it told her sharply and hurtingly that she was alive.

Presently the chill left her flesh and the blood ran warm again. She sat quietly, enjoying the very fact of living. She poured another cup of tea. Holding the cup close to her face, she allowed the steam to bathe her and its fragrance to fill her nostrils.

Thoughts began to stir out of this creature contentment, and they were troubling ones. To die, to leave Makaniloa, never to see or smell or feel it again. . . . A bitter thing! Besides, matters were not settled enough for her to die. Kaupena and Lucia were probably bound for their deepest conflict, and she was not at all sure of their ability to meet it and find the harmony they must have.

Her reflections now moved upon the deeply passionate motive of her life for the past forty years. She had had cold, shocking instants of doubt about this motive, instants in which her entire life seemed to have been wasted. But now brought from the very brink of death, as she was convinced, it seemed wholly good and noble. What would allow greater contentment in the face of death than the work she had done to strengthen her racial pattern? If her life had served to rescue from extinction some of the ancient strands, it would be woven for all time into the Polynesian design. Her influence would live long after her, subtly and anonymously; it would contribute to the vitality of her people.

She remembered the day many years ago when she had taken up the task laid down by Hoopai. The neighbors had gathered on a cold blustery January afternoon to watch by the bedside of the dying man. Hoopai had been for all Makaniloa the counselor, the father-confessor, the helper. His wisdom ran deep and instinctive, and he seldom faltered in his decisions. His mind was filled with the ancient lore which he had had from his father. Unfortunately there were secrets he had taken to his grave. How often she had wished she had pressed the dying man for those secrets to add to her store.

In her mind was a clear picture of the little house where Hoopai lay. It had a hewn wooden frame, but the walls and roof were of thatch, and the sweet smell of the grass permeated the room. Hoopai had clung to the old idea of a separate house for sleeping. He lay on a pile of mats in a shadowed corner, and she had sat on a stiff koa chair nearby. In another corner stood a small bureau, which had on it only a faded yellow photograph of his wife. The room had been filled constantly with people coming and going, greeting Hoopai, wishing him health, sitting silently with him for a while and then going out to join the rest of his family in the big house. During a moment of loud confusion he had called out, "Let everyone leave me now."

His tone had rung like a bell warning of disaster. The people had stopped their chattering and stood for a moment like a frieze. He continued softly, "I will speak to Lokalia Waiolama."

Lokalia was not surprised at this. After the death of her husband, she had become Hoopai's student; he had helped her shape that first glimmering she had had in the crater days with Joseph, her husband, into a reverent sense of dedication to Hawaiian lore. Hoopai had hinted often that when the time came for his death, he would pass on to her certain bits of knowledge. Her heart beat painfully as she felt the people glancing at her as they filed out. When they all had gone a deep silence settled into the room; even the wind seemed to have abated, and the sea sound was faint and mellow. Hoopai was lying on his bed with his hands clasped across his breast, his eyes staring up into the mistiness of the thatch. His face was thin and pinched, the nose bony, the mouth sagging. The neck of his sleeping muumuu was cut low and revealed the deep hollow of his throat. She heard the breath come harshly from his chest, and she saw death already settling on his face.

When he spoke finally, his voice was low and pitched in a tone of sorrow. "Lokalia, you know what I have worked for; you know how I have given my strength for these people. I have for years thought that the important thing was to perserve the old. But I was wrong."

Tears came from his eyes, rolling down his cheeks and onto the bed mat where they stood full and glistening as though they rested on an oiled surface. His face was shining with tears. She waited.

"The young no longer understand many things. With the

alii gone, so much of the old loses its power. What do the young care for the old days. Auwe! They are not worthy of receiving the secrets or of learning the ancient chants and hulas. It is better that such things die with us who have understood the full power of them."

"Hoopai," she said tenderly. "It may be that you are wrong. The young are confused now. But the day will come when they will need what you are denying them."

"I knew, Lokalia Waiolama, that you would say that. I know too how you have felt as I have felt, that you have honored the things of the past. That is why I am speaking to you now. I want to give you two chants. One is very sacred; it is addressed to Lono and is to be used only at Pohaku Lono. The other is to Laka. This chant was used only in Makaniloa by my family who trained the young dancers devoted to Laka."

He paused as the breath came in gasps from him; the emotion of the moment had strained his old body to a tension it could scarcely bear. When he was somewhat quieter, he continued, "You must not write these down. You shall memorize them. If you write them down, their power will be gone."

So in the stillness of the little house he taught her the chants, and she spoke them to him over and over again until he was certain that she knew them. Then he admonished her, "But remember, Lokalia Waiolama, most of what you will do in your life will be useless. We are a dying people. The memory of the young does not stretch into the past, for they have not been trained. They are the children of a dying people. These secrets must go out with us—not be passed on to unfriendly, skeptical minds. I shall die carrying with me many things I would prefer to go on. You will die carrying with you almost the last of Makaniloa secrets."

While he spoke in this mood of despair, she had felt a contrary fire blaze up within her. There was a way of giving these old secrets to the young. And she would find it! Pride must be stirred in them.

"I see the fire in your face," Hoopai said feebly. "Auwe! You too will have to learn in pain." These words brought a spell of choking coughs to him. His face grew red, then purple, and his eyes stared in agony. She started to go for help but he motioned for her to stay. She cried into his ear that she would teach the young to love and understand the old and would give them a pride in it. Then solemnly she promised her grandson, Kaupena, to that cause.

He tried to speak, but there was only a horrible noise in his throat. Finally a stillness came to his body, and she knew that Hoopai was dead. She closed his eyes, smoothed back his hair, set his hands peacefully at his side, and laid a piece of tapa over his body. Then she went to the doorway to announce that he was gone.

The little house swarmed again with people and the air soon hummed with wailing. She slipped through the throng to make her way homeward. But before she entered her own house, she had sprinkled herself with salt as was the custom for one who had ministered to the dead.

Lokalia now sighed. Kaupena had been dedicated at the deathbed of old Hoopai. But it seemed as though the dedication had worked too well. He had strayed too deeply into the darkness, so deeply that he could be duped by the hysterics of that foolish girl, Hallie Kepelino. She hoped that Lucia could be kept from knowing of Kaupena's association with Hallie. It would be enough to make any woman turn in scorn from her husband.

Hallie was a tall, thin, ugly girl who was so unattractive in spirit and body that she lived a lonely life. At dusk two weeks ago she had been walking near the site of a heiau when an old woman had approached her. The woman told Hallie that if she wanted to become beautiful and give up being lonely she need only come and sit for five days in a row on the large rock which had once been part of the heiau. As Hallie watched, the strange woman shuffled off toward the sea, and then like a puff of foam wind-scattered along the beach, she suddenly vanished. Hallie realized that the apparition must have been Pele, goddess of the volcano. Glowing with excitement, she ran home and cried out her story to her credulous family, and they spread the tale quickly over all Makaniloa. Pele had been seen again! So great was the faith of the people in Pele that at the end of five days of Hallie's sitting on the stone, they found the girl to be growing in beauty. She had begun to care for her stringy, dark hair, washing it and brushing it. Her eyes were filled with the warm light of her faith, and her manner took on this warmth. Other women tried sitting on the rock—some to be cured of ailments, some to find wealth, some to beget sons. In ten days the excitement had grown so that the rock was credited with the most amazing powers, and the young people gathered gleefully and excitedly around Hallie. Hallie now allowed herself the thrill of hysterical displays during which she claimed that Pele visited her almost daily. She could not foresee that in another fortnight her rock would be abandoned, her incipient cult all but forgotten. It was the old way in Makaniloa, this sudden mushrooming of supernatural events and then an equally sudden decline in interest in them.

Lokalia could remember in her lifetime seven or eight such periods of excitement. None of them ever lasted very long because they had no roots; they were pitiful imitations of what someone thought must have been the ways of the ancients. She recognized that they rose from ignorance, hysteria, and love of excitement; they filled her with a growing sense of anguish for her people. And now to think that Kaupena was one of the followers of Hallie! He was still far from understanding the ancients if he could be so easily duped. . . . Oh no! She could not die yet! Kaupena must be set back firmly on the right path, and Lucia must learn to find her happiness with him.

Lucia sat alone one warm gray evening on the lanai. Mele was in bed asleep, and Kaupena had, as he so often did now, slipped out without a word on one of his mysterious activities. It was probably to the Hui, she thought, or to Hallie's Rock. She seemed in the past two weeks to have lost all touch with him and had the curious feeling that he was someone she had known intimately some years ago, and that time and a divergence of paths had made them like strangers. He no longer even slept with her in the big koa bed, but made his own on the hikie in the living room. She did not know just when he ate or slept; she suspected he often stayed in the bunkhouse for the night or at times even out on the pastures. But she and Mele continued the regularity of their lives and had become in truth mother and child. She was deeply moved when she realized that Mele had come to depend on her for decisions in many of her little problems, and confided her thoughts and feelings. "Mamma," she said one afternoon, "Kaupena has grown so strange. I don't like him anymore." Lucia tried to excuse Kaupena, but Mele persisted. "Why can't we live without him?"

This suggestion had an appeal to Lucia, which made her uneasy, and it dwelt in her imagination. If she and Mele could have a little house together and live their placid days, ruffled only by occasional picnics, or church suppers, or birthday parties, then Kaupena could keep to his mysteries, and they would be untroubled by him. Her love was being strained dangerously. Ten long difficult months had passed since Joe's death, and he seemed now to be completely engrossed in the fanatical concept of being utterly Hawaiian. He had gone so far as to make himself ridiculous by following Hallie Kepelino!

But this evening on the lanai, her mind was wearied of the growing entanglement of her life, and she turned to the placid vista about her. The sky had been opalescent just before dusk, giving a tone of unreality to the landscape as though it were suspended in a painting or a dream. This dreaminess entered her, giving an impression of changelessness and quietude.

Thus the car lights moving up the driveway startled her, and she rose quickly from her chair and moved to the balustrade. Who could it be, she wondered vaguely, still half immersed in her mood of peace. As the car turned to park on the grass, she saw that it was Paul's, and a stir of friendliness warmed her. They had often in the past few months spent pleasant evenings together. It was a comfort to have Paul at hand now that he had gotten over his insistence on being in love with her. Of course he still was; she could see that in many of his little gestures toward her. And she knew that deep within her she was thankful for this love. It gave her an anchor in the confusing tide of Makaniloa.

"We're going out tonight," he said as he came across the lawn.

"But Mele!"

"Don't worry. I've already told Julia. She's sending Lei and one of her friends over to sit."

She smiled. "You seem to have made my mind up for me. Where are we going?"

"This is going to be a great night in Makaniloa!" There was excitement in his manner. "Do you mean to say that Mele hasn't told you of it?"

"She's said nothing."

"I suppose she's reluctant to speak of it because of Kaupena."

"Kaupena?"

"Yes, that's why I'm taking you. To see him in action. We're going to eavesdrop! So put on your slacks and your heavy shoes."

She questioned him with her gaze. He laughed finally. "Darling, I ain't tellin'. So hop into your old clothes."

She put on a pair of blue jeans and one of Kaupena's palaka shirts. Then she went in to peek at Mele, who slept soundly.

Out on the lanai Paul announced, "The girls are here."

She told Lei and her friend that there were cokes in the ice box and cookies on the shelf. Then she followed Paul into the car.

"Why are you so mysterious?" she asked.

"I want you to see some of the goings-on of Makaniloa. And this is an unusual occasion, for two very esoteric events are being held tonight." His voice was faintly mocking. "Momi told me about it and went cheerfully off to attend both. It gives her the excitement she needs and a chance to be part of the gang. So I got Mrs. Yamato to come in and sit with the boys. It was too good an opportunity for you and me to go spying."

"Why spying? Why not just go with Momi and the others?"

"Because we'd spoil their fun. They know how I feel. They probably suspect you."

His eyes glowed brilliantly and there was a smile twitching on his lips. He laid his hand tenderly on her knee for a moment. She wondered if he was hoping to reach her through exposing Kaupena's behavior.

After Paul had driven for ten minutes along the narrow, black road, he pulled the car to the side and parked it. "We walk from here. I daren't drive any closer."

He guided her to a well-trodden path that curved through a guava entanglement. The scent of rotting guavas hung in a savory sweetness in the air and struck her with a stab of anticipation; the scent of guavas always stirred in her a little thrill which she could not explain. They heard a chatter of human voices and saw a glow of yellow light ahead.

"There's a big bush at the end of the path," he whispered. "We'll crouch under that."

He took her hand and pulled her down under the laden

branches of a guava bush. She breathed again of the heavy fragrance, and her heart pounded.

"Look!" he whispered.

She saw in an open space about ten yards beyond them some twenty-five or thirty people; most were young, in their teens or twenties, but a few were of middle age. Behind them rose Hallie's Rock, and beyond it the crumbling walls of a heiau, thickly overgrown with a spindly, dry-looking shrub. A torch burned at either side of the boulder lighting weirdly the gangling figure of Hallie standing on top of the rock.

"Hallie!" Paul whispered. "She's gone wild over this!"

The girl was harranguing the crowd in a shrill voice, waving her arms violently and tossing her head in a curious stiff way. The little of her talk that drifted to them seemed to be a muddle of phrases from Christian sermons and the time-worn accounts of the appearances of the goddess, Pele. Young people, clustered at the back, snickered among themselves. A large middle-aged woman watched Hallie with the concentration of a devotee, and from time to time frowned at the young people. Some of the throng moved restlessly about as though searching a spot to hear better. Others had frankly turned away and were conversing among themselves. There was in most of the gathering a mood of skepticism and mocking. Hallie's day was almost over.

A man leaped suddenly to the rock beside her and shouted in a powerful voice, "Pele is watching! She sees your laughter. Beware! For Pele has her ways!" The effect on the crowd was instantaneous. They froze in their positions and stared at him; Lucia could almost feel the fear move into them. They were all vividly aware of stories of Pele's vengeance, and Kaupena understood their psychology as the fumbling Hallie did not. For the man was Kaupena.

"He knows how to do it," Lucia breathed to Paul.

"Momi says he's Hallie's right-hand man. He's kept this alive longer than it normally should last."

Kaupena began to chant in Hawaiian an old song to Pele. Others joined him, and the crowd in its newly found unity began to sway and move with a vague suggestion of dance gestures. Kaupena's voice continued harshly resonant, and the movement of the crowd took on a primitive spellbound quality. Hallie clapped her hands and stamped her feet to the rhythm of the chant, and every now and again she cried out, "Pele, Pele!" When she did this Kaupena threw back his head and thrust his hands, the fingers spread wide, into the air.

Lucia tasted bitterly the nausea rising in her, and slipped from under the sheltering guava. Paul followed quickly after her.

He said, "I'm sorry if this upset you."

"Such stupid, hysterical abandon! How can he do it!"

He tried to soften it for her. "Remember, darling, this isn't unique. There are exhibitions like this all over the world—cheap, sensational, semierotic expressions of a kind of pseudo religion."

"But how can Kaupena? He's not like that."

"Darling, such things lie dormant in all of us. When we're upset sometimes . . . And these people! It's easier for them to go back."

She spoke to herself. "It's all part of this plunge of his. He can't distinguish right now. Oh, if he only could!"

Her mind was full of Kaupena, and Paul had the hurt look of one who has been shut out.

"I try to understand him," she said. "Sometimes I almost do. Then something like tonight . . ."

"They have channels of raw feeling we can never know," he said sententiously.

"Then we've just got to dig deep enough into ourselves. We're all the same at the bottom."

He took her hand. "Don't fool yourself, darling. You'll only be hurt. Face things as they are—the primitiveness, the wildness—it's hard for us to take."

They reached the car, and she opened the door and climbed in. The vision of a completely repulsive Kaupena in all his hysteria hung vividly before her. She welcomed the presence of Paul as he slid into the driver's seat; a scent of tobacco and of oiled leather was about him, good familiar scents which she had associated with men from her childhood. She moved closer to him.

"Now we have another place to go," he said lightly. "There's a to-do up at Pohaku Lono."

"Pohaku Lono!"

"Yes, the stone at the back of Lokalia's valley."

"I've never known just what went on there. I've often wondered."

"You mean the old gal hasn't told you yet? With all of your Hawaiian lessons?"

"No, she hasn't."

"I guess she's afraid. She's wise about haoles. She knows the things that make them condescend to Hawaiians."

"She goes to Pohaku Lono?"

"Sure, she's the high priestess. She's training Kaupena to take her place." He started the engine. "This time we've got to get there ahead of them. It's a long walk, and then we'll have to hide in a very damp cave. We can't be seen there, but we can see very well. Can you take it?"

For a moment she thought of refusing. Seeing Kaupena on Hallie's Rock had been alarming. To see Lokalia in the same kind of thing—Lokalia whom she loved and admired—would be too hard. And then even as she recognized the anguish it might be, she knew she must go. "Yes, I can take it," she said faintly.

He drove to the mouth of Lokalia's valley and hid the car in a clump of trees. After they had climbed out into the dew-heavy grass, he locked the car, first taking from the back seat a knapsack which he slung over his back.

He guided her through the tall grasses to the path up the valley until they rounded the curve that gave a view of Lokalia's house. The front of the house was dark, but at the back there was a faint flickering glow as though a candle might be lighted. They moved into the woods and made their way cautiously. Paul had a small flashlight. The darkness sharpened their sensitivity to the noises of the woods, the rustlings, thuds, delicate little cries as of mice or stricken birds, leaf crunches under their feet, the ghostly squeaks of rubbing branches, the swelling murmur of the falls, and high above them the night wind booming in the top-most branches of the trees.

"It's spooky," Lucia whispered with a little laugh.

"Yeah. It's strange just how frightening these woods can be even when you know there are no snakes, no animals, or wild men, or even poisonous spiders. I never can understand my fear. It's so irrational."

"Ah, but, Paul dear!" Her voice was teasing. "It's the primitive raw fear of the dark."

"Strike one!" he said with good nature.

When they neared the back of the valley, he took her hand, and led her to the bottom of the cliff. "We'll have to climb along a slippery little ledge here. I'll go first with the light. Hold tight to my hand. You wouldn't fall very far, but it might hurt."

They stepped slowly, one foot at a time. Thick oozy moss grew on the ledge and in places little trickles of water coursed over it.

"There must be a continual slow drip from the top. I've never seen it dry here," he said.

He ducked suddenly into a black hollow. "Here we are!" One hand drew her and in the other he held the flashlight to show her the way.

The cave seemed opaquely black and forbidding. The sound of the falls was dulled like the distant roar of the surf.

"We'll have some time to wait. So I've brought all the comforts of home." From the knapsack he took two folding stools and two plastic raincoats. "Here, put this on!" he commanded, handing her a raincoat. "Your clothes will get damp through in this air if you don't." He set the stools at the mouth of the cave. "Now," he said, "the cup that cheers! I have coffee and some brandy to put in it, and some very choice cheese and liverwurst sandwiches. We need a little refreshment."

He poured her a steaming cup of coffee and added a jigger of brandy into it. She sipped it slowly, feeling the warmth creep down deep into the marrow of her bones. She took the sandwich he handed her and nibbled at it. The cave was no longer so black as it had been when she first entered. It seemed now to have a faint luminosity, and she could see clearly the profile of Paul as he held the cup to his mouth. She smiled; she was reliving the old childhood feeling of being in a secret cosy shelter away from prying eyes and the uncertainties of weather.

"You have been here before," she said.

"Many times. As a matter of fact, I did an article on one of these Pohaku Lono things for a Pittsburgh paper. I don't think anyone here ever saw it, for which I'm grateful."

Lucia peered out into the valley blackness, which was so dense that she could not distinguish a thing beyond the line of tree foliage against the sky. "It's terribly dark."

"Yes, the dark of the moon."

"Why should there be two ceremonies tonight?"

"I think Lokalia is trying to show Kaupena the difference. She doesn't approve of the Hallie business, you know. Of course the difference lies only in her mind, poor old lady."

"I can't always make out just where you stand, Paul."

"I'm torn between my love for these people and what my mind tells me."

"Look!" she interrupted.

A light was approaching from the distance. They watched in silence until they could make out the figure of a woman carrying a large basket in one hand and a lantern in the other.

"It's Lokalia," Lucia whispered.

"Yes. She's getting things ready. Keep your voice in a whisper. This cave acts a little like a band shell."

They watched as Lokalia set her lantern at the base of the tall rock and then fumbled in the basket. She pulled out a long plumeria lei, which she twisted about the base of the rock. Then she took a maile lei and, standing tiptoe, threw it up several times, aiming at the top, until it caught and she could festoon it down the length of Pohaku Lono. She stood back to gaze at the effect and then made slight changes in both leis. When she was satisfied, she took a can from her basket and poured kerosene into two torches which stood ready at either side of the rock. Then she stooped to lay a little basket of fruit at the base of the rock, and rising, paused for a while, her hands clasped, her head bowed. She was dressed in a black silk holoku and on her hair rested lightly a yellow feather lei. Around her neck hung some strands of maile.

People came presently, a large group, and seemed to take appointed places around the rock. She lighted the torches, and as though it were a sign, Kaupena appeared out of the darkness and walked slowly and with dignity toward the rock. He had around his shoulders a yellow feather cape. When he was a few feet from Pohaku Lono, he raised his arms above his head, the palms facing the rock, and chanted to the God Lono.

It was a long, poetic verse describing the benefactions of Lono to the harvest, calling upon him for the cooling, refreshing rains, for the germination of the seed, the growth of the plant. Kaupena's voice was rich and deep, resounding with the dignity and liquid rhythm of the Hawaiian words. His manner was calm, his body motionless. When he had finished, Lokalia stepped to his side and chanted of Makaniloa, how beautiful it was because of Lono, and how Lono watched over this land and its people, the chosen ones of his heart. She then took the maile from her shoulders and laid it across the fruit she had placed at the rock. The rest of the people now filed past leaving their tokens, flowers, fruit, or vegetables at the base of Pohaku Lono. They spoke no words, performing their oblation in silence. Then they went slowly down the path toward Lokalia's house, keeping strictly in the line of their procession. Lokalia followed immediately after them, but Kaupena lingered long enough to put out the torches.

The whole ritual had taken no more than twenty minutes. Yet in its simplicity and in its assumption that these words and gestures contained a profound secret and power, the ceremony had religious dignity and sincerity. Lucia was shaken by the psychic need it showed among these people of an approach to God, which was their own, deep-laid in their racial memory. But Kaupena! How could he share in this and in the other too? How could he on the same night be two such different people? Her whole being suddenly cried out against him. She could no longer go on in this misty wood he had made of her life, filled with strange distorted creatures. She must take Mele and find a house where the two of them could live alone in the sun and the wind.

She felt the cold creeping into her flesh through the raincoat and the damp oozing up under her feet. She shivered partially from cold and partially in reaction to her revulsion from Kaupena. "Oh, Paul," she whispered. "It's so puzzling!"

He moved close to her and put an arm about her shoulders. He did not speak, but she felt the shelter and strength of his presence. His warmth became her warmth, and she moved closer, her body and her heart crying out for peace and for the familiarity and at-homeness he gave to her. Kaupena had deserted her; his desertion was actually more complete than if he had left the house, because he had fiercely cut all the strands of communication which in spite of his behavior had lingered on between them. And Paul! Paul was hoping, waiting for her. In her weariness and her need, she turned to him and fastened her arms tightly around his waist.

On the following day when she awoke she wondered at first why happiness was singing in her. Then abruptly she remembered, and turned over in bed and hid her face in the pillow to stifle the pure laugh that rose in her throat. Then she flung the covers off and walked to the window. The wind of Makaniloa blew, pressing her nightgown tight across her hips and close around her breasts. Her body had a tingling warmth in it, a sense of anticipation which again brought the laugh bubbling to her throat. She let it come this time and then began to sing softly *Flow Gently Sweet Afton,* a favorite song of hers from childhood.

She went in to awaken Mele. "Get up, lazy!"

Mele rolled over, hiding herself in the folds of the sheet.

Lucia bent down and tickled her across the back of her neck and then probed gently along the lines of her ribs. Mele doubled up in a spasm of laughter. "Don't, Mamma," she cried breathlessly.

"Get up!" Lucia sang out.

Mele squirmed out of bed and threw her arms around Lucia. "Mamma, you're so different today."

"I feel happy, Mele. Really happy. Come on, darling, take your bath and get dressed."

Lucia squeezed her tightly and kissed her cheeks. "We'll have hot cakes this morning. So hurry."

At noon Paul came to have lunch with her, as they had planned in the cave. She was shy at first. Emotions which came more easily in the shelter of the night seemed terribly exposed by day. She met him at the doorway and held out her hand for shaking. He grinned at her. "My dearest darling, you're so formal this morning." And he took her into his arms.

Finally she pushed herself away. "Paul, you almost hurt." And she laughed.

She spread out on the table a luncheon of fried chicken, potato salad, and hot rolls with guava jelly. He ate heartily. "I haven't tasted a meal like this in ages." He reached for her hand. "Darling, we do belong together. Even in the simple daily affairs you know instinctively what I like, what I've been craving."

She smiled, basking in his appreciation, expanding under the generous, steady, certain love he was lavishing upon her. No one had ever given her such love, not even Ted who wanted their love to appear other than what it was and who was afraid of the conflicts which were necessary to keep love refreshed and thriving. And Kaupena! He was too many people ever to be steadily in love; he lived for bursts of passion.

She didn't want to think of the future with Paul; she wasn't ready to cope with that. She simply wanted to enjoy the love he was giving her. She rose impulsively and walked around the table. She laid her arms about his shoulders and kissed the top of his head. "Oh Paul, how I do love you!" Then she moved away from him before he could touch her and brought to him the coconut cream pie, which had turned out so beautifully and of which she was proud.

"Lucia, Lucia!" he cried. "I think I'll move in tomorrow."

His words startled her, and she was aware of an undercurrent of uneasiness.

He must have seen the look on her face, for he said, "We must do things easily, gradually, darling."

She sat down and started to eat the piece of pie she had cut for herself. Then she reached across the table, her fingers touching his. "Darling, why did you want to live in Makaniloa?"

"I told you at our first meeting. That still holds."

"I know. But something in me tells me it's more than just that. Oh Paul, I want to know all about you!"

He grasped her fingers tightly. "Someday I'll tell you more. I'll tell you everything about me. But let's just make today for you and me and Makaniloa. The three of us."

15.

ON THE morning after the two ceremonies, Kaupena awoke as usual at dawn. There was a bitter taste in his mouth, and in his mind the troubling sensation that he had done something wrong, something, perhaps, faintly disgusting. He got up from the hikie, pulled on his trousers, and went to the lanai. Makaniloa was a diffusion of gray and black, gray in sky and grass and sea, and black in tree foliage and rock. He gazed for some moments at this drabness and then went in to put on his shirt. He tiptoed to the kitchen and drank a cup of the cold coffee he had made the night before. When he had finished he listened for any stir in the house, but there was none; he felt a vague disappointment. So he left the house immediately and walked to the stables. Panini seemed impatient to be out in the field, and his champings and pawings did not help in the saddling.

Kaupena rode to the embankment overlooking the village where Joe lay buried. A pale gold had now come into the sky and the sea, and the grasses had turned green. The soft wind carried the scent of dawn. He pulled Panini to a stop and dismounted. The strong coffee taste lingered with the morning bitterness in his mouth, and nervously he lighted a cigarette. But he had only one puff from it before the wind snatched it from his trembling fingers. He walked to the edge of the embankment. Joe was lucky, he thought. He had found his resting place; he lay securely among his own people, and his bones were blending with island earth.

Again the thought of last night rose into Kaupena's mind like a wave af nausea. In an effort to destroy it, his eyes concentrated on Joe's grave. He knew it like a well-loved painting that had been hanging on the wall for years, and his glance lingered on the soft lines of the grassy mound and then on the twisting dark form of the young plumeria tree planted by Lucia. The fence he had built of round black stones from the beach neatly enclosed the little spot. He had never put a marker on it, for that did not seem to fit in with this old place. After all, the Hawaiians had always hidden the bones of the dead.

He looked away from the grave to the kamani grove where he had first taken Lucia, and his mind turned nervously upon her. He reflected now that he should never have taken her there; it had given him the illusion that she too belonged in Makani-loa. But how could she? She was part of all he wanted to escape. That is, he corrected himself uneasily, she had seemed to be in these last few months, anyway. . . .

Last night! The unpleasant memory of it persisted in blotting all else from his consciousness. And he saw again the expressions on the faces as he stared into them from his eminence on Hallie's Rock: the fleeting smiles of derision and mockery; the skeptical curiosity vainly masked by firmly closed mouths and round eyes threatening laughter; the whisperings behind hands, and the furtive pointings. These people had come for excitement, to be amused. He knew that now. They didn't care at all about Hallie or her vision of Pele. Why should they? People all over the islands were always seeing Pele in some form or other; the goddess might beg a ride in a car and then suddenly disappear from the back seat, or she might knock at a door at night and ask for food, or possibly she would appear briefly on a woodland trail and then disappear mysteriously. Why should anyone take Hallie and her vision seriously? Why had it drawn him? Hallie was a queer hysterical girl, and of course that made the situation great fun for the people gathered at the Rock. It was double fun for them that he, Kaupena Waiolama, should be taken in by it.

He lit another cigarette, filling his mouth with the mordant smoke and holding it there as though it might have a cauterizing effect.

He recognized that the deep and powerful cause of his awakening was not, however, in those mocking smiles. It was in the Pohaku Lono ritual, so soon after the travesty at Hallie's Rock. He exhaled the cigarette smoke in a thin stream, which was at the same time the latter part of a sigh. Pohaku Lono, he mused, and the ancient chants devoted for generations to that slender shaft of stone, the quiet dignity of the offering to a god of the harvest and the rain—all of this, after the cheap hysteria of Hallie! He remembered how the followers of Lono had gathered in Lokalia's house and how he had seen on their faces the repose of quiet hearts and the happiness of people who have acknowledged by personal dedication that there is spirit behind the life force.

Slowly Kaupena was being driven to admit his fall into blindness, a blindness that had come upon him at Joe's death and had thrown everything out of perspective. It had made such things as Hallie's Rock possible for him. It had made him turn from Lucia. . . . How could he ever again trust his own judgment?

"Oh, Lucia!" he said aloud. It had seemed so clear to him that he must give her up, in spite of his love for her, in spite of the remembrance of the sweetness of their past embraces. Often he had seen the sadness on her face and wanted to open his arms to her. But stern and harsh against this impulse was his sense of mission for his people, his desire to show them in his own life how to make their being Hawaiian count. A haole wife, a stranger to the islands, was not the way. He was embracing one of the very group that had destroyed them. He had kept firmly to this in the face of Julia's love for Lucia, of

Mele's love, Lokalia's love, and even the recollection of Joe's love. What force had driven him?

He mounted Panini suddenly and rode swiftly across the brown-green pasture toward the ranch. At the bunkhouse he found Johnny and told him he would be gone for several days in the crater, where he would work on a method of piping water from the spring to the dry pastures. "Tell Hallie, I'm pau. Break it as easily as you can. Tell Lucia not to worry." He stuffed a box of hardtack and a handful of chocolate bars from the pantry into a saddle bag and started on his way.

When he reached the crater he dismounted and threw himself down on a grassy plot. There he slept until sunset. It was the first deep dreamless sleep he had had since Joe's death. He had been awakening some nights as often as five or six times, with his throat choking, his nose constricted, his head shooting with pain as though he were drowning in the turbulent sea off the Point. Some nights he could even taste the salt of the water on his tongue and feel it burning in his eyes, so strong was the illusion of drowning. On other nights he had dreamed of the ancient gods; they came to him in the form of the wooden images, with great grinning mouths and staring eyes of pearl, which once had stood in heiaus. He would awaken with the image still in his eyes, and seeming to move toward him out of the darkness. Only by burying his head in the blanket could he drive the vision away.

So he was grateful for this dreamlessness in the winds of the crater. His mind when he awoke was clear and at peace, and he sat up, watching the pale iridescent blues and violets of the cinder cones deepen into solemn grays as dusk came on. He rose and, going to the spring pool, took off his clothes. He dipped water with his hands and poured it over his body, rubbing his flesh until it burned. Then he stood in the cold rough wind of the gap to dry. When he put on his trousers and shirt again, his body felt smooth and clean as it had not for months. He took a chocolate bar from the saddle bag and ate it, following it with a long cold draught from the spring. Darkness had come and he could see a few lights twinkling up from Makaniloa. He unsaddled Panini, and taking the saddle blanket lay down in the grass and pulled it over him. Quickly he was asleep again.

He spent three days in the crater. He slept a great deal, bathed often in the spring, ate sparingly of his hardtack and chocolate, and carried on monologues with Panini as his audience. He reviewed his whole life from childhood, in an effort to understand himself and the world in which he found himself. He watched the shapes and colorings of the clouds, the advance and withdrawal of shadows, the flickering, shifting moods of the broad sweep of grassland and lavaland and bare red earth down to the sea. He read the wind in its every shift and gust, and distinguished its tones and roars. The hours went rapidly, intensified as though they were in a dream.

On the morning of the fourth day he started down again, going through a forested area to gather ieie blossoms for Lucia. When he reached the house he called out to her. But there was no answer. He went through the living room to the kitchen, where he lay the blossoms on the table. There was no sound in the house but the wind. He went into Mele's bedroom and then into his and Lucia's. A note was lying on Lucia's pillow. He snatched it, his heart pounding. But the handwriting was that of Mele.

It read, "Dear Mamma and Kaupena, I have gone home. I don't think you want me any more. But when you do, I shall be at home. Your daughter, Mele."

He ran into Mele's bedroom, opening the drawers and the closet door; she had taken all her things with her. "Mele, Mele!" he cried as though his voice could force her back. He ran to the lanai and gazed around the garden, hoping that she might be hidden there. Mele gone! Gone home because they didn't want her any more! Mele, little Mele, his heart cried.

He knew that he had neglected her recently. But Lucia! Lucia had devoted her whole life to the child! They did everything together, sewing, cooking, visiting with Julia, going up to Lokalia's, swimming, crabbing, picnicking. He rubbed his hot damp palms together. He pulled from his pocket the note and re-read it. He must go at once and bring her back.

He took Lucia's yellow coupe and drove down to the highway, turned toward Hana, and sped until he came to a small pebbly beach enclosed between sharp barren headlands. The pebbles were silvery gray and heaped in a long curving mound, which was constantly reshaped by the sea. A small lagoon, its water a deep and shining brown and shaded by puhala trees, lay just behind the beach. The valley back of the lagoon was no more than a tiny glade shut in by barren rock cliffs. Just back of the crest of the pebbly beach was perched a small wooden shack, seasoned by the salt and the sun. The boards had a pearly glow against the background of dark cliffs and brown lagoon.

Kaupena left the car and started swiftly down the pathway to the shack. When he was close, he called, "Mele!"

The girl plunged from the shack and hurled herself into his arms. She sobbed convulsively, and he held her tightly to him and kissed her cheeks and her hair. Mrs. Poepoe came from the house to stand near them. The wind whipped at the gray ragged muumuu she wore and sliced the thin mass of her hair into streamers which lashed about her face. Every now and again she patiently drew her fingers across her forehead and cheeks, picking up the strands of hair and twisting them at the back of her head.

"Why did you go?" Kaupena asked when the little girl had quieted.

"I didn't think anyone wanted me."

"You know we love you."

"But you're never home. And Mamma's never home any more—or when she is Paul is there."

215

"Paul!" His face went suddenly hot.

"Yes, he comes all the time now. Every day. Mamma and I don't have times like we used to."

Mrs. Poepoe interrupted. "Kaupena, if you don't want her any more, she can come home. We miss her."

"Oh, but we *do* want her."

"She likes it at your house. And she's grown so fat."

"We love her, Mrs. Poepoe, as though she were our own."

"Come in, Kaupena, I have some fresh opihis. The kids just brought them home."

It was the first time he had ever gone into the Poepoe shack. Always before he had sat on the beach talking to them. The house, even in its smallness, seemed bare. There were mats for the family to sleep on arranged in the most sheltered corner. Three or four pillows were stacked neatly on them. Against the back wall was an unpainted wooden shelf, which had on it a few cracked dishes, three battered pans, a tin labeled rice, and two cans of salmon. A calabash hung from the roof that contained, he knew by the smell, fermented sweet-potato mash. There were two chairs made from orange crates and a small table covered with a crocheted cover on which stood the family photographs. There was no wall on the sea side of the house, but a coconut screen, very dried and tattered, stretched a third of the way across. When Kaupena was seated, Mrs. Poepoe brought him a handful of opihis. He thanked her and ate them with appreciation.

"Mr. Poepoe isn't home today?"

"He went down the beach fishing with the boys. You know when it's warm this way he feels better and his bones don't hurt so much. He can walk a little and even stoop."

"Your life has been pretty hard, Mrs. Poepoe."

"Yes, we have a hard life. We never know what's going to happen. Yes, it's hard. I'm glad Mele can get out of it a little."

"You've had bad luck." He knew she wanted to talk about her unhappiness.

"Yes, the Poepoes always have bad luck. My family's not so bad. It's a funny thing. When you're poor out here it doesn't seem so poor. Now, my sister in Wailuku, she has a really hard time. When she has to move it isn't like here: empty houses around where you can go, and someone to give you a can of fish for the kids to tide you over. Sometimes I tell her she should come back to Makaniloa. But she says waste time. She gets lonely out here."

"Yeah," he said, his eyes upon the sea. "It's lonely here all right. But there're worse things than loneliness."

"I guess what you say is right. I like to sit here and watch the sea. I always think I got my kids. I'm lucky." She shrugged her shoulders. "The sea is full of fish—if you can catch them."

"Yeah," he murmured. "And there's always limu and opihis. These are big opihis."

"The kids know a special place to get them. They keep it a secret."

Mele climbed onto Kaupena's knee and tugged at his hand. "Let's go home now."

He teased her. "Are you sure you want to go? Maybe I should leave you here."

Her face paled. "Oh no!" she gasped.

He put his arms around her. "O.K., baby dear."

When he and Mele were in the car, he came back to the subject which had been simmering just below the stream of his spoken words. "You say Paul comes to see Mamma?"

"Often! Especially the last few days! Sometimes they stay home and talk and play with me. Sometimes they go off. When the Hui meets, Paul usually comes."

"Why did you think we didn't want you?"

"You're always away. And when you're home you're so strange. And now Mamma, I think, likes Paul better than me."

Kaupena stopped the car suddenly. It was no longer safe for him to drive, blinded as he was by jealousy. He got out and started pacing up and down the road. Lucia and Paul! Just as Lokalia had foreseen. God, how the old woman always knew! He tried to think back over the past week. But he had paid so little attention to Lucia's movements that he actually didn't know how she spent her days. Why, he didn't even know whether or not she came in at night! He pounded a fist in the palm of the other hand.

And as though that gesture were the valve relieving the pressure, his rage was gone from him, and he sat limply on a rock. He had pushed Lucia from him, cruelly, harshly! Again he asked himself how he could have done it. She was all he wanted in a woman, gentle of manner, tenderly passionate, soft in all her ways like a sweet delicate animal. He began to weep for her hurt and her loneliness through these long months. He had pushed her away from himself—to Paul! Paul had been waiting, watching. Paul who had found out what Kaupena had known long ago, that Momi was a foolish, jealous, possessive girl. Paul had been waiting for Lucia, and he had taken her. Kaupena's anger was beginning to rise again.

He jumped into the car and drove home at reckless speed. Mele cowered in the far corner. The knowledge that she was cowering pricked at his nerves. He was seeing himself as he was, completely on the outside of things. In the effort to plunge himself into the warm core of the life of his race he had only isolated himself from his family and his friends. He had taken up with ghosts and unreality.

As he went up the driveway, he saw that Lucia was on the lanai reading a book. "Mele baby," he said, "go over to Aunty Julia's for a while, yeah? I don't want Mamma to guess that you went home. She'd be hurt. She can see you've been crying. So you scoot, O.K.?"

"O.K.," Mele replied sadly.

"Now, baby dear, you be sure and come back. We love you. We want you."

"Yes, I come back."

In the darkness of the garage he kissed her and sent her on her way. Then he moved slowly across the lawn toward Lucia. He saw happiness and content on her face, and it whipped his jealousy. Lost as he had been in his imaginings it had not escaped him that her face had taken on melancholy in the past months; this happiness was new. He mounted the stairs and sat in a chair opposite her.

"What is it, Kaupena?" she asked, seeing at once the tension in him.

"It's Paul."

She blushed, but her gaze did not waver. "Paul?"

"Yes, Paul," he repeated slowly and ponderously. "You're in love with him, aren't you?" He felt his calm going, and desperately he tried to control his voice.

"Why do you say that?"

"Mele ran away today."

"Mele!" She leaned forward in her chair, and he saw the paleness of anxiety on her face. "But I just saw her with you."

"Yes. I brought her back. She went home."

"Home! But why? Why did she do it?"

"She said you had forgotten her." And then his voice could be controlled no longer, and he rose and lashed out at her. "You spent your time with your lover. She thought you didn't care! That little girl left alone! How could you do that to the child?"

"But I never left her alone. Always I thought of her first!" Lucia's voice was high and quivering. She too rose.

"Ah, you're admitting it!" he cried. "You thought of her first! And when she was settled you went out with your lover. But she was lonely. How could you do that to Mele? How could you do it to me?"

Lucia's voice was under control again. She gazed steadily into his eyes. He had never seen so powerful an emotion in them. "And if I fell in love with Paul what difference does it make to you? You have given me nothing. No love. Not even companionship for months—for almost a year. There are times, Kaupena, when I nearly hate you. For your selfishness. For the way you shut yourself off from me. For the cruelty of your words."

She turned and walked from him, down the stairs, across the lawn, and onto the driveway. He watched her in a turmoil of desolation and anguish.

For some way along the road Lucia trembled in reaction to the emotion which had shaken her. She was proud of the way she had struck back at him, and she was pleased that he had shown jealousy. She suddenly felt herself the stronger, and mixed with her anger and her pride and her hate was a kind of soaring jubilation. She began to laugh.

She was not at all surprised to see Paul coming toward her on the road. It was the fitting, predetermined moment for him to come.

"He knows now," she greeted him. "And I'm glad!"

Paul grasped her arm. "How did he find out?"

"Through Mele. She ran away, saying she was lonely."

"Oh God, we've got to talk this over!" He grasped her arm and pulled her swiftly down the road. "Come on, there's an old abandoned house not far. No one will see us there."

"Yes, we must talk," she said. But her mind was not on this talk. It was on Kaupena's jealousy. The jubilance stayed with her, and she walked with a lilt; every now and again a smile broke out on her face.

"Darling," he said with concern. "You seem happy about it."

"I am," she said. "I feel freed. I feel as though a dam had broken. Or as though I'd escaped from a prison. Too long I've been shut up in worry and fear and a strange sense of being lost. Now I'm free!" She gaily swung her hand, clasped in his.

"Oh! I see," he said awkwardly, unable to respond to her lyric mood. "Here," he pointed. "The trail goes in here."

She followed, the hono-hono grass catching at her ankles and guava twigs switching at her face. "Watch your eyes!" he warned.

The lanai of the house was completely overgrown with twisting vines. Paul looked at the thick stocks and drew out his slender pocket knife which he thoughtfully tossed in the palm of his hand. Then he shrugged his shoulders and slipped it back in his pocket. He led her to the back. There was a large outcropping of flat pahoehoe lava on which the back entrance opened. The door had fallen from its hinges and lay cracked and termite-ridden in the earth. They entered cautiously. Directly across the room was the front entrance opening out onto the green-shadowed lanai. There was no door at the front, either, and no glass in the windows. The straw matting on the floor was still quite clean. The walls were pasted with pictures cut from Japanese magazines, once brilliantly colored but now faded and insect stained. An old battered straw hat that looked as though it had been carelessly tossed there only yesterday hung on a hook in the wall. On a nail spindle near the back entrance were some yellowed grocery bills from Oshiro's Store. Lucia leaned down to examine them. The most recent date was August of five years back and the name was K. Yamashiro.

"Isn't it strange?" Lucia asked. "It's as though they had walked out only yesterday. Yet it was five years."

"Look at the poles," Paul said, pointing to the ceiling. Stretched across the rafters she saw several slender bamboo poles. "I think fishermen must use this place—maybe when they come down from Hana or Kipahulu and want to stay the night."

"That may be it. It's awfully clean for a house empty for five years."

"I noticed a place in the back where there had been fires recently."

The sense of mystery and of unknown lives lingering on, which one has upon entering an abandoned house, gripped Lucia. She was startled and displeased when Paul drew her to him. "Oh, Lucia darling," he whispered, "what kind of a mess am I leading you into?"

She smiled absently. She continued to be under the spell of the house. She felt strangely as though she too had come and gone in Makaniloa, as these people had, as her great-grandmother had. Paul's kiss even, though she could feel it still warm on her lips, was a part of the past. Everything was remote but the house with its faint, musty odor and its ghosts.

"Let's sit down," she said and bent down cross-legged on the matting. He moved close to her.

"Darling," he urged, "we must decide things now that Kaupena knows."

"There's no rush."

"But he might—he might hurt you! Jealousy in Hawaiians can be very cruel."

"No. He won't hurt me. Something happened today. I don't know just what. But I feel strong now. Stronger than Kaupena."

Paul moved so that he could watch her eyes. Presently he ran a tender finger down the side of her face, feeling the cheekbone, the delicate hollow beneath it, the soft rounding of the jaw. "Don't change, Lucia."

She laughed lightly, trilling her voice. "I'm too old to change. . . . Darling, tell me why you came to Makaniloa."

"Oh, Lucia!" He was startled and moved his fingers in irritation. "Something certainly did happen to you today. Darling, we've got to be serious."

She smiled. "I'm very serious."

"We've got to decide about Kaupena."

Her voice took on gravity. "These things take time. I've got to know how Kaupena really feels before I can know what we are to do. Don't rush it, dear. And don't worry. I can handle Kaupena. You know, after this first bit of hurt pride is over, he may not care at all—he may not even be concerned with us."

She leaned down and kissed him. "This is a moment to ourselves. There may be fewer with Kaupena on the watch. Let's make the most of it."

He took her in his arms, laying his cheek against her breast. "Oh Lucia, I want time to hurry. I want this whole thing solved so that we can be together."

She stroked his hair gently, thinking that it was soft and fine like a child's. The skin of his forehead was smooth and firm and brown, unblemished by a wrinkle or a line. For a man in his middle thirties to have no lines . . . Perhaps she didn't really understand what he was like underneath; she certainly knew little enough about all those years before he came to Makaniloa. He was in some ways a complete stranger to her. Oh, she knew the taste of his lips, the fire of his embraces, but except in the mood of lover she hardly knew him. "Darling," she said with gentle insistence, "tell me about you."

He moved so that his head lay in her lap. "You asked me why I came here," he said thoughtfully. "Sometimes I almost wonder myself."

He caught the fingers with which she had been stroking his forehead and kissed them.

"You know how we lived back there. The snobbishness. The superstition. I was never really successful in that life. I didn't like the friends of my parents. Even at the age of fifteen I was a social misfit. And because I was an only child, I was already making it difficult for Mother and Dad. I spent a good deal of time at school in Switzerland, and I continued to be lonely. As I look back now I can't quite understand why I couldn't make friends. The boys seemed to expect me to be someone other than I felt myself to be. And I wasn't quite sure what it was they wanted of me.

"Then one day—I was seventeen then—I read a passage in a book. It was in a college preparatory course on world religions. We were touching upon Buddhism, and I read how Buddha told his followers to rely on themselves. I remember still some of the words. 'Be ye lamps unto yourselves. Look not for refuge to anyone besides yourselves.' Perhaps that doesn't sound like much to you. But it was the right psychological moment for me. I learned then that there was no refuge except in yourself, and that true value comes from within. I must be my own lamp.

"I went through college remembering Buddha's words and trying to be self-sufficient. It worked pretty well. I only did those things I thought were of value. I learned to have the strength for independence. And so it was not hard for me to break with the old life I had hated as a child, and had been afraid of, and come to Makaniloa where values are simple, perhaps, but where they are honest."

She let the silence move in upon them, while she absorbed his story. Then she said softly, "So Paul, this is the real you."

He ignored her words. "I saw Momi as someone simple and beautiful and honest. I didn't know then how she was torn with jealousies and fears. That, of course, was my big mistake. I have simply tried to make the best of it. But now . . ."

She stopped his mouth with her hand. "Don't let's speak of it now. It will be easier to do our settling with one at a time. First, Kaupena."

After Lucia had disappeared in the distance, Kaupena's anguish goaded him to action. There was only one thing to do, to go to Lokalia. But he must stop at Julia's and reassure Mele. Before he had reached the steps, Mele rushed out to him. He kissed her and told her he would be back to get her supper. When he felt the warm little body in his arms, he knew suddenly and poignantly how much he had been missing, shut away from this affection by his ghosts and gods. It came over him that in a sense he had been betraying Joe's memory and not serving it. He gave Mele a kiss for Joe and another for Lucia. Then he put her down.

"How's everything?" Julia asked with a stressed casualness.

"You've guessed, yeah?"

"Sure. You're one pupule kane."

"Yeah, I know. I go see Lokalia."

"She fix it up . . . Sometimes I want to give you hell these months. But Lucia tell me shut up."

He found his grandmother asleep on a mat in the grass, and he sat down near her. Her body was the frailest he had ever seen it: the flesh had grown strangely transparent and the eyes were sunk deeply in their sockets, the nostrils skeletal. Her fingers were thin and looked as brittle as dried twigs. But even in this frailness he could feel her strength; it was as though an almost palpable aura, a delicate diffusion of light and of fragrance, emanated from her. As he watched, a lizard moved cautiously up her arm, across her chest, and then rose on his back legs and tail and gazed into her face. Suddenly the little creature turned and ran as though in terror. In that moment the thought struck Kaupena that his grandmother would die soon. It filled him with a profound sadness.

She awoke; her naps were never long. "Kaupena!" she exclaimed.

"Yes, I came to see you."

Slowly and with difficulty she sat up. He noticed then for the first time a stiffness on the side of her face. "Have you been sick, grandma?"

"No. But I fell down some time ago. I must have hurt something. My left leg doesn't work so well."

"Grandma, you must come down and live with us!" he exclaimed with sudden fervor. "You shouldn't live alone."

"I'm not really alone. And I want to die here."

He took her arm and slowly they made their way into the house. He settled her in her rocker and spread the afghan over her lap.

"And now, Kaupena, you have at last come to me about Lucia."

"Yes. You were right about Paul. And I have lost her."

"You have played the fool."

He went to the window and gazed up at the thrashing mango foliage. "What can I do?"

She did not answer immediately but abandoned herself to memory. Then her words came almost imperceptibly and he had to bend close to hear. "Once I too . . . It was a dark experience though now I'm glad of it. After your grandfather died I was drowned in grief: I could not seem to work my way out of a sense of being lost—abandoned. He died of a childish thing, measles. We Hawaiians had not had such a disease until the haoles brought it. And that disease became a symbol to me of the decaying touch of the white man. They were like a blight on us, physically and spiritually. So I buried myself in the old: searched out the old ways of curing with herbs, of cooking, of weaving, of praying to the gods. I guess I was a little crazy for a while. I refused to use anything western.

"Then one day you got sick. I tried all the ancient ways and you only got sicker. Your mother came and took you away to a haole doctor. He put you in the hospital at Hana and cured you. Then I knew there was some good in the West. I learned that we must mingle and exchange ideas." She paused as her voice changed from a tone of revery to one with emotional timber. "I hope you've come around to that again. That you're out of the darkness." She gazed sharply at him. "Because if you aren't you can never win her back!"

"I'm out. I must be! I feel strange, as though I'd been away for a long time. . . . But what am I to do?"

"Do you love her?"

"Yes. Very much. I go mad at the thought of Paul!" He set his teeth against the anger flaring in him.

"You must be kind to her," she said sternly. "Love her, be tender to her. You have been a stranger too long. She'll not accept you at first."

He leaned against the arm of Lokalia's chair and trailed his fingers along the grain of the glowing koa wood. "I've been a stranger too long," he repeated. "Not only to Lucia but to myself—to you, to Mele, to everything clear and normal."

"You'll never be a whole man, Kaupena, until you have pride in yourself. Pride in the life you are leading. You have always moved uncertainly, feeling your way. You must find something in which you are superior, something you can hold up to Lucia with pride."

"But what? But what can I do? I can ride a horse. I can fish. I can sail a canoe. What's there to be proud of in that?"

She gazed enigmatically at him. "You have something in you. You'll have to find it out for yourself. Dedicate your life, Kaupena. Then the way will always be clear."

He moved toward the door. "You've always made things hard for me. You've always expected too much. That's why I've been uncertain."

"I've only expected what I've known is there."

He walked slowly out of the house, his mind full of what she had said. He idled along the path, searching himself. Whatever could he dedicate himself to? He laughed briefly. That wasn't the Hawaiian way. The Hawaiian way was just to live. What did Johnny live for? Women mostly, and getting drunk. And Julia? For her kids, and just sitting comfortably on her mat. And what had he, Kaupena, lived for? Mostly for the ideas he had had of what Hawaiians should do and be. He wanted his people to remember they were Hawaiians, with their little niche in humanity.

And then as he walked among the overarching trees, an idea emerged and grew. He would record the ancient lore of Makaniloa, gather it in a volume. He would devote his life to preserving the old in the hope it would have something for the new. He would translate the old chants, the records of the churches and the Hui; he would gather the stories of the old people and write them down. Lucia could help him with the material she had from her great-grandmother. They could dedicate their lives to Makaniloa.

When he reached home Lucia was there. He wanted to blurt out his thoughts to her, but when he stood before her he was suddenly embarrassed. So much of feeling and uncertainty lay between them. He noticed that she watched him furtively, and when his back was turned he felt her eyes upon him.

At the supper table Mele talked about her afternoon at Julia's. Kaupena said that he had seen Lokalia and that she looked very frail. Lucia did not speak except to urge Mele to eat her vegetables and to ask Kaupena if he wanted another piece of cake.

After supper he silently wiped the dishes for Lucia. He wanted desperately to say something, for he was afraid she would regard his silence as a further punishment for her affair with Paul.

Finally he said, "Mele's growing up. She's almost as tall as you are."

"Yes."

"Do you think we could—uh—tuck her in together to-night?"

"She's outgrowing such things, you know. She reads to herself."

"Oh, she is a big girl!"

When the dishes were done, Lucia went in to Mele. He heard the squeak of the bed springs as Lucia sat down by the child. Then there was a soft murmur of tender, responsive voices. He moved to the doorway and saw Mele locked in Lucia's arms. "I'm glad I'm back, Mamma. I'm glad you really want me."

"Darling, you mustn't ever doubt that."

He came into the room. "Good night, Mele."

"Are you going to kiss me tonight, Kaupena?"

"Tonight and every night." He bent down to kiss her. Lucia moved swiftly from the bed and hurried out of the room.

"It looked like Mamma was going to cry!" Mele exclaimed.

16.

IT WAS a sultry day, and Lokalia found it difficult to breathe. Drops of moisture gathered on the gray walls of her house and dripped down the rough hewn boards. Her hair and clothes were dank from perspiration and humidity. She had spent an active morning in putting to order the things in the chest, labeling each quilt with the name of the person who had made it and the date, wrapping the genealogy chant in a clean sheet of paper and marking it with Kaupena's name, putting in a fresh envelope the two chants Hoopai had given to her. In spite of his admonition not to write them down, she had done it when she felt her memory growing weak. At the bottom of the trunk she placed the little box that held her few bits of jewelry, a polished kukui nut necklace that had belonged to her mother, a jade ring that had been her mother-in-law's, and a cameo brooch that had been given her by her husband. She wrote a little note to Lucia and put it in the box. She sprinkled some camphor crystals in her three feather leis and among the folds of the quilts. She did these things very slowly and with much pain.

She sat down at noon to a bowl of poi and a cold laulau which Julia had brought her the day before. But she was not hungry. She nibbled on small shreds of pork from the laulau, and scooped up a little of the poi with her fingers. After lunch the wind ceased entirely, the sun beat straight down, and the cliffs shut in the steaming heat. Her head began to ache. She went out to the mat under the mango tree, hoping to find some coolness from the green of foliage and grass. She lay down and watched the waves of heat corrugate her house. But her eyes could no longer focus, and she shut them. Doves called in the heavy silence. Occasionally there was a crackle of twigs and leaves drying in the intense heat. Without the wind of Makaniloa, the air seemed taut, and the blood throbbed in her ears.

Presently she was aware of a growing numbness in her feet and fingers. A strange compound of feelings—this numbness in her limbs and the excruciating pain in her head. It came to her that she was going to die, and for a moment she was frightened, calling out to Kaupena and Lucia. Then a wind began to stir in the mango foliage, and the sound of the falls grew loud and humming like a bee in the jasmine. There is rain on the mountain, she thought. And with that her fear ebbed. Makaniloa was quietly taking her to its earth. Lono was bringing rain to cool the parching grasses. She would lie with her people, her bones feeling the rain, knowing the long wind which swept from the crater. If only Lucia and Kaupena were settled. . . . A sharp stab of pain seared her eyes, and she lost consciousness.

Lucia and Mele found her lying under the mango tree. They had come up to see how she was, for Kaupena had decided that someone must look in every day.

Mele ran to her calling, "Tutu, Tutu! We've brought you a pudding." She stopped suddenly as she reached the edge of the mat. "Mamma, hurry! I think, I think— Something's wrong!"

Lucia ran to the mat and knelt beside Lokalia. She laid a hand on her forehead and found it quite cool. Then she took her wrist, but there was no pulse. She turned to the child. "Tutu has gone, Mele."

"Dead? Really dead?"

"Yes, darling."

"But why? She wasn't sick."

"She's an old, old lady."

"Oh Tutu!" Mele cried out and threw herself across Lokalia's breast. She started to moan in the ancient manner of wailing.

As the sound of the child's grief poured in upon Lucia, she was seized with trembling, and in spite of herself tears flowed from her eyes. "Oh, Lokalia, why did you have to go now?" she whispered softly.

Lucia's mind flew to Kaupena. With Lokalia's death would there be another seizure of darkness? Would his returning kindness and love be shattered? If so—she trembled slightly—there would be no reason not to go to Paul.

"Oh Lokalia," she whispered again, "why couldn't you have waited a little longer? Even a week . . ." She gazed moodily at the aged woman with the child sobbing on her breast. Then she knelt on the mat and kissed the gnarled hand. It came to her how empty her life would be without Lokalia. She had loved the old woman as she had loved the remembrance of her great-grandmother. In each generation there arise a few women such as these two who live with fire and determination and magnetism and so leave their marks on the following generations; their influence descends quietly, firmly, and a child of Waiolama or Appleton blood fifty years hence might wonder why it was in him to hunt out the ancient Hawaiian ways, why Makaniloa stirred in him such a flush of emotion.

"Mele, darling," Lucia said, stirring from her sorrow, "we must hurry and tell Kaupena. He must know right away."

She pushed the tears from her eyes with the backs of her hands, and rose from the mat.

"We will take her in the house first. Open the door for me, darling," Lucia said. She picked up the frail body and carried it into the house and laid it on the bed. She smoothed her hair and laid the arms neatly at the sides, and took a quilt from the chest and spread it over Lokalia, who in the shadows had the look of one sleeping.

"Come, Mele, we must hurry!" They ran all the way down the valley.

Kaupena was at home. He must have been watching for them, for he came onto the lanai, calling, "What's the matter?"

"Tutu's dead!" Mele cried before Lucia could stop her.

He appeared to go limp and, whirling about, went back into the house without waiting for them. Lucia found him seated on the hikie, his head buried in his hands.

She said quietly, "Her death must have been peaceful. She was lying in her favorite place on the mat under the mango tree. Her eyes were shut, and there was a look of repose on her face. She may have passed in her sleep. I took her in the house and laid her on the bed and spread a quilt over her."

He looked up. "You did all of that, Lucia?"

"Yes."

He rose. "I must go and be with her. Would you mind telling Julia about it? She'll know what must be done. My sister should be informed."

"I'll do that, Kaupena." She glanced anxiously at his face and saw there the dark brooding of his eyes. It was, she thought, the same as when Joe had died, and a great despair came over her.

As she walked through the woods to Julia's her mind turned with relief to Paul. She felt for a moment a pang of happiness at the flood of affection for him which filled her. There was little use now in denying this love, in struggling for the improbable reconciliation with Kaupena. She and Paul were indeed much more suited. It would be a different Makaniloa she would share with him. She and Paul would always be the watchers, not the sharers.

Kaupena sat on a chair by Lokalia's bed, whispering the lines of the genealogy chant. These words, he reflected, were what she would have liked to hear as she lay dying. Somehow he felt that even now it was not too late.

When he had finished, he let his mind move slowly along the details of Lokalia's life: how she went from the warm dusty Lahaina hut of her father to the missionary's home, where she learned English and the Bible and haole living; her return to her father's banana-shaded place and the heart of Hawaiian ways; then the long, cool, thrilling days in the crater with her lover, and her marriage and those happy natural years; Joseph's death and her passionate reversion to Hawaiian ways; how she had taken him, Kaupena, and all the long, sweet, and sometimes difficult days he had shared with her in this very house with its musty fragrance, its cleanliness, its remoteness. Her long life dipping with sensitivity and awareness into two civilizations, shadowed by the deep-laid hurt of all Hawaiians that the great vital world of the West should look upon them as wayward children, though proud and charming; her long years strengthened by the deep welling-up of devotion to men and to life which she knew to be the Hawaiian way of standing up to the West; her long life given to the people of Makaniloa . . .

Once she had tried to explain to him what had happened to her in that week with Joseph in the crater. "There was such a peace in our days, a peace in spite of the passion of our love. We had to live much as they did in the past. Joseph had built a little grass house, and I cooked outside on some stones. Each evening we sat and looked down the slope of the mountain, and he pointed out where the old heiaus had been, and the villages, and the taro patches. He told me much of the history and legend of Makaniloa, for he wanted me to love this place I had never before seen. Somehow living the way we did, talking so much of the past, and expressing our love so constantly, it came upon me that the old life had something to give to the new; it would be a tragedy to let everything old go. After all, our people had paddled their canoes from the southern seas and found these islands. They had adapted themselves to Hawaii, and they brought with them ancient racial memories of the lands from which they had come. This life was of their own fashioning and it was good because it was one stream in the flow of the long, veiled history of the Polynesians. In that crater I grew proud of my people and was stirred by the mystery of their origin and by the greatness of what they had done among these small lost islands of the Pacific."

Kaupena saw now the one course open for him: to fulfill the expectations of Lokalia's life. He would carry on her work and pass it on to Mele and to any children he might have. His collection of the lore of Makaniloa was a start. Only the other day he had spent two hours with old Mr. Clarke helping him to unravel the memories of his childhood. Mr. Clarke had told him how the grass houses had been built and how the sands and pebbles for the floor were chosen with such care that when the mats were spread upon them for sleeping, the effect was soft and plushy like a heap of thick, dried grass. He had told of the outside ovens kept at a safe distance from the house so that a flying spark would not endanger the thatch. He told of the stench from the calabashes in which were stored sweet-potato mash, dried fish, and dried goats' meat. Old Mr. Clarke had loved this conjuring up of his youth, and had invited Kaupena to come as often as he wished. Kaupena had planned to tell Lokalia that very evening and to show her his notebook.

Now there was left to him only watching her through the night. It came to him that she belonged in his book. It need not be confined to facts and customs and beliefs alone. Vivid personalities had always been a part of Makaniloa's history. And Lokalia was the very spirit of Makaniloa. Tonight he would write of her. He rose and found writing paper, and took his pen from his shirt pocket. He sat again in the chair near Lokalia, and moving a candle closer he began to write.

Some time later Lucia came in and found him still writing. "Everything is ready," she announced. "She is to be buried tomorrow noon. Julia is taking charge of the food. She thinks it's better to serve it at our house. Your sister says her children have the whooping cough, and she can't come."

"I'll stay by Lokalia tonight. You'd better go home and be with Mele."

"I think the Hui is forming shifts of watchers and also the Pohaku Lono group. So you'll not be alone."

"It wouldn't matter one way or the other," he said and went back to his writing.

Shut off again, she thought. A gust of wind and rain lashed at the window, flickered the candles, and filled the house with melancholy. She watched him, his back hunched and his pen moving steadily across the page. Lokalia would not like his shutting her out again. Lucia looked at the still figure. "Oh Lokalia," she thought again, "you went too soon!"

After casting one more glance at the absorbed figure of Kaupena, she left him, and in her loneliness turned from the homeward path to the one leading to Paul's office at the ranch. She told Paul that Lokalia had died and asked him to come late to the house and sit with her for a while. "Be sure it's late," she warned him.

It was close to midnight when he came. The women preparing the food had left the kitchen; Mele was asleep, and the rain sang in a quiet murmur from the eaves and the foliage.

"Day after tomorrow," he said, "I am taking you on an outing to a hidden valley. You will need to get away then, and this is just the place to refresh yourself."

"Yes," she said faintly. "I shall need it. Kaupena has gone off again just as he did at Joe's death."

At breakfast on the morning after the funeral, she told Kaupena quite frankly that she was going to spend the day with Paul. She had not expected him to react one way or the other and therefore was surprised when he flared angrily.

"My God, Lucia, what do you think I am? After all, you are my wife!"

She felt anger rising in herself. She was not going to let him spoil this excursion, which was the only thing that had made it possible for her to endure the lamentations at Lokalia's funeral and his own coldness and withdrawal. Her words came crisply. "When you keep it constantly in your mind that I'm your wife, perhaps I can be one again."

He caught her in his arms. "Lucia, what are you trying to do?"

She struggled free. But a strong emotion had taken hold of her, and she could only stammer, "I'm trying to find a little happiness somehow."

He turned to Mele and drew her to his side. With hands outstretched he stood dramatically before Lucia. "Don't leave us!"

Still caught in the wave of her emotion and repelled by his histrionics, she whispered fiercely, "Go back to your ghosts and your broodings. You have shut me out quite successfully. I remember only too well how it was after Joe's death. I'll not go through that again!" Her last sentence was spoken aloud and with passion. Strength was coming into her again.

"You won't have to," he cried huskily. "Lucia, you won't have to."

"I saw the darkness in your eyes at the funeral," she said bitterly. "I feel it closing in on me. I see the tension growing in Mele. This house will again become a place of emptiness and fear." She took a step toward him. "My grief is cast in a different mold. It wants warm sympathy, and a little coming together—not drawing apart."

When she had finished all feeling seemed to be drained from him, and he looked at her with blank resignation. "Mele and I will be waiting," he said dully.

She reached the cove where Paul kept his canoe under a shelter of woven coconut fronds. Paul had not yet come. She lay back on the black sand and let the sun beat upon her face and arms. It was good to feel the bright yellow heat driving all thought and all emotion from her, and slowly the muscles, the cords, the nerves began to relax until she felt her body molding itself easily to the undulations of the sand. It was as though she were something drifted upon the beach by the sea and left there long enough to be a part of it, long enough to be wind-silvered into the beach tone. The sun was entering her veins and flowing with her blood. After all, she thought, it was the sun of Makaniloa she wanted to live in, not the shadow.

Paul awakened her with a kiss. "I'm sorry, darling," he said. "I was held up. Poor Jackie had one of his attacks."

She jumped up and helped him launch the canoe. He had already packed it with two large knapsacks lashed securely down and an extra supply of gasoline. When she saw the supplies, she laughed. "It looks as though we're going for quite a voyage." She hesitated and then flung out romantically, "Across the trackless seas into the path of the sun!"

"It'll take us all day. And it's better to be prepared for emergencies," he said matter-of-factly.

She took a paddle and did her share in maneuvering the canoe through the surf. The open sea was glassy, mirroring the clouds in meticulous detail, and distant reflections took on faint color tones of mauve and pink and beige. Mauna Loa and Mauna Kea were not in their usual ethereal disguise but were definitely of earth and rock in the crystal atmosphere—cloud shadows, even, were distinct upon them. But Makaniloa seemed bathed in a faint opalescent haze, and in the crater of the mountain a few purplish clouds hung heavily. "The day has a look of heat," she said. "But strangely it isn't hot."

"The air is stuffy, though. Humid, perhaps."

"Tense, as though waiting," she murmured to herself.

He started the motor and motioned for her to come close to him. She moved so that she could lean against his knee. He kept his eyes on the water, but from time to time he stroked her hair or cupped his fingers under her chin. Again she knew the peace she had felt on the hot black sand of the beach. She was aware of the warm comfort of being with Paul.

She stretched and yawned. "Oh, Paul, I haven't known such restfulness in a long time." But immediately a vision came of Mele and Kaupena standing hand in hand in the kitchen. Mele's eyes had been dark and clouded with hurt, and her little mouth had drooped in despair. Kaupena's eyes had been concentrated in sorrow—strangely, not the grief of bereavement, she thought, but sorrow brought by misunderstanding and love. She shut her eyes and rubbed them vigorously to rid her of this vision. Then she sat up and concentrated her gaze on the shore. They were passing the old village where Joe lay buried, and she turned her glance up to the crater where the purplish clouds were continuing to gather quickly. They had a dull, water-heavy look. "It may rain this afternoon."

"Oh, those clouds mean nothing. I've seen it look as though a deluge were coming from the crater, and yet never a drop fall."

At the confidence in his voice she settled back again, her head on his knee, her eyes on the mingled cerulean of sky and water. But with the remembrance of the clouds in the back of her mind, the peace was gone.

"A cigarette, darling?" Paul asked.

"Oh yes!" She spoke too eagerly, and he glanced questioningly at her. She smiled.

"You'd better light your own. The wind is pretty strong."

She took his lighter and managed to get her cigarette lit.

"Are you happy?" he asked.

"Happy," she sighed.

"In a few minutes we'll be able to see the valley." There was a quiver of excitement in his voice.

She peered along the shore line, but there seemed to be only the desolation of lava flows and vast fields of scrubby grass and panini, punctuated by patches of bare, reddish-brown earth. Higher up the mountain lay a gray, brooding ohia forest. "I think your valley is in your imagination," she teased. "I can't see the remotest suggestion of one."

"It comes as a surprise. That's part of its beauty."

Then abruptly they saw it. The flank of the mountain was cut as though a slender triangular slice had been taken out. Lucia saw the coconut trees rising from the valley floor, the movement of their fronds voluptuous in the wind. There was a greenness of grass and foliage that was all the more vivid for the surrounding desolation of dark lava; about the whole spot was a sense of promise and an enticing invitation to man.

Paul explained, "The valley gets its water from the forest above, and I think too there is something about the wind currents and the shape of the mountain, which brings more rainfall there."

"It looks beautiful," she said. Here was the ancient dream, she thought, of all those who yearned to get back to the simple life. Here hidden from the casual curious eye was a valley, well watered, lush, almost inaccessible, waiting for Thoreaus and Rousseaus and Paul Rittens.

"Did people once live here?" she asked.

"Oh yes. There are lots of old walls."

"I wonder why they left," she mused.

"This kind of life went out a century ago." His voice grew

suddenly bitter. "We are too busy making atom bombs and thrusting ideologies down each other's throats to think of living simple lonely lives in a spot like this. People have become afraid of loneliness. They huddle together in masses, finding a sham security in the touch of sweaty shoulder to sweaty shoulder."

"Paul, do you really hate people so much?"

"I don't hate people. I hate what they've made of themselves —through cowardice."

He cocked the motor up suddenly and motioned for her to move to the bow. They were now opposite the dark shining beach of the valley. "We're going to take a wave in!" he shouted. "Paddle hard when I tell you."

He maneuvered the canoe so that its bow faced the shore. Then he turned to watch the incoming waves. They rose and fell gently in the long undulations of the surf, and she thought how pleasant it was to sit offshore and contemplate the valley. Out here it maintained its quality of mystery and the remoteness of its beauty. Out here it was still the enchanted, the unfulfilled dream.

Suddenly Paul shouted, "Paddle!"

She paddled with deep strokes and they caught the wave which carried them into the quiet water just off the beach. Paul jumped out and dragged the canoe up onto the sand.

"Here we are!" He lifted her and held her tightly in an embrace. "This is our valley," he murmured.

As they walked hand in hand across the sand she felt something vaguely familiar about the valley. The shape of the small lagoon near the cliff with pandanus foliage and sky reflected in it; the smooth lawn of green out of which rose mossy-backed coconut palms; the cliffs brooding in a blue-green haze—she had at some time looked on all these. "Paul, I feel as though I've been here before."

"Darling, a valley like this haunts the dreams of many of us.

When we explore it, you'll be even more certain that you've been here before."

They wandered slowly along the beach and the open grassy area behind it. A little coolness came into the air; the wind freshened and ruffled the waters of the lagoon. They moved into the coconut grove. The air was softer there and fragrant with green scents rather than salt. The light was a diffused green-yellow haze. The fronds lashed in the strengthening wind, shedding a crackling sea sound; underfoot the rotting coconut husks were spongy. When they reached a spot where hau trees began to spread their mesh of twisting, impenetrable branches, Paul paused. "I suppose in the old days one could reach the back of the valley. But unless you wade up the stream it's almost impossible now. The boys and I once brought a little rubber boat and paddled up to the back of the valley. It's very beautiful with forests of koa and lehua. There are strange big rocks and nearby a rocky enclosure that I'm sure must once have been a heiau, although I can find no account of it."

He moved closer. "Well, darling, how do you like my secret valley?"

"It's beautiful," she said trying to fill her voice with enthusiasm. The uneasiness about the weather, which had come upon her in the canoe, had grown into an inexplicable uneasiness about the valley. Amazingly, she found herself wishing Kaupena were in Paul's place. She did not trust Paul's reading of wind and clouds, nor could she feel, in his presence, the Polynesian quality of the valley; it was still like a painter's or a poet's romantic fantasy. Through Paul's eyes the valley was a place of escape from life, a place to hide and enjoy your own lonely freedom. But for Kaupena it would have been rich in the sense of lives lived and of lives to be lived. It was part of the Polynesian pattern of feast and famine, desolation and beauty, desertion and rediscovery.

Paul kissed her, holding her with a passionate insistence. "Lucia, darling, this is our world." His fingers pressed tenderly around her breasts, and he put his lips to the little hollow of her throat.

Slowly and subtly she disengaged herself and started toward the beach. "It's beautiful!" She drew out the words, filling them with a tenderness and response she did not truly feel.

He followed her closely. "If you're hungry we'll have lunch now. There's a lovely little spot by the side of the lagoon. It's already after twelve."

"Oh I'm hungry!"

He took her to a place where the grass grew to the edge of the dark water. An old hala tree, its spreading foliage high in the air, cast a blur of thin shade on the grass. She stretched out at full length. "This is lovely. I'll be lazy and let you get the lunch." While he went back to the canoe, she explored with her eyes the cliffs shutting in the valley. Seaward they were bare and rocky, but as they moved up the mountain, they reached eventually into the straggly end of the forest area. A little point jutted out on the Makaniloa side; it must give, she thought, a marvelous view of the valley. Then remembrance struck her, and she sat up suddenly. She stared hard at the cliffs, at the falls plunging down them, and at the coconut grove and the grassy place which had two spindly palms rising from it. This was Lokalia's hidden valley! There was no doubt! Her heart pounded violently, and warm tears clouded her eyes. Lokalia had understood the true life of this valley; it was a place like any other which had known the anguish and hope and happiness of man. And Paul shamed it by making it a Western escapist dream. In that instant it came to her overwhelmingly that it was not Paul's life she wanted to share but Lokalia's and Kaupena's.

By the time Paul returned she had regained her composure,

and she helped him unpack the food and spread it out. As soon as she dared, she thought, she would suggest their going home. The clouds were now pouring out of the crater and that could be her excuse for leaving. She would pretend fear.

"This is where the kids and I've come sometimes to camp," he said happily. "Momi came once too. But she couldn't stand it. Said it was too lonely. I think she was a little afraid of something—perhaps ghosts and spirits."

"I imagine at night it is a little ghostly."

"The noises are so different, so filled with possibility. . . . The trouble is, these people too are afraid of being alone—just like the rest of this crazy world. They haven't learned that solitude is necessary for refreshment."

He held out a browned piece of chicken breast for her. "Thoreau was for a while my constant companion, and I learned a lot from him. I remember he says in his quaint way that no 'exertion of the legs' can bring the minds of two people closer to each other. One might even add the hearts. It always amazes me that people don't learn that more easily. He has another passage I shall never forget; I've recited the words so many times that I can almost quote them." He paused reflectively. When he began it was with a voice scarcely above a whisper. " 'In the midst of a gentle rain I was suddenly sensible of such sweet and beneficent society in nature, in the very pattering of the drops, and in every sound and sight around my house, an infinite and unaccountable friendliness all at once like an atmosphere sustaining me, as made the fancied advantages of human neighborhood insignificant.' " He stopped and gazed moodily into the waters of the lagoon. Their clearness was frosted by a cat's paw of wind, and the sky hazily reflected was grayed with clouds. He smiled and said, "This is, perhaps, my *Walden*."

Lucia watched him and wondered what emotion of the past

had welled up in him. The wounds of his childhood still festered, and solitude, as he had learned in boyhood, was the only balm. Momi's jealousy, her fear that she was losing him, was understandable. He never really gave himself to Momi or to anyone, for he was afraid of doing so. He had learned the peace and strength of loneliness, and he would not give it up easily.

She said, "Then you came to Makaniloa really to enjoy solitude."

"I suppose so. I had to get away from the thousand petty demands of living in a complicated society."

Her mind was suddenly fired. "Do you know what I want, Paul? I want to throw myself into the life of Makaniloa!" She hesitated and then plunged on. "I don't see Makaniloa only as it is today, a place of great beauty with a scattering of wonderful, difficult, deep-feeling human beings. But I feel it as it was in the past and as it will be in the future. I feel the flowing of life through it. It isn't really lonely and remote. It's as much in the mainstream as any place where life is lived."

He looked at her and smiled. "You're being quaintly mystical, darling. You still have to learn the hard lesson that I did. Rely only on yourself!"

"But I like to forget at times that I have a self!" she continued fervently. "I want to be a part of this flowing."

He reached over and rumpled her hair with his hand. "What strange little emotional ideas you have."

She laughed, then, playing his game, and leaned down to cut the cake. They munched in the silence drawn awkwardly between them, and when he had finished, he stretched back upon the grass, his elbows beneath his head. "This is really where I'd like to live. I admit that I need beauty in my solitude. So you see I'm vulnerable."

The sky by now was completely overcast. Out at sea there were two or three rain squalls. "Look, Paul! I really think we'd

better go. There may be a storm." She filled her voice with ex-
aggerated worry.

He sat up. "Oh, that doesn't look so bad."

"It does to me. Already there are squalls. Please, Paul, let's
go."

He gazed questioningly at her. Slowly his face became grave
and his fingers began to tremble slightly. "It's more than the
storm, isn't it?"

"No!" She blushed. "It's just that I'm worried. It's a long
way to go, and with only a canoe——"

He moved close and took her in his arms. "Don't spoil our
day, darling." He began to unfasten the buttons of her blouse.

She turned her face away and with a sob said, "I've made a
mistake, Paul."

His hands fell from her, and he cried, "What do you mean?"

"I'm sorry about it. I was discouraged. I didn't think clearly,
and you were so good to me."

"Oh, Lucia!" She saw the shadows pass into his eyes and the
lines of strain mark the corners of his mouth. "But why? Why
this sudden change? What have I said? What have I done?"

"It's nothing you've done or said. It was my selfishness, my
stupidity." She stood up. "Please, Paul, don't make it too hard
for us. It's my fault. I'm bitterly sorry."

"You mean you don't love me?" he asked bluntly.

"I'm afraid so. I——I was confused by my own difficulties."
She could no longer face him.

"Can't you explain better than that?"

"That's all there is! Oh, Paul, it was horrible of me to do
this!"

Silently he packed up the lunch and carried it back to the
beach. She followed and helped him push the canoe away from
the sand. He jumped in ahead of her and left her to get in as
best she could. She was soaked to the waist in the process. He

took the boat expertly through the surf without her help. The water beyond was uncomfortably choppy. He started the motor and headed the canoe for Makaniloa.

"Look at the clouds, Paul," she said in an effort to bring things back to normal. "It's pouring at home. We're going to get it, don't you think?" The slope of the pastureland was completely blotted out by a gray curtain of rain. The top of the mountain was engulfed in sodden, impenetrable clouds, and the sea to the east was both white with froth and dark with rain.

"I guess it's a storm all right," he admitted. He smiled with a perverted happiness. "We'll have some rough going. Perhaps the proper climax . . ."

She felt a little pang of fear. His mood, the weather's mood . . . Oh Kaupena, she cried to herself, why aren't you with us? You know the temper of Makaniloa; you are part of its ebb and flow. . . . The many tales of canoe drownings flooded in upon her. Drowning! To drown with Paul! It was unthinkable. To drown with the watcher and the stranger! "Oh Kaupena, Kaupena!" she cried into the wind.

They moved at retarded speed through the rough dark seas. Paul's attention was riveted on the water, but Lucia watched the island with rigid intensity. She was afraid it would completely disappear in the shroud and then how would they find their course? Clouds now seemed to be pouring in from every direction, flinging themselves across each other's path and creating shapes and dark colors of great beauty. There were moments in their progress through the water when she forgot the fear and thrilled to the wildness of the storm.

Time, in a way, ceased to be, and she was startled when Paul called out, "We're half way home!" She knew from the tone of his voice that his moodiness had passed. She smiled briefly at him, and he responded.

"Paul, I'm despicable!" she cried.

"Forget it!"

The words were no more than out of his mouth when the wind suddenly rushed down upon them; a wave lashed over the bow. "Bail!" Paul shouted at her as he struggled to keep the canoe on its course.

She snatched up the can in the bottom of the canoe and scooped the water with a frantic haste. The wind grew stronger minute by minute. Now every fifth or sixth wave washed into the canoe, and the outrigger seemed to be constantly under water. The rain came as suddenly as the wind with a steady, flooding downpour, swelling the water in the boat. She bailed more and more frantically. All that she could see—her whole world—was the water inside the canoe, the dark rhythmic toss of her can and its plume of spray caught by the wind. Her clothing was drenched and her arms and shoulders ached with fatigue. She glanced once or twice at Paul; his teeth were clenched as though he were in pain and his eyes remained steadily on the sea and the path ahead.

The moment came when she felt she could not raise her arm another time, and she slumped momentarily, her back bending until her head nearly touched her knees.

"Bail!" came Paul's voice fiercely through the wind noise and the rain noise.

She started again. Her fingers were numb, her arms stiff with pain. But slowly and jerkily she bailed. She no longer watched the water inside the canoe, but rather the waves. Her head began to throb and her eyes burned. The salt taste was strong and acrid in her mouth. And she began to have visions of curious shapes in the waves and to hear sounds as of people calling. Fatigue traveled in long surges through her, distorting her vision and her hearing.

The wind now shifted, coming in gusts of great speed and power, which were strong enough to buffet her slightly from her seat in the canoe bottom. It was in recovering from one of these buffets, which knocked her against the side of the canoe, that she saw clearly in the waves an image of Joe; his eyes were dark and frightened and his mouth open with calling. She blinked her eyes, but the image remained. She could almost hear his voice asking for help. And she called softly, "Joe, come in the canoe." She stretched her arm for him, and in that moment he vanished. Then the idea flashed on her that it had not been Joe but Kaupena—Kaupena swimming out to help her. She commenced to sob, calling on Kaupena, when a wave washed over her stinging her face like a lash and crushing her breath. When she recovered, she began to bail again, frantically. Her mind had shed its hallucinations and grown calm. She forced a rhythm into her bailing, and her muscles relaxed somewhat. The determination had settled upon her that she must get home safely to Kaupena and Mele—she must share their lives intimately and passionately. If there was to be sorrow she would learn to share it with them. She would break down the racial barrier, and chart a faint little trail toward the world of harmony that might be.

Paul's voice broke through her reflections. "Can you hear anything?"

She looked up and realized that no land was visible. There was only the sea and the pall of rain. She turned a frightened look at Paul. "How do we know when we're there?"

"Do you hear anything?" he shouted impatiently. She listened, but she could not distinguish anything but water and wind.

"I don't know," she cried.

"I think I hear horns. We'll turn and go in here."

"But the rocks!"

"We've got to risk it. I've been watching the time, too. We're about due home—even with the storm."

After he had turned the canoe, she bailed with a renewed vigor. And then she heard distinctly the noise of horns. "I hear it!" she cried. "We're home!"

He grinned at her.

In a few minutes they could see the beach of Makaniloa. The rain had lifted slightly so that the Protestant Church was visible on its low cliff. When Lucia saw it tears rolled down her face, and she sobbed quietly. She could see the cars lined up beyond the beach, each blowing its horn and blinking its lights. On the shore there was a scurrying of figures. A man stood in the waves. Behind him a little girl watched tensely. Nearby a woman clutched three small boys close to her skirts.

Paul cocked the motor and cried out to her to paddle. The moment the canoe struck the sand, she jumped into the water and ran toward Kaupena, who was wading out to her. He took her in his arms and carried her to the sand. Mele clasped her about the waist.

She sat down with Kaupena and Mele to a supper that Julia had kept hot and waiting. She was warm from her bath and dressed in an old flannel muumuu that had been left by some-one unknown in one of the drawers. Kaupena put around her shoulders Lokalia's old Scotch sweater. Her wet hair was bound in a towel. Mele moved her chair so that she was close to Lucia, but Kaupena took his usual chair across the table.

Mele put her hand on Lucia's arm. "Mamma, we were afraid you would drown."

"I guess I was too, darling."

"Kaupena said we must love you and be kind to you so you wouldn't go off that way again."

Lucia gazed at Kaupena. No tension strained in his face, no darkness lay in his eyes. There was only love and concern for her. She stretched her hand across the table, and he took her finger tips, massaging them in the way she had seen Hawaiian mothers massaging the fingers of their babies. Outside the ebbing storm wind lashed against the house, rattled the windows, and rubbed the mango branches together.

TALES OF THE PACIFIC